PLAIN JANE

PLAIN JANE

BY

Schledia Phillips

THREE KEYS PUBLISHING

UNLOCKING WORLDS, HEARTS, AND MINDS

THREE KEYS PUBLISHING

www.threekeyspublishing.com

Schledia Phillips

www.schlediabenefield.com

like her on Facebook at Schledia Benefield Phillips, Author

or follow her on twitter @Schledia

or follow her blog at www.schlediabenefield.blogspot.com

Dedication

For the One who shined His light into the darkness that shrouded my life. Thank you for stretching forth Your strong hand and pulling me from the depths.

Acknowledgments

To my editor, Lynn Thompson, without you I would have never had the courage to have this novel published. Thank you for your encouragement and for allowing me to use your name. To my mom and daddy, thank you for teaching me to believe in my abilities. Brooklyn, Colby, Trenten, Hudson, and Trinity, thank you for sharing me with my characters; also, thank you for your forgiveness when I was stressed to the max! Thank you, Anthony for painting exactly what I wanted. The cover design is perfect. Thanks to Dandyart for taking Anthony's design and making it into a wonderful cover. Thank you to Eddie Parsley of Parsley's Photography for the gorgeous picture you took. A special thanks to Raquel Torres and Donna Huber for their reviews for the back cover.

CONTENTS

PROLOGUE

I crawled onto my bed with a bottle of sleeping pills in one hand and a bottle of vodka in the other. *This way won't hurt, and it shouldn't take too long,* I thought to myself. I could no longer endure the pain, the pain of being completely alone in the world. Sure, others existed around me, but that didn't matter—they weren't a part of me. How can someone be a part of you when they barely recognize your existence?

I had been abandoned, plain and simple. Everyone I had ever loved had abandoned me. My dad deserted us all, which caused my mom to turn comatose. Sure, she didn't leave the house, but she abandoned us nonetheless. My sister dove into her world of friends and college, and my best friend left me to finish high school elsewhere; it wasn't long after she left me that my world came crashing down around me. The last one to forsake me was the one I least expected. He was there with me through all the rest, and his departure hurt the worst.

I poured the pills into my cupped palm, brought my hand to my lips, and hesitated...

CHAPTER 1

PLAIN

Plain. That was a word I knew quite well. The word described *me* perfectly. I embraced it as a part of who I was. I had eyes—I could see. I was an average-size girl with drab brunette hair. It was dark and dreary in my mind. My skin was milky white; my sister's was as well. People always referred to her as looking like a porcelain doll, but, of course, I had to carry the badge of sun-kisses, freckles, scattered across my nose and cheeks. My eyes were big and blue. I suppose that was my only redeeming feature, the only physical feature that ever drew anyone's attention. If my eyes were my best feature, my mouth had to be my worst. My mouth was small, but that wasn't the most deplorable part—that would be my lips. They were devastatingly thin, so thin, in fact, that to me it appeared as if I had none; they were simply nonexistent in my mind, and standing next to my beautiful sister with her full, plump lips always made me feel worse.

Plain was the best I could expect of myself. Ever since I was big enough to refer to myself in descriptive words, I called myself *Plain Jane.* My name is not Jane, of course. My name is actually exceptionally pretty. It never did match. Aralyn Paige Liddell, that's my name. My parents called me Ara; my sister, Laila Elise, called me Air. I preferred Aralyn. I insisted upon it, in fact. It was pretty, my one pretty attribute. I determined to hang on to the one thing about myself someone could refer to as pretty, and people always did comment on the beauty of my name.

I was born in southern Mississippi on July 31, 1976. We lived in the small town of Escatawpa not far from the coast. The town inherited its name from the Indian name given to the river running through it. The history of that name was a story the people of our little town always told with an air of pride. The Choctaw Indians traveled yearly to the area because cane grew abundantly on the outskirts of the river. They cut the cane to use in weaving their baskets—hence the name Escatawpa, which means to cut cane. I'd heard the story repeated throughout my life, and I was quite fond of it myself. I took on the pride of it all.

My father, Robert Liddell, grew up in Escatawpa. His

father had been the post master in our little town. My dad had three brothers and three sisters, Sean, Brian, Evelyn, Derek, Nicole, and Traci—in that order. My father came after Nicole, so he was next to the baby. With a family of eight, the pay of a post master did not go far. While my grandpaw Jack worked hard, they barely scrapped by. My grandmother had died giving birth to Traci, so things were a little more than strained. The older three took care of the little ones while Grandpaw worked; it was an expected responsibility.

The small town lacked entertainment and recreation. The school had a couple of dances a year, but other than that, a bunch of teenagers would gather together, jump into someone's big car, and head down to Lake Drive-in, a drive-in theatre on the coast in Pascagoula, and that is where my dad met my mother, Meredith. She came from a small, well-off family. Her father owned Daisy's, a popular department store in the city. He named it after my great-grandmother Daisy, his mother. My mother was a beautiful woman. Her hair was raven-black, and her skin was milky-white—minus the sun-kisses. She had rich, mahogany-brown eyes lined with long, thick, feathery lashes. Her features, with the exception of her full lips, were petite and perfect.

My father bumped into her at the concession stand. Their eyes met, and my mother looked into his bright-blue eyes and blushed from embarrassment. Courteously, Daddy insisted on replacing the drink and popcorn my mom had dropped. He introduced himself, and that was that. From that moment on, they were always together. They spent most of their time at J & J's Restaurant on Market Street. It was the place to be, and it was there on August 17, 1970, that my daddy proposed to my mom. Daddy and Momma both told the story so many times in such detail that Laila and I felt we were watching it take place on the big screen.

Talking to his buddy Tony Phillips about the decision he had made, Daddy slipped the ring from his pocket and discreetly showed it to him. "I'm gonna do it tonight, right here," he said as he looked to Tony for his reaction.

Tony gave him a firm pat on the shoulder and laughed. "Congratulations man. I'm sure she'll say yes." Daddy let out a slight sigh of relief and headed toward momma. As he approached her, she was laughing with her friend Lydia Broadus. Both girls were set to start their senior year in high school and were excited about the concept. Daddy had just recently graduated and went to work immediately at a small automotive shop as a mechanic.

As he came near to Momma, he reached out his hand to grab hers. "Lydia, do you mind if I borrow Meredith for a few minutes?"

"Yes, actually I do, Robert. You'll have to make your requests in advance in the future." She chuckled.

Daddy held her hand tight and led her to sit down in a corner booth. His hands trembled as he reached in his pocket. "Meredith, I've been thinkin' 'bout my future. I'm never gonna be wealthy, but I'm a hard worker. I know I can't give you the kind of home you're used to, but if you'd marry me, I'd do my best to make you happy." He slipped out the box and opened it, revealing a small diamond ring.

My mother's eyes flooded with tears as she screamed, "Yes!" and threw herself across the table into my daddy's arms.

My grandparents threw a hissy fit—that's what my mom refers to it as—when she said yes to my dad's proposal. They felt she deserved a better life than the one he could give her, so as soon as momma graduated, they ran off together, eloping.

It seemed to be a very romantic story. They rented a small apartment for the first couple of years, saved money, and bought a small piece of property. My dad, with the help of his brothers, built a small framed house in Escatawpa. He worked lovingly on it in the evenings and on weekends. When it was done, they moved into a small two-bedroom house, our home.

Before long my father came home to my mother with fear spread across her face and tears in her eyes. She was pregnant and scared. My grandparents hadn't spoken to her since she had run off to marry my dad, and she longed for the comfort only a mother could give. Daddy went to their house to try and make amends for Momma's sake and to tell them they were going to be grandparents. Grandma and Grandpa weren't happy about it until the day my sister was born. She looked so much like their precious little girl that they both broke down and cried. Laila softened their hearts with her beauty and brought a broken family back together.

My grandparents insisted they be allowed to provide the clothing for Laila. She was the best-dressed baby around. Two years later I came along, and the offer extended to me as well. For my whole life my grandparents have taken Laila and me on four shopping sprees a year at Daisy's, so while we lived in one of the smallest houses in town, we were very well dressed. For my sister that, combined with her beauty, meant popularity. For me it meant I had access to pretty clothes.

In the beginning I picked out fluffy, frilly dresses because I was attracted to their beauty, but that changed the day I realized I was plain and my sister was beautiful. I was five years old. Laila and I had been helping Mom pick up pine cones in the yard. We had worked extremely hard that day; loads of pine cones covered the yard. I had quite a few pricks in my fingers from their pointed scales. After I started school, I made sure I found out the name of my stabbing enemy that seemed to enjoy inflicting pain upon my hands. Umbo. That was his name. He sat at the tip of each scale waiting for his prey. Of course, he was really trying to protect the seed from predators, but (considering that our yard was full of pine trees, and it was my job to pick up their by-products) I took his attacks personally.

On this particular day Mom decided to reward us

by taking us to TG&Y. "You both did a really good job today," she said as she kissed us both on the forehead. "Go inside and clean up, and I'll take you to TG&Y to pick out a toy for all your hard work." We both took off in a flash, washed up, and headed to our favorite store.

Laila and I stood in the aisle and rummaged through the Barbie dolls. From the corner of my eye, I caught a glimpse of a woman as she approached my mom. "Meredith? Is that you?" she asked.

Mom turned to see who belonged to the voice. "Vicki?" my mom questioned in return.

"Yes, oh my gosh! I haven't seen you since high school. How are you?" Vicki asked, grabbing my mom and squeezing her in a tight bear-hug.

"I'm great. How are you?" Mom choked out through windless lungs.

Vicki released her grip and answered, "Wonderful. I just came into town to visit my brother and his wife. He has a little boy now, so I stopped here to pick him up a gift for his birthday. My husband is a lawyer at a firm in New York, so we don't make it down too often." She caught a glimpse of my sister in her peripheral vision and turned to gaze upon her. "Oh, my gosh! Meredith, this has to be your daughter. She is without a doubt the most beautiful girl I have ever laid my eyes on," she gasped. "You should seriously consider taking her to a modeling agency. This is a girl who should be in magazines," she said as she caressed the side of Laila's face.

A bright smile crossed my mom's face, and an air of

pride radiated like a sheen through her eyes and over her cheeks as the corners of her mouth stretched to meet her eyes. In that instant I saw very clearly that my mother felt the same way—to her Laila was the most beautiful girl in the world. So, who was I?

"Thank you," she replied. "This is my Laila," she said as she wrapped her arm affectionately around my sister's shoulder and squeezed her tight. "And this is my youngest, Aralyn," she said as she tousled my short, matted hair.

"Aralyn, what a pretty name," Vicki replied. My heart sank as I realized the only nice thing she could say about me was that she thought my name was pretty.

"We call her Ara," my mom said, informing her friend of my nickname.

I quickly interjected, "I like Aralyn better." If my name were the only thing about me she could see as deserving a compliment, then I was going to insist that it stick.

The following week Mom took us to church to see Grandma and Grandpa. They went to a Methodist church in Pascagoula. I stood at the closet door and examined my dresses trying to decide which one to wear. Laila never picked out frills; she didn't like them. She always dressed stylish and looked beautiful, but she preferred simple dresses. I daydreamed about living in the movies Mom and Dad watched where the ladies wore big, beautiful dresses. *Gone with the Wind* was my mother's favorite movie. I climbed upon her lap late one night to watch it with her. "I want to live in that house, Momma." I pointed to Tara.

"Yeah, that would be nice, wouldn't it, dear," she replied with a sigh.

"Oh, Momma! Look at the pretty lady with the beautiful dress. I want to wear dresses like hers. What is it, Momma?"

"It's called *Gone with the Wind*," she answered me. For the longest time I thought the dresses were called Gone with the Wind. The dresses were what I was referring to, and that was Mom's response. I used to tell Grandma I wanted to go to the Gone with the Wind section of the store. Grandma always laughed and took me to the section overflowing with lacy, frilly dresses.

That Sunday I picked out a yellow dress. Tacked with a beautiful white bow right at the waist line, the front of the skirt gathered from the hem and revealed layers of white ruffles underneath. The same white ruffles trimmed the short, puffy sleeves. Smaller white bows lined the bodice, starting at the neckline, and ran down the center of the bodice until they met the bigger white bow that held the gathered skirt in place. *This is the one you will wear today, Plain Jane,* I said to myself.

I stepped into the dress and pulled it up over my shoulders, slipping my arms through the sleeve holes. "Laila, can you button me up?" I asked.

"Sure," she mumbled back as she glided toward me with her graceful gait. "You look pretty in yellow," she commented as she straightened my yellow headband securely in place.

A bright smile glistened across my face. "Thank you," I whispered. The dress made me feel pretty. Not that I was pretty at all; I knew better than that, but wearing a beautiful dress detracted from my plainness. In my mind my plain features were overpowered by the luxurious beauty of the dress. A lovely dress covered with lace and frills could enhance even the plainest of girls, and I was plain.

That day at church a rich elderly lady who knew my grandma approached my mom. "Meredith, look at you, all grown up with children of your own. Your mom is so proud of these girls," she said as she hugged my mom.

"Yeah, Mom really adores 'em," Momma responded.

Then the lady did something that stuck with me and made me realize for the first time one way I could combat being plain. She placed her hands on either side of Laila's face, bent over, and looked into her eyes. "Look at those eyes. You have got the most beautiful eyes I have ever seen, and with that complexion, you should be in pageants, dear." Then she turned her gaze upon me and ran her hand gracefully down my dress. "You look so cute in that dress, dear," she proclaimed. She glanced at my mom, patted her on the shoulder, and said, "Hope to see you again soon." She strolled off toward the next unsuspecting family, or maybe they were expecting her, who knows? What I did know was she thought my dress made me look cute, and cute was better than plain.

My clothing was my secret weapon—a defensive weapon, of course. Deflecting people's attention away from my plain features, my outfits shrouded me with beauty and grace. I would never be able to hear the word *beautiful,* but as long as I had my grandma and the clothes from Daisy's, I could camouflage my plainness and maybe even be considered cute. At least that was what I thought until I started school.

CHAPTER 2

THE INVISIBLE INTELLECTUAL

School was a different story. I imagined other children would think in the same fashion as the elderly lady from Grandma's church, but I was destined to find out otherwise.

I woke up extremely early on my first day of school—an internal alarm clock, I suppose. I didn't sleep well that night. I tossed and turned all night long. Aside from the occasional visit to Grandma's church, I was never around people, and if I ever were, I froze in fear—not knowing what to say as incompetence ran over me like hot oil being poured on my head and slowly and painfully oozing its way down over my entire body and finding its destination at my feet. It always left a burning heat in its wake. The sheer idea of being around people made me excruciatingly nervous. My stomach, contorted in a horrendous tangled mass, felt like the huge knot in the rope that hung from the big oak out back that Laila and I swung on all the time; the longer we wrapped our feet around that humongous entanglement and swung each other around, the more taut it became. That's how my stomach felt. The closer the hour hand on the living room clock got to 7:00, the tighter the lump felt. I swear it looked like the minute hand was flying by at the speed you would imagine a second hand to be doing.

I stood at the closet and contemplated what to wear. I knew I wanted to use one of my secret weapons, a pretty dress. I picked out a light-blue dress with dusty-blue trim work. A dusty-blue, circular collar embellished the rounded neckline. I adored short, puffy sleeves, and of course, it had them. A wide dusty-blue sash wrapped securely around the bodice, and a dusty-blue ribbon laced its way through the hem of the gathered skirt. *This is pretty. The blue will match my eyes; of course, no one will be looking at me; they'll be looking at the dress for sure,* I thought to myself. I ran a brush through my short, blah hair and waited for Laila to finish dressing. While I waited, with huge, wide eyes locked on the clock watching the time race by right in front of me, I stood as still as stone in the living room.

Since it was my first day of school, Mom walked me to my class. The school was small compared to the ones in Moss Point or Pascagoula. A large sign stood in front of the school that read "Escatawpa Elementary."

The red brick building had three sets of double doors standing side by side at the front entrance. Mom had to pry me from the back seat of our sky-blue, four-door 1975 Plymouth Valiant. Once she won the battle of pulling me from the car, I silently gave in. I was a big girl, so I held back the tears and took it like a champ. Entering the building, I eyed my surroundings and saw the door to the attendance and principal's office tucked in the wall to the right of the entrance. Three tables sat in the middle of the large walkway with poster board signs hanging from each one. My mother approached the lady sitting at the table that read first-and second-grade classes. Mom gave her my name. Shoving her glasses to the bridge of her nose, the woman quickly looked through her small stack of papers. Giving my mom directions to my class, she pointed through the line of double doors at the opposite end of the walkway.

As we approached the class room, I slipped my hand from my mother's and quietly walked through the door. Looking at my feet, I hesitantly stepped toward my new teacher. With my head hung down, I glanced up at her through the shades created by my thick, dark lashes. She was a short, rather large woman wearing a huge grin that spread from ear to ear. "Hello." Her eyes glanced upward to my mother while her face continued to smile toward me.

"Aralyn," my mom answered her unspoken question.

"Aralyn. What a beautiful name you have, dear. Why don't you come with me," she said as she held her hand out to me, gesturing for me to take it and follow her.

Oh, no, another 'what a beautiful name.' Not even a 'what a beautiful dress. You look so cute in it.' Maybe I can shoot for total invisibility, I mused.

"My name is Ms. Beck," she informed me as she led me to a desk at the front of the classroom. Placing my spiral notebook and my pencil on the desk in front of me, I quietly took my seat. Afraid to look around at the others in the class, I sat and stared at the notebook.

It seemed like forever passed before Ms. Beck stepped to the front of the class with a roll book in her hands. She proceeded to call out all the names from the list, making sure to make a seating chart as she went through. Being sure that my voice stayed silent, I gave a timid gesture when my name was called. "All right, children, remember where you are seated today. This will be your assigned seat for the year," she insisted in a friendly yet stern tone.

The day was filled with the mundane task of the teacher issuing us our books. We received the very basics: a reading book, a math book, and a Grammar book. Ms. Beck reviewed the colors and shapes that those who went to kindergarten knew well. Those, like myself, who didn't attend a nearby kindergarten paid close attention. We did a finger-paint project that included three circles—one red, one yellow, and one green.

"This is a red-light," Ms. Beck explained. "This tells your mom and dad whether they can go, if they need to slow down, or if they have to stop when they are driving a vehicle."

It took what seemed like a century for the day to drag on. I enjoyed the finger-painting, but that was about it. A wide grin crossed my face when I realized the day was over and mom would be picking me up soon.

The second day of school started out much the same—twisted mass in my stomach included, but the one major difference was the ride to and from school. Mom decided I could ride the bus with Laila. It wasn't so bad; Laila allowed me to sit with her.

"You can sit with me for now, but as soon as you make a friend, you need to sit with whoever she is, okay?" she insisted with a hard stare, studying my eyes for my comprehension level.

Being the pretty, popular girl was important to her already. She didn't want to be embarrassed by the fact that she had to babysit her little sister on the bus. She loved me, but she loved her friends more. She was the total opposite of me, beautiful and confident. Her confidence kept her talking and making friends non-stop. She never met a stranger. She talked to anyone and everyone. She was friendly to all, but, of course, she stuck with the popular crowd when it came to friends.

On the other hand, I had not spoken to one person the previous day. My name was adored by my teacher, but my dress didn't seem to draw anyone's attention; rather, I seemed to be overlooked all together— nonexistent. My plan had worked; I was the Invisible Woman. I kind of liked that idea. The Invisible Woman was one of my favorite cartoon characters. She used her invisibility to fight evil. *Maybe someday I could do the same,* I thought to myself. Besides that, I was comfortable with invisibility. Despite my apparent transparency, I still clung to my theory that pretty dresses could camouflage my plainness. Then the thought occurred to me, maybe my dress was the cloak that hid me.

Weeks later when I got to school, I walked quietly to my desk never looking up from my feet. I sat and waited for Ms. Beck's instructions to begin. I moved rather slowly when it came to pulling out my work, but I finished each task with more speed and accuracy than any other child in the class. Considering the swiftness with which I picked up on each new concept, I was surprised and anxious when Ms. Beck sent a note home with me informing my mother that she desired a conference. It simply stated that she was concerned about my leisureliness in class.

My mom walked into the empty classroom with deliberate caution. I sat down in a chair by the door. Mom looked warily toward the teacher and braced herself for a rebuttal in her parenting skills. She had frequently seen teachers treat young mothers with disdain, reproving their inadequacies in rearing children correctly. Mom knew most teachers weren't like that, but ironically, it seemed to be the aged spinsters who never married and never had any children of their own who seemed to think they knew the formula for rearing the perfect child. Mom had already reprimanded me for daydreaming in class rather than paying attention to every syllable that departed the teacher's lips. I tried to assure her that I had, but she just gave me a look that pierced through with the warning of an impending spanking.

When the meeting ensued, Ms. Beck informed my mom that I had the highest average in the class. "My concern for your daughter is not with her grades or abilities; she has the highest average in class in every subject," she said, pulling out her grade book and placing it in front of my mother. "She is obviously a brilliant child, but she moves so slowly. When I ask the children to pull out a book, she stands to her feet, kneels down beside her desk, pulls out all of her books, goes through them one by one until she finds the proper one, and then she places that book to the side, assembles the remainder of them back into a neat stack, places them in her desk, and slowly stands to her feet before sitting back in her desk."

"I don't understand," my mom uttered. "What seems to be the problem?" she questioned Ms. Beck.

"It's not that there's a problem necessarily for her. You see, I have to wait for her to retrieve her book before I can begin instructing the class. She is actually wasting my time, Mrs. Liddell. I've tried to talk to her and make her understand that she needs to quickly pull her book out, but she insists that she must do it properly." Ms. Beck looked at my mom with concern. "I don't want to offend you, but your daughter is using up five to seven minutes every time I have them pull out a book. Perhaps this doesn't impact her grades, but it can cause negative consequences on the other students' grades if they do not have sufficient time to grasp the lessons."

Awareness of the situation flickered across my mom's face. "I see," she responded. "Robert and I will have a talk with Aralyn tonight, Ms. Beck. I am sorry about your time being wasted. We'll see what we can do to alleviate the situation. Is there a particular structure you use when teaching? What I mean is, is there a set time that you begin certain subjects?"

"Yes, there is actually. Maybe that will help. Here is a list of what time I begin each new subject." Ms. Beck scribbled a quick series of words on a teeny piece of paper and passed it to my mom. "Maybe you and your husband can help to train her to prepare herself ahead of time. It would be no problem for her; she seems to be finished with each task with time to spare."

"Thank you. We'll talk to her tonight. Again, I'm sorry for any problems this has caused for you or any student."

"Think nothing of it, Mrs. Liddell. That's what the conference is for, to deal with problems swiftly. Have a nice evening. I'll be in touch soon."

That was that. My mom stood and left the room, grabbing my arm with a slight jerk as she pulled me along with her.

That night after my dad got home from work, Mom called him to their bedroom immediately after supper. I tiptoed to their locked bedroom door and placed my ear gently to it. "I'll go to TG&Y immediately and buy her a watch so she can keep track of the time," my father said, his voice stern. "Meredith, don't you dare be harsh on her. It is who she is. She has always moved around slow and done things in a particular fashion. Apparently it has no bearing on her intelligence level. All ninety-nines and one-hundreds! She should be rewarded not scolded because you were embarrassed by the fact that you had to have a conference with the teacher." My daddy was taking up for me. My mom had given me a couple of stark looks during the meeting. I had sat quietly with my head hung low.

"Rober..." I heard my mom spout out before being quickly interrupted by my superhero dad.

"I know you, Meredith. You hate it when someone makes you feel that you're not the best at everything. Aralyn's being slow paced is *not* a reflection on your parenting abilities, and just because you may feel that part of her personality caused you to feel inadequate as a parent...well, I'm not gonna let you take it out on her."

With that I heard my dad's large footsteps bearing down on the wooden floor boards, heading in my direction. I swiftly took off on my tiptoes running across the room like a flash of lightning. I caught my breath as I came to an abrupt halt in the living room. Dad passed by me with a solemn look on his face. He turned to face me, his eyes full of warmth and pride. He gave me a slight smile and headed for the front door.

I realized as the door shut behind my father that there was another weapon at my disposal; I was intelligent. A brainiac! I set my mind at that moment to utilize my new weapon. There was more to me than being just plain; I was not just a simple girl in a pretty dress who happened to be overlooked by all her peers. I was an *Invisible Intellectual*. I devoted myself to the development of my secret weapons. The Invisible Girl (I wasn't quite to the woman stage yet) had an arsenal that could defeat any attack. I was quite positive of that fact until during my fourth-grade year when I received the blow that knocked the wind from me and left me wounded and bleeding on the cafeteria floor. The wound was the gaping hole in my courage, and the blood that ran freely from it was all of my new-found confidence.

CHAPTER 3

THE UGLY DUCKLING

By the time fourth grade rolled around, reading was one of my passions. The more books I could get my hands on, the more information I could fill my mind with, and the more information my mind held in its many folds and creases, the more intelligent I became. My mind was quickly becoming a huge data base filled with facts that helped Daddy and me defeat Mom and Laila when we played Trivial Pursuit, but facts were not the only thing I desired for my brain to pass from neuron to neuron and store somewhere in the cerebral cortex.

I loved to read and write great stories with happy endings. I desired to live amongst the fairytales where the nobody became a somebody. My most treasured story was one I had recently penned myself; it was the tale of a heroine who had lived her life looking into the cracked mirror that hung above her dresser. She had only been able to see the distorted reflection that shimmered in the looking glass. One day as she strolled through the woods she came across a small creek. As she bent over to scoop her hand into the water and drink, she saw her true reflection. She was not disfigured and plain as she had thought, but rather she was beautiful. That was the storyboard I had conjured up for my life—well, the one I hoped my life would play out.

From the world of books, there was the story of a peasant boy finding an old lamp with a genie hidden inside whom, after being freed from his horrid prison, was thrilled to be able to grant a few wishes. There was also the triumphant story of an orphaned boy finding a magical sword buried in a stone. He was the only one able to remove the sword from its permanent residence, and, of course, there was the fable of the giant Irishman, Finn MacCoul, who defeated the much larger giant through the wit of his wife, but my favorite of all was *The Ugly Duckling*. I suppose the story of the beautiful swan born believing he was a duckling grabbed my heart and ran away with it from the moment I read the first few pages. You see, even the duckling's mother, who loved him dearly, thought he didn't compare to his siblings who hatched alongside him. It seemed to mirror my life because I knew my mother thought Laila was the most beautiful of all. The story gave me hope that one day I would find a group in which I could fit and belong; then maybe I would spread my wings and realize *that amongst those with whom I belong, I AM beautiful.*

I found myself submerging in the worlds of these ordinary characters who turned out to be extraordinary people with amazing gifts, abilities, and talents. The stories, along with my own intelligence level, gave me hope, a hope that made me feel my lack of beauty could be overridden by a combination of my intelligence and fashion, but deep inside of me, a seed of doubt concerning it all lay dormant.

Doubt formed the hard shell of the seed and encapsulated the life of a fragile little girl, and locked securely away inside that hard shell lived the soul of a little girl who *desperately* wanted to be pretty. She knew in her heart of hearts no matter how fluffy and ruffled her dresses were that the feelings of confidence that arose from those defensive weapons could never replace the elation of knowing someone thought she was pretty. They could only protect the little girl hiding behind the thick, strong walls of doubt. The light and essence of her soul that lay trapped in fear and rejection often pondered the idea that *if just one person believed she was beautiful, then maybe she could believe it herself.* Believing it of herself was the key to cracking the hard shell of doubt and allowing the light of the little girl inside to burst forth and shine with complete confidence and a bright smile of joy.

Joy was missing from my life. I wasn't happy with myself, so joy could not reside within me. Yes, I felt occasional pleasure and momentary happiness, but these feelings came as I left my own reality and entered the worlds that awaited me inside the pages of the books that sparked tiny flickers of hope. It usually didn't take too long after closing the hard covers encasing my fantasy worlds before reality once again set in. I determined within myself that I would use my defensive weapons to hide my insecurities and enter the fourth grade with the confidence that came from wrapping the invisibility shield around the seed of doubt. After all, if no one, including myself, could see the little girl I called Plain Jane hiding beneath those walls, then she could be ignored and the only girl seen would be the smart, confident Aralyn.

When I woke up on the first day of my fourth-grade year (which happened to fall two weeks late because of Hurricane Elena which hit on Labor Day of 1985), I went about finding the perfect dress for the new year. I found a red dress trimmed with white lace. I was quite positive my mother would give me "the eye," the look she often gave when she was displeased with something, and I felt certain she would be displeased with me dressing up on the first day of school after a hurricane. Life had yet to return to normal, and a fancy dress guaranteed a more difficult wash day. A wave of guilt hit me as I contemplated that fact, but the need to be invisible was more powerful.

As I pulled the dress from the rod, I whispered to myself, "Okay, Sue, do your stuff. It's time to use your super power of invisibility. We have to work together to hide Plain Jane. She needs your protection."

I often talked to my dresses as if they embodied Sue Storm, the Invisible Woman. By cloaking myself with her, I became the Invisible Girl. I felt a surge of power as I slipped the dress over my head and absorbed her super power—the ability to be invisible. Sue was my best friend. She had saved me on a daily basis since I had found her.

"Laila, can you tie my dress, please?" I hollered from the closet.

Dressed in her new pink Converse high-tops, tight-rolled gray trousers attached to pink suspenders, and a pink top, Laila rushed in and quickly pulled my sash tight with enough force to knock the wind from me. "Huhhhh," I heaved. "Ouch, Laila," I spurted out breathlessly. "What was that for?"

"I don't have time to help you dress, Air. Learn how to do this for yourself or else get Momma to do it."

"Jeez! Sorry, you've *always* helped me," I responded; then I filled my tone with sarcasm and added, "Fine. I won't ask again. Sorry I bothered you." I rolled my eyes and heaved a heavy sigh.

"Good. I have to hot roll my hair. I'm starting the sixth grade. I have to look my best. It takes time to fix your hair stylish, Air. I know you probably don't understand it all 'cause you're not really in my class of friends, but I have to roll my hair, spray it down with hair spray, let the rollers sit for a while and cool, then I have to take them down, brush it out, tease it, and spray it some more. It's very complicated, but everybody who's anybody knows the bigger the better, so I want my hair to be the biggest!"

"Oh, big hair is what's pretty?" My mind swiftly tucked away the need to learn all the details of how to hot roll and tease my hair. I decided then and there to follow Laila to the bathroom to watch and learn.

"Yeah, it's like totally awesome!" she squealed with an unusual accent. She sounded like she was trying to be someone else or somethin'. She was definitely not using proper English; that's for sure.

"Why are you talkin' that way? It's not correct English to say 'like totally awesome.' You should just say that it's awesome. It sounds much better that way."

"It's valley-girl talk, Air. Uhh, never mind." She rolled her eyes in a mocking way. "My geeky little sister would have to harass me about my grammar," she whispered under her breath as she walked away.

I tiptoed my way to the bathroom and stood silently outside the opened door. I watched closely as she separated her hair into sections and combed through small pieces before wrapping them around the fat rollers she pulled from the white tray. She rolled each one close to her head and stuck metal hook-looking things through them to secure them in place; then she sprayed over her entire head with a *lot* of hairspray. After she emptied what seemed to be an entire spray can on her head, she turned to exit the bathroom; I ducked back and slipped away without her noticing me. Laila would have kicked my butt and made fun of me if she had caught me spying on her. She was nice to me most of the time, but over the summer before entering the sixth grade, she had gotten all into her friends and doing cool stuff and looking *fine*. She gave me a hard time about following her around, especially if her friends were at the house. They usually sneered and asked why I was around. She always responded to that with a shove and a shout to mind my own business.

When I arrived at school, I found out quickly that my homeroom teacher, Mr. Barnett, believed in giving a challenge. I was ecstatic! It was a class I could thrive in. He was a stern teacher who gave demerits for infractions and disruptions in class. Once a child reached the much-feared ten demerits, it was off to the office to get a paddling. Of course, I knew I would never be in need of his strict discipline; I had already disciplined myself. A bright smile crossed my face as he scribbled across the dark green chalk board the words *Extra Credit*. Under the words was the title of a book we could read and write a short report on for extra points on our overall grade. I knew I wouldn't be in need of the extra points, but reading was one of my favorite pastimes—I loved it.

Mr. Barnett set the standard of the book a little higher than what our reading level should have been, and that thrilled me all the more. The book was *Anne of Green Gables*. I sighed at the thought of it as I pulled my pencil from its groove on the wooden desk and sketched the name of the book on the first sheet of blank paper in my seventy page spiral notebook; then I looked up with a smile and prepared myself for the intriguing day that lay ahead of me.

Two months had passed, and the year seemed to be moving along smoothly. I kept to myself as always. I still in all my years in school thus far had not reached out and made a friend. I just couldn't seem to get past the feelings of inferiority that ran over me like hot lava every time I even imagined approaching one of the girls in class. The Invisible Girl didn't give me a sense of boldness; she just did a good job of masking me over with a protective shield—being friendless didn't bother me as much that way.

Half-way through my first grade year, Laila had given up on me finding a friend on the bus and left me to sit by myself. Every once in a while a kid would sit next to me out of necessity, but I kept my focus forward and my mouth shut. They were usually older kids who kept their bodies facing the walkway so as not to pay attention to the plain girl sitting next to the window. Occasionally I would pivot my head to peer out the window and view the surroundings of huge oaks and tall pines as we passed in order to imagine away the person sitting next to me. It was there in the reflection from the window that I would find Sue, always sitting next to me. It filled me with confidence to know that her gift of invisibility surrounded me, and after realizing her presence, I would resign myself to the idea that I simply wasn't seen by my neighbor because Sue was protecting me.

My weaponry, Sue's invisibility (infused into my

dresses) and my brain, had given me a new measure of confidence that had kept me strong since the day I realized I had them both at my disposal. Of course, my confidence was never the type that allowed me to speak or to be noticed; it was simply the ability to quietly exist amongst my peers and know that I could endure. I could walk into class with my head held high and smile at the teacher when he commented on my paper as he handed me back my ninety-eight or ninety-nine, very seldom did I make below that.

One day as I stood in the long line in the cafeteria awaiting my tray of yucky food, yucky was really the only way to describe the cafeteria food, I looked across the cafeteria to the line on the other side of the room. I spotted Laila and watched as she laughed and giggled with her mesh of friends surrounding her. *It must be nice to have a slew of friends to laugh with,* I thought to myself.

I wish I was as pretty as her, I reflected. Then from out of the blue I heard a familiar voice speak from somewhere in my mind. "You just read *Anne of Green Gables.* Don't you remember what Diana Barry said to Anne? Remember, she told Anne that being smart was better than being pretty," Sue encouraged me with her usual gift of wise words from the stacks of books we had read. "And who did Gilbert Blythe fall in love with?" she added, giving her words an extra punch of inspiration. I thought of her words, and then looked back across the room and set my eyes upon my sister.

As I gazed upon her and her friends having a good time waiting in the lunch line, my mind drifted and imagined myself in her position. I saw myself beautiful, much like Laila, *and* smart. It felt good to fantasize something that surpassed even Laila's experiences. Sure, she was beautiful, but she was not smart. She was average when it came to grades.

It was at that point, while my mind was fixated on imagining away my awkwardness and plainness and seeing myself popular like my sister with friends who adored me, that I received the blow that knocked me to the cafeteria floor. From the corner of my eye, I saw him approach wearing a pair of tight-fitting, shiny, black parachute pants covered with zippers. The boys who wore those pants were usually the super cool guys who liked to break dance; they were one of the trademarks of break dancers. He had the sleeves of his loose white t-shirt stylishly rolled. He was obviously a sixth-grader and a popular one. He just had that look of superiority that often radiated through their countenances like high-pitched sound waves screaming out their superciliousness. His height was average, but his shoulders were very broad. He had the kind of stature that shrieked, "Don't mess with me unless you wanna get stomped to the floor!" He carried himself with a particular strut that whistled by with an air of arrogance with each stride.

When he reached me, he came to an abrupt halt, turned to face me, and peered directly into my face with his beady eyes. His round face and his narrow eyes intimidated me. He stood there for what seemed like an hour and scanned me over, just staring. Frightened, I inhaled a sharp breath. His fists clenched as the oscillating fan blew our way and ruffled his dark-brown hair. Being shaken from his intense stare, his black eyes wandered around the room, quickly viewing the witnesses who encircled us.

His eyes cut back to my face and caught me in their glare. A trance suddenly came over me, and I could no longer move. My breathing stopped as if it were cut off by some invisible monster that attached itself to my face and sucked all the oxygen out of my lungs in much the same way that a vampire would drain the blood from a body, but this monster lived off the breath of life rather than the blood of its victims. No matter how hard I tried, I couldn't breathe. My face turned ghostly white as I stood under his menacing glare unable to catch my breath.

Once he sensed my weakness and helplessness, he pulled back the fist of words that he was about to unleash and pound right into my gut; then from his curled lips he spewed, "You're *UGLY!*" As the two powerful words flowed from his mouth with all their force and might, their punch cut through me, leaving a gaping hole in the center of my body.

The cut ran so deep that all the confidence I had mustered from my cloak of invisibility and my intelligence drained from my body like blood flowing from a severed jugular. The flow was rapid and unstoppable. My forehead wrinkled in pain, and I was finally able to muster a soft, "Huh." At the sound of my weak gasp of air, my eyes filled with tears. The mystery sixth-grader sneered, turned, and walked away. As I watched him amble back to his side of the cafeteria through the well of water that distorted my view, I whispered to myself, "I will never turn into the beautiful swan, will I, Sue? I will forever be just an *Ugly Duckling.*"

At that precise moment Sue rose up. She gathered the torn pieces of my body and patched me back together. The pieces were being held together by one tiny thread. Sue reminded me as she placed each piece back in its proper position that we had seen the answer to beauty on the first day of school. "All we have to do is incorporate big hair into our life," she whispered as she threaded the strand of hope and then stitched me back together with the only remaining possibility either of us could see.

CHAPTER 4

HUMPTY DUMPTY

The next morning I woke up an hour early and crept out of bed; I tiptoed my way to the bathroom and opened the cabinet as quietly as I could. Right up front sat the object of my desire—Laila's hot rollers. A bright grin stretched across my face. Tilting my head out of the bathroom, my eyes shot toward our bedroom door while my ears perked up and listened for the sounds of Laila's soft snores. Hearing the signal all was well, I set about my task.

I gently set the rollers on the counter and plugged them in as I whispered to myself, "If we're quiet enough, Sue, Laila will never hear us, and if she never hears us, she'll never know we used her rollers." I paused for a moment as I contemplated the fact that my fashionable hair would most definitely give me away. "I wonder...Come on, Sue; I need your invisibility to sneak into Momma and Daddy's bathroom. If Momma has rollers, then Laila can think I used hers. She'll never know the difference."

Much to my surprise, Momma didn't have a set of hot rollers. She must have given hers to Laila. She was always good about giving us her things if we needed them or even if we simply desired them. I suppose that is what a mother does. I decided then and there that Laila screaming at me was worth being beautiful if I never had to experience the trauma of being called ugly again. I timed the rollers (remembering that Laila, in telling me of how time consuming being beautiful was, had mentioned that they took about twenty minutes to heat up properly).

When twenty minutes had passed, I set about combing and parting my hair. I attempted, as best I could, rolling my hair the way I had seen Laila roll hers. As I pulled each roller from its heating element, I felt the stinging heat burn its way through my digits. When I finished, the tips of my fingers were red from it. I stood staring at my blistering tips and deliberated if it was really worth the pain or not. Every stinkin' roller had burnt me. It's not exactly easy to be quiet and invisible when you want to scream "Ouch" every minute or so.

When I finished setting the rollers, I sprayed my hair all over with her purple can of Aqua Net extra super hold hairspray. *Boy, extra super hold...Big hair must need a lot of sticky stuff to make it stick up and out,* I thought to myself. After another twenty minutes had passed, I hesitantly reached the tips of my fingers to one of the rollers to see if it had cooled down. As I quickly tapped the roller several times, I estimated from the warmth that another five minutes should be sufficient.

I thought about it and decided that now was a good time to go to the closet and pick out a dress. I picked out a colorful dress, a simple one with a layered skirt and printed with rainbow colored flowers. Since it was not as dressy as I usually wore, I found a pair of purple jelly shoes to match. After my five minutes expired, I slipped back into the bathroom. I very gently took down each roller. When I opened the drawer to retrieve the teasing comb, I eyed the clincher—the tool that would seal the deal. Tucked under a box of tissues, I spied make-up.

Laila would know that I used it for sure, but she was my sister; surely she would see my need to improve upon myself. I pulled out the case of eye shadow and imitated Laila. "This will be simple. She just makes a rainbow on her lids using these colors. What color should we use first, Sue?" I questioned my best friend as I peered at her through the mirror that hung above the lavatory.

I started with purple, stretching a thin line of it just above my eyelashes; then I dipped the sponge applicator in the royal blue and swept it across my lids just above the purple. Using the same sweeping motion, I applied the lavender and then the baby blue; then I finally topped it all off with an arch of pink. My eyelids glimmered with a rainbow of colors!

Slipping the shadow back into its place, I found a small tube of light pink lip gloss. I brushed it across my thin lips, blotted them together the way I had seen my mother do many times, and smiled. Time had raced by as I worked to make myself pretty. I looked down at my watch which always sat securely on my left wrist.

Daddy had purchased me a new watch every Christmas since my second-grade year. He had decided it was close enough to Christmas when I received my first watch, the watch he bought to help me stay ahead of the rest of the class so that no one got behind because of my "pokiness" (as mom referred to it), so when he came home from TG&Y that night, he suggested it was part of my Christmas as he wrapped it around my wrist and explained to me how to read it. He patiently gave me the instructions I needed to execute Mrs. Beck's plan for me.

"Here is the list showing you what time you will need to have what book on your desk," he said as he signaled for Mom to hand over the piece of paper from the meeting. "You start preparing for each lesson ten minutes ahead of time, all right?" he suggested.

"Yes, sir," I responded with my head hung low.

Daddy placed his thumb and forefinger on my chin and lifted it with a gentle tug. "Chin up, girl. Mommy and Daddy are not fussing at you, Aralyn. We are both very proud of you. You're very smart. We're just trying to help you. Understand?" he inquired while he peered into my eyes.

"Yes, sir," I answered. Daddy's eyes lit up, and a smile crossed his face. He leaned over and tenderly kissed my forehead. The memory of that night will forever be branded in my mind as the night my dad became my superhero and a special tradition was set in motion.

As I glared at the face of my watch, I was brought back to reality by the ticking of the long hand. "Five minutes!" I gasped. "Sue, Laila will be up in five minutes, and we still have to tease and spray our hair and...and...and then put everything away! We have to hurry. Boy, I sure wish you could give me the power of super speed," I whispered as I hunched my body over, hanging my head towards the floor. I grasped the teasing comb and ran it through my hair, teasing away at the roots. When I was certain I had done the best I could at it, I erected my head. I stared in the mirror and combed out the curls. I did my best to imitate Laila. Teasing my hair as I went, I would pull the comb through each curl.

When I finished, my hair was the biggest; that's for sure! I grabbed the purple can of spray and topped it off with a nice, thick coat of sticky goo. "One minute to go," I mumbled as I began frantically slipping the hot rollers back over their rods. I stuck the medal pins securely in their slot and put the lid back in its place; then I shoved the rollers back in the cabinet. As I turned to exit the bathroom, I froze in fear as I looked intently into my sister's eyes.

Sluggish and barely awake, she stood before me. I watched as she glanced me over, and awareness hit her in the face like a breeze of fresh, cool air on a hot summer day. Her groggy countenance rapidly contorted into an angry glower as she used her furrowed brows to aim and began shooting darts at me through her narrowed, black eyes. Her smooth, milky-white face flushed a brilliant red; then folding her plump lips over her teeth, she pressed her mouth into a hard line.

She inhaled a large gulp of air and lunged. "Aaaahhh, you put my make-up on and used my rollers!" she screamed as she wrapped her hands firmly around my shoulders, gripping so hard I was certain I would bruise, and shook me back and forth.

My head dropped. My eyes darted to the floor as tears streamed down my face. A lump formed in my throat, but I managed to mumble, "We just wanted to be pretty like you. We're sorry."

Laila knit her brows. "We?...Who is we?" she asked as she released her grip and softened her fierce glower.

"Me and Sue Storm—you know, The Invisible Woman. She's my best friend," I answered with full assurance as I raised my head to peer in her eyes.

"The Invisible Woman is your *best friend?*" she quizzed me with bewildered eyes as she folded her arms across her chest.

My eyes lit up like stars on a clear, crisp night. "Yes. Actually, she's my only friend. She helps me."

With worry-stained eyes she asked, "Have you ever told anybody about her? And how does she help you exactly?"

I looked up at my sister and assessed her disposition. Upon finding no anger or jest in her eyes, I answered, "You're the only person I've told...,and I'd like to keep it that way if you don't mind. Please don't say anything to Momma or Daddy, please, Laila."

"Don't worry. I won't, but you didn't tell me how she helps you, Air."

"She helps me to be invisible. People don't notice The Invisible Girl—that's who I am when I use her superpower. She doesn't have the superpower of speed though. Boy, I sure wish she did; that would definitely be helpful. Her invisibility shield usually does a good job of hiding how ordinary and plain I am, but it didn't work very well yesterday." I dropped my head and shook it. "Neither one of us are quite sure why." Lifting my head, I stroked my chin. "We're thinkin' that maybe he had some sort of amulet with a dark source of energy that radiates like waves of light. The light waves must hit the invisible shield that surrounds us. I figure an explosion of color must take place when the invisible cloak is struck by the light; it must leave the shield detectable. This would make it very easy for him to use some sort of evil x-ray vision to see through it."

"What happened yesterday, Air?" she pressed.

"Well, some sixth-grade boy told me I'm ugly. That means he saw me. If he didn't have some sort of evil power, then her shield must've been down, but she helped me hold back the tears and reminded me that you said big hair was the best. That's what makes a girl pretty, right? Oh, and make-up, too, so I decided to wake up early and use your stuff. I figured you'd be mad at me, but I decided that being pretty was worth your screaming at me. I am sorry. I should have just asked you, *but* it didn't occur to me to use your make-up until I saw it stickin' out from under the box of tissues in the drawer."

My sister stood speechless, which was very unusual for her. For some reason that morning we seemed to have walked through an energy field that reversed our roles. For the first time ever words spewed forth from my mouth like a raging river that reached its edge and the only thing left for it to do was to plunge head long off the cliff side creating a mighty waterfall full of force. My words were just that —forceful—, and they seemed to burrow themselves down into Laila, leaving her almost completely without words; that in itself was a miraculous event. I wondered if we had switched bodies like Jodie Foster and her mom in *Freaky Friday*.

Laila stood before me, her mouth agape. A state of shock had taken over her, freezing her in place. She stared at me with eyes of pity and disbelief. After a motionless moment or two she pulled the drawer open and grabbed the tease comb and a brush. "Here, let me help you with your hair. I can make it real pretty," she assured me.

I went to school that day with very big, pretty hair.

Laila sat with me on the bus that morning; it seemed that a bond had formed between us. My wounds from the previous day seemed to be healing rather nicely. I was able to step off the bus with a hint of confidence and assurance that all would be well. With Laila's and Sue's help, I felt I was facing my first *real* day of school.

All too soon lunch time rolled around, and my confidence started to seep from my stitched up wounds. A tight knot formed in the pit of my belly as I thought of the impending threat awaiting me in the cafeteria. *Will he be there? Will he approach me and glare as he did yesterday? Will he be able to see past Sue's obscure shield again? If he sees me, will he still think I'm ugly?* My mind raced with these thoughts as I entered the cafeteria and walked to the back of the line.

As I waited in line, I felt a surge of pain run through the lacerations left from the previous day. I realized my heart had begun to race at an accelerated speed. As my heart rate shot through the roof, it seemed as if I could feel the exact entry point of each gash. I squeezed my eyes shut and whispered, "Sue, you still there?" I felt a slight tugging at the incisions and decided that the stitches must've loosened from the pressure of my racing heart, and Sue was pulling the threads taut. Then without warning, I glanced across the room to see Laila and caught a glimpse of the dark-haired villain approaching. My heart began to pound!

Suddenly my arms and legs stiffened, and my

breathing became shallow and rapid. A great pressure closed in on my chest like the weight of deep, dark waters that trap you beneath their encumbrance and force. I was instantaneously trapped in the nightmare of being entombed under water and unable to find the surface no matter how vehemently I kicked and paddled my way upward. Eventually the nightmare ended as I was forced to inhale, breathing in the cold water and feeling it rush through and fill my lungs. Straightaway my breathing was utterly cut off.

My eyes, the only movable part of my body, glanced up from my solid state only to see him once again standing before me. Giving me a once over, his beady eyes started at the top of my head and worked their way down my body as he scanned over my new appearance. A slight grin broke out on his pudgy face. I stood as still as a stone still unable to breathe. He inhaled and let out a pleased sigh, "Hmm. You're pretty," he uttered as he continued to look me over.

At last I was able to breathe. The weight and burden of the dark waters lifted from my chest in an instant. The water that saturated my lungs only moments before seemed to dissipate in a flash. I silently sucked in a quick gasp of air, relieving my oxygen-depleted lungs. A feeling of victory washed over me, and a sense of power infused my veins. A rush of adrenaline found its way to my muscles and fortified them with strength. A gentle smile flitted across my face. It was the first time I had smiled at school without a teacher handing me a paper with a bold **A** scribbled across the top.

I felt a sense of worth rise within me. I detected warmth trickling through my wounds from the inside, sealing the tissues together as it ran. As the wounds began to heal (leaving no scars in their path), it felt as if the warmth carried with it a sense of elation, and the elation left behind a residue that could only be described as *joy*.

I quickly shifted my eyes to remove them from the sight of the white-clad knight situated in front of me wearing white pants and a white sports jacket covering a pale-blue shirt. The sleeves of the shirt and the jacket were neatly rolled together. He was sporting his Don Johnson look with pride. He waited until I glanced at him again; then he smiled and spouted, "Pretty *Ugly*!"

My eyes grew huge and instantly filled with pools of water. There was no holding back the tears that time. They burst forth as the dam of my lids crumbled under their pressure. A sinister smirk covered his face as he watched my reaction. He was evil! I had heard in Sunday school that the devil will try to appear as an angel of light and make you think he's good. Surely beneath his thick head of hair, two tiny horns were growing.

This time he didn't punch a hole through my belly. His target was my heart, and he ripped it completely out. I turned cold as the blood no longer pumped through my body. I was positive I was dead. I had to be; you can't live without your heart. I searched my mind for Sue's whisper, but it was not to be found. At that moment I thought of an old nursery rhyme—"Humpty Dumpty." I imagined Sue had left because she realized that like Humpty Dumpty, I could not be put back together again.

CHAPTER 5

THE WALL

To prevent the wails from coming forth, I threw my hands over my mouth and ran as fast as I could from the cafeteria. I burst through the office door squalling. "I...I...I...," I tried desperately to speak, but no more words were uttered. It felt as if they were trapped in my throat, which was being constricted by an unknown force.

Mrs. Natalie, with her bobbed, silky-black hair, came from behind the tall desk and wrapped her arms around me. "I'll call your mother, dear," she whispered in my ear as she tried to calm me down with her gentle pats. "Come, sit right here while I call her," she kindly insisted as she led me to the wooden bench leaned against the back wall facing the entry door.

I sat down and began to mold two huge bricks in my mind. I had already built many of them in the past and set them in a perfect circle encasing me. Each brick had its own name. In many ways it was as if I were accumulating and naming my own army of guard dogs, except my dogs didn't bark; they simply lay still as one was laid upon the other with the intention of guarding and protecting the weak, fragile girl hidden behind them. *Ugly will be your name,* I thought to myself as I etched the word into the cold, hard stone. *And your name....hmm, I will need to find out the name of the evil villain you represent before I can give you your name.* I scowled at the imaginary block.

I had read once about the Great Wall of China; they began building it around 221 B.C. as a defense against the raids of nomads. (Nomads were people who traveled from place to place, but had no permanent home. Not all nomads were bad, but some of them were. There were those who would attack and steal from peaceful villages full of innocent men, women, and children living as a community). When it was finished, it was fifteen-hundred miles long. The fortification was situated with watchtowers for guards to keep an eye out for approaching enemies. When I read the story, I realized I had already begun to build a Great Wall of my own. The story of the three-hundred-thousand enemies buried within the wall, although said to be false, inspired me to name the bricks I used to build the protective wall after the things that brought me harm.

The foundational stone in the gigantic wall I had

been building was a rather large block with a simple word scribbled across it, *Plain*. It represented the first negative thing I knew about myself. Right next to it was a smaller stone with a name written upon it, *Vicki*. It belonged to the lady friend of my mom who clued me in on the fact that I was indeed very plain. There were numerous other bricks of different shapes and sizes with many different tags and titles carved into their solid forms. Some of those tags were simply descriptions of myself that I became aware of just by looking into the bathroom mirror while standing next to my beautiful big sister.

There was a big block titled *Leopard*. Encircling it were bricks tagged *splotchy, spotted, sun-kissed,* and *freckled*. I had heard my grandpa say once that a leopard never changes its spots. That was the day I molded that stone and carved its name therein. I knew in my heart my spots would never change. I was doomed to carry them with me all the days of my life. There was also a humongous block representing my most hideous and deplorable characteristic; it simply read *lipless*, and to depict my hair were three small blocks stacked side-by-side that said *rat's nest, murky,* and *blah*.

In the heart of the wall sat an accumulation of etched rocks symbolizing *my* heart which had been engraved with the emotions hewn into its stones as only words. *Lonely, sad, hurt,* and *alone* all described the feelings that wrapped themselves around me like a dark shroud. These impressions stretched from the heart of the wall and touched the stones that read *friendless*, alone, *withdrawn*, *isolated*, *overlooked*, *transparent*, and *invisible*. Stacked vertically next to that cluster of stones were three enormous bricks that said *outcast*, *incompetent*, and *afraid*.

Just yesterday I had formed a stone and carved out the title *ugly duckling*. Now, next to it sat the brick that simply stated *ugly*; it was secured in place by the only nameless brick which filled the only remaining hole in the wall. I determined in my heart at that moment to seek out the name of the devil who covered himself with white to try to appear as an angel of light. I had read plenty of the *Nancy Drew* books. Surely, I could hone in on the information filed away in the data base of my brain and pull up some of her skills to initiate my search for clues to his true identity.

As the tears continued to rush over my cheeks like a raging river running swiftly over the smooth surface of river rocks which had all the rough edges chiseled away by the force of the water, my face turned a splotchy red, and my cheeks became raw and sore. I slowly gained some form of control over my breathing, which had run away from me like Peter Pan's shadow. I felt as if I had been senselessly chasing after my breath, unable to catch it no matter how diligently I tried; I needed a Wendy. At last I inhaled one large gulp of air, and my lungs leapt forward, ensnaring the object of my desire—oxygen!

I held the oxygen in my lungs allowing it to saturate the tiny air sacs inside; then I slowly released the exchange my lungs had made with the oxygen, replacing it with carbon dioxide. As the heavy, warm gas left my lungs, my mind sifted through the information stored away in its folds. It came across an interesting fact concerning carbon dioxide being in soft drinks, and I began to contemplate why we would put something into our bodies that was obviously meant to be excreted as a waste product. It was during this moment of heavy thought that my enemy entered the room.

The door opened in what seemed to be slow motion; I heard every creak of the hinges as they swiveled. I felt as if all sound waves had been sucked out of the room by some huge vacuum or black hole; or rather, the swirling vortex had extracted all air from the room leaving the sound waves no medium in which to flow. Everything seemed hollow. As the door opened, a small amount of air must have leaked through because the only noise was that of the door, followed by the loud echoing of his footsteps.

Gradually, he reached the front desk. He glanced my way and viewed his most recent victim. I imagined he had many victims before me. Someone so brutal and inhumane must inflict their cruelty on more than one. I was certain he couldn't have just picked me to wound and leave dead to the world. There are many people who are called collectors because their hobby is to fixate on a certain type of object and then accumulate many different varieties of them. Surely he must have been a collector of hearts. He probably had a dark and creepy attic full of large mason jars where he kept his prizes—the actual hearts of innocent girls.

His stout physique frightened me. He kept his head

low so as not to be seen staring at me by Mrs. Natalie. His eyes pierced through me like daggers. Squinting, he narrowed his eyes as he took in my splotchy face and overflowing tears; then without warning he released a vicious smile revealing his nature. His teeth could have easily been sharpened to razor-sharp points and dripping with my blood. It was his mouth that had unleashed the death blow. His words had sharpened his teeth into fangs worse than any vampire ever thought of having.

The saying, "Sticks and stones may break my bones, but words will never hurt me," was the farthest from the truth. Words, as I had just found out for myself through my own bloody experience, cut deeper than any dagger, knife, or even any double-edged sword could ever go. The lacerations of those inanimate objects may at times leave wounds that result in physical death, but the gashes left through words cause a much more agonizing demise—the death of the soul. Physical wounds which are survived heal over time, but the injuries suffered from the tongue, the most vile member of the human body, leave a person with only one option, to build their own "Great Wall" to protect themselves from future invasions; unfortunately, if the stones are laid in front of the wounds, they will act as skin and seal the wound off. As a result it appears healed, but underneath it oozes with infection and disease.

The wall I had been building from the stones molded by words was almost complete. I lacked only the name to the last stone that sealed me in. The sculpted bricks sat in an orderly fashion (that's the way I liked things, orderly) in a perfect two-foot diameter with me as the center point.

Before the wall came into existence, my life was wrapped up like a seed. Doubt surrounded me on all sides like a hard seed-coat. Inside the lonely monocot seed lived a delicate little girl surviving off the endosperm of hope. Hope was the only nutrition I had, the only source of dormant life, and that hope was derived from my pretty dresses, which camouflaged my plainness, and Sue. Sue had left me; I could no longer hear her thoughts, and I had just discovered that even pretty dresses couldn't camouflage my hideousness because I wasn't just plain; I was *ugly*! In *Anne of Green Gables* Diana Berry had given me the hope of intelligence. She was wrong. Being smart wasn't better than being pretty.

I'm not sure exactly how it happened, but at some point the seed and the wall morphed together. They decided, without my mental consent, to fuse together and become one. The seed's job was to keep me protected until the wall was finished and sealed. At that point I could root myself down and begin to flourish. The clincher to it all—In order to be protected, I had to stay hidden from the world around me.

Mrs. Natalie hung up the phone and turned to check on me. It was at that moment that she eyed the wicked villain. "Thad, what do you need, dear?" she inquired.

Ah, ha, Thad's his name I thought to myself as I

etched the missing name into the final stone that fit securely into the hole in the wall which was situated directly in front of my eyes, sealing off all vision and light. It was a name I would never forget.

"I'm not feelin' very well. Can you call my mom to come get me?" he moaned as he squinted his eyes and grabbed his belly.

"Sure, dear. You go sit over there by Aralyn, all right," she uttered while pointing in my direction.

My eyes shuddered, and I began to tremble. Intimidation gripped my gut, but I determined within myself not to let him see any more of my tears; he had seen enough of them already. I drew the tears back, holding them within the walls of my eyelids. As the tears seeped back, they ran down over the perimeter of the "Great Wall" surrounding me. Leaving a hardened mass of pitch behind, the trickles of water ran through the crevasses between each stone; the tears miraculously sealed the stones together.

The tears dribbled their way down from the top of the wall all the way to the foundation. Upon reaching the bottom, they began to fill the base. Before long the seed was submerged in the tears that were destined to germinate the life that lay dormant for so long, but unfortunately, the wall had covered many wounds that were filled with sacs of gangrenous infection. With no place else to go, the bitter infection bled down the inside of the wall and dripped into the well of tears. As the two mingled together, the seed drank them both in.

CHAPTER 6

THE FRIENDSHIP PIN

Time had passed extremely slowly in my mind. I suppose that being alone with books for the majority of one's life can make it seem that way. On top of the many books I had read, I began to write poetry; it was the medium in which I could allow my feelings to flow from behind The Wall. It was only a small trickle of relief as the hurt mingled with the gangrenous, oozing infection and found its way on the other side of the wall through the tiny portal made through the poetry which tossed in waves inside my heart. At times the tossing was violent with anger and hurt, yet there were times when the waves would calm and stream through my heart with gentle movements that brought with it a sense of melancholy.

It had been two and a half years since Sue had left

me, and much like a hermit crab, I had hidden myself securely away from the world revolving around me. Feeling pity for me and knowing what I had been through the day before my tears and pain sealed the wall around me, Laila stood firmly by my side for a time. She sat next to me on the bus and talked to me at school, but eventually her need for her friends outweighed her concern for her sister, so she gradually returned to her normal routine which excluded me. At home she would try on occasion to get me to talk, but speaking was a thing of the past for me. I never did very much of it, but at that point in my life, I would not have recognized my own voice because of the infrequency of its use.

I never told my momma what happened when she picked me up that day. I sat quietly in the car as she drove home. I went straight to the bathroom, washed my face, and crawled in my bed. When Laila got home from school and saw me, she told my parents what had taken place the day before but insisted she didn't know of anything happening that day.

My parents, never knowing for sure what had taken place to cause the near catatonic state, had taken me to a counselor. She seemed to be a nice lady, but I never spoke to her either. My hero, Daddy, increased his tradition with me by purchasing several watches a year. Laila had informed him of the swatch watch craze (Of course, she was informing him for herself.

She always had to be in with the trends, and she was sure to let him know that you could *not* wear just one!), so he had purchased Laila and me two for Christmas. I was very proud of my white watch with a green and red face and my red one, sporting colorful geometric shapes on its yellow face. Laila had one with a black band and white designs on the face and a neon yellow and pink one to match her new fluorescent outfits.

School had just let out for the summer, and I was looking forward to our trips to the beach park in Pascagoula. We always made at least three trips over the course of the summer. We would pack a picnic lunch and head down to the park early on a Saturday morning. Daddy would always come with us. Grandma and Grandpa lived nearby, so they would meet us there. It was a huge family event. Grandpaw Jack died when I was only four; however, he was never far away from our celebrations. Every year Daddy would always bring him up and tell us the stories of how he would play with us on the beach building sand castles. Daddy worked hard to keep his spirit alive on these joyous occasions. Despite his best efforts, I couldn't dredge Grandpaw Jack up from my memories. To remedy this problem, I would stare at his picture for a long time before each trip, and when Daddy told his stories, I would squeeze my eyes shut as tight as I possibly could and imagine the Grandpaw Jack from the picture doing all of those wonderful things with me. I learned that with a little imagination I could create memories.

Laila had decided several years before that she was too old to play on the playground swings and make sand castles. She would get Momma's permission to go strolling down the beach, and of course, she always pre-arranged for a friend to meet her there. We shared a room, so there wasn't much she could keep secret. She had just hung up the phone with her boyfriend Brad. She skipped back into our room full of glee, prancing around and going on and on.

"Da, da, da, da...," she hummed the tune to "Girls Just Wanna Have Fun" as she danced around the room; then she pulled a tiny purple bikini out of her drawer. It was strapless with a large ruffle across the entire front of both the top and bottom pieces. It was cute yet frillier than she usually wore, but it wasn't a swimsuit I suspected Daddy knew about or would even allow.

"Laila, is Daddy gonna let you wear that?" I inquired, eyeing the two small pieces.

"Daddy won't be there today, Air. He had to work. I'm gonna be goin' on a trip this comin' year in school, so he's gonna be workin' a lot of Saturdays to pay for it. I overheard Momma telling Lydia about it on the phone earlier."

"Oh!" I responded with large, round eyes. I had used up my words for the day.

When we were all packed up, we drove down to the beach park. Laila, wearing an over-sized Coca-Cola t-shirt, darted off to the pier immediately. I assumed Brad was to meet her there. I imagined how nice it must be to have a boyfriend and to think someone might actually love you. That was a feeling I was sure I would never be able to experience. It was all the pretty girls at school who had boyfriends. The plain, smart girls were ignored. Real life was turning out to be nothing like the world I lived in—the world described through the pens of creative minds. I wondered if they created those perfect imaginary worlds because their worlds were too unbearable.

"Momma, can I cross over to the beach? I wanna build a sand castle," I petitioned in my even voice which reflected no emotion. Monotone had become my norm.

"All right, dear," she granted. "But you make sure to look both ways before crossing the road," she insisted. As I walked off, she noticed the pad and pencil tucked away securely under my arm. I hadn't even worn clothes suitable for making sand castles. She shook her head and sighed. "I don't know what I'm gonna do with that girl," she whispered to herself, yet I still heard the worry in her words.

I turned to look over my shoulder. "Yes, ma'am," I whispered in a barely audible voice.

Unhurriedly, I found my way to the cross walk, looked both ways to make sure the coast was clear, and slowly crossed over to the other side. I glanced up at the pier and noticed Brad jogging over to meet my sister. As they embraced in a kiss that I really didn't care to see, she spotted me approaching the pier entrance. She pulled away from Brad and yelled, "Air, go away! Did you come over here to spy on me, you brat?" Then she grabbed Brad's hand and darted toward the end of the pier.

"No," I answered as I passed the entrance and walked toward the water. My reply was so soft she would not have heard it even if she hadn't been briskly walking to the end of the pier.

I sat down in the sand, looked out over the horizon, pulled out my pad of paper, and wrote.

"Sand Castles"

Sand castles are made by little boys and girls,
Creating for themselves imaginary worlds.
They start out with a bucket and a shovel or two,
They dig up the sand and add water for glue.
Placing patty upon patty,
They stretch their tower to the sky,
Carving out windows way up high.
Once the tower is erected and tall,
That is when they start on the wall.
As they mold it and shape it,
Securing it in place,
They add to the wall—one large gate.
A moat is then dug all the way around,
To keep out the beasts that cannot be bound.
The sand castle is protected by a moat and a wall;
Unfortunately, a world made of sand
will eventually fall.
~ Plain Jane ~

I finished my short poem for the day, slid the pen into the spiral binder, and placed the pad in my lap as I imagined the sand castle I had created in my world. I knew one day the sand would give way, and my world would come crashing down around me. In my peripheral vision I saw a blonde-haired girl walking toward me, wearing a huge grin. She sported a red t-shirt and wildly colorful jams.

With fierce boldness she walked right up to me and stuck her hand out for a shake. "Hey, my name is Laurie. What's your name?" she inquired.

I looked into her eyes for a brief moment; then I stared back over the water. "I'm Aralyn," I answered.

Laurie glanced toward Laila and Brad on the pier. "So, big sis suspects you're spyin' for mom and dad, huh?"

"Yeah," I answered.

"I'm a big sister, so I know how bossy we can be at times," she continued. "Sorry, I just saw and heard what went down a few minutes ago. You looked busy writing for a while, so I waited 'til I thought you were finished. So, what were ya writing?" she pressed in an uplifting, non-pushy way.

"A poem," I said, my answer short and simple.

"A poet, huh? Do you ever let anyone read your poetry?" she asked with a smile.

"No."

"Oh, okay. Maybe one day you'll let me read your work. I'm prepared to wait. So, you wanna go walkin' down the beach, looking out over the Gulf so that your sister will see that you are otherwise occupied?"

I turned to look her in the eyes in order to see what deception was lying in wait, but there was none to be found. What I did see was a brightness shining in her eyes that glimmered as the sun reflected off them. She was wearing a huge smile that practically spread from ear to ear. What I saw was something I had never seen in anyone outside my immediate family; I saw friendliness. Fear gripped at my heart, and hesitance was a natural recourse.

She held out her hand to me and said, "Come on." Assessing my reluctance, she gave a nod of her head in the direction for us to go and added, "I don't bite."

I glanced at her hand and watched as it dropped back to her side; then I drew a deep breath and stepped toward her. We walked side by side up and down the beach for what seemed like an hour. She did all the talking, which was perfect for me. She was bright and cheerful. She went on about her little brother whom she adored; his name was Timothy. She lived on Briarwood Circle in Moss Point. She had just completed the seventh grade at Magnolia Junior High, so she was between Laila and me. She was ecstatic when I briefly mentioned I would be attending Magnolia that coming school year.

She was obviously brilliant, which made a place inside me smile and wonder: *After all this time, have I finally found a friend?* Immediately after that thought passed through my mind and heart, I tagged it as a hopeless dream, something that could never be true. I assured myself that the false idea was a result of misread signals. She couldn't truly *like* me; no one had ever liked me before. I was plain; who could like a plain girl when there were so many pretty ones in the world? Even friends liked to have pretty friends. I was not sure why, but it was a definite observation I had made. Pretty, popular girls didn't want friends who were not pretty and popular. I had noticed one exception to the rule—money. Boys and girls who had money could make themselves attractive with it. I wasn't sure exactly how they did it, but it was a reality I had observed first hand. Like a scientific experiment which must test a hypothesis and show a clear and absolute result before a conclusion is made, I had a firm conclusion: money could buy beauty and most definitely popularity.

I decided to place my tagged thought in a safe place and observe the situation before I totally discarded it. Of course, my wall was securely in place. Obviously I would not allow the thought to penetrate my security, but I had made a firm decision to "chew on it" for a while as some say. Laurie was bubbly and uplifting. There was a part of me that yearned for a friend just like her, but I felt certain that vast amounts of time would be involved before she would be able to dig a hole through the wall which surrounded me.

I wasn't sure she would be willing to put forth the effort which would be needed on her part to cultivate a friendship; nevertheless, after two hours of non-stop talking as we walked the beach and created a beautiful sand castle together, she led me to the huge beach towel laid out with her stuff on it.

"I have something I would like to give you." she

smiled. "Come on."

We stepped over to her beach towel and sat down. As she opened her beach bag, she explained, "Before you got here, I was just sitting here making friendship pins. I know it might seem kinda silly, but we learned how to make them in my art class this past year." She pulled out a group of colorful safety pins. From a large pin hung five smaller ones decorated with colorful beads slid side by side. "I don't know why, but when I saw you cross the street, it was like I could see some things about you. The colors have meanings. The white means you are gentle; the red means you are strong. The yellow means you are intelligent; that's why I put four yellows in a row. I could tell that you are very smart. The turquoise means you are sensitive, and the black means you are sad."

I glanced down at the pins and saw more black mixed in amongst the other colors than anything. She had truly seen I was sad. The yellow was the only color not tainted with the black or mixed in with any other color. I wondered to myself why she had done it that way. Was it possible that my intelligence was the one place sadness could not touch or hurt me?

"Here," she uttered as she handed me the friendship pin. "You wear them on your shirt or your shoes. I expect to see you wearing this on the first day of school. I'll be trackin' you down, all right?"

"All right," I answered, taking the pin in my hand and allowing a gentle smile to cross my face.

I don't know how or why, but she saw something about me that caused her to want to be my friend. In order to express that to me, she was willing to read and examine me and make that pin. She wanted me to wear it in public where others would know she had given it to me, and I was not friendless. She had dug a small hole in my wall and given me hope through a friendship pin.

CHAPTER 7

LEAN ON ME

As summer rolled to an end, I wondered if Laurie would really find me on the first day of school. We had exchanged numbers that day, and she called me at least three times a week. Our conversations were usually one way. I sat and listened as she filled me in on all of her latest adventures with Rachel, Andrea, and Milt. She informed me that she had told them all about me and how they could not wait to meet me.

I still loved pretty dresses, but Laila had sat me down the day before we were to do our school shopping with Grandma and insisted she be allowed to help me pick out my clothes. "Things are different in junior high, Air. Girls only wear dresses on occasions. You should really think about letting me help you with your wardrobe for the year. I'll pick out the stuff that's in style. I promise I'll get your approval before I force you to make a decision. *Pleeease!*" she begged.

I stood silent for a moment and thought about life without my defensive arsenal of dresses. "Okay," I answered. It came out very hesitantly, yet it came out. It had been almost three years since Sue had left (taking her super power of invisibility with her), and I had managed to survive. Of course, my survival was not much of one. Life without Sue *and* my dresses would most definitely not be a pretty sight.

That night Laurie called, and I told her we were going shopping for school clothes at Daisy's the next day. "Laila insisted I allow her to help me pick out my clothes. She doesn't really care for the way I dress," I murmured.

"Oh, well, maybe she's just trying to help you in her own way. She knows how things are at Magnolia. Guess what? We're doing our shopping tomorrow too, so maybe I'll see ya," she enthused.

"You shop at Daisy's, too?" I inquired.

"No, not usually. We go to Mobile a lot, but I've been in Daisy's a few times. I really like their stuff. Maybe I can talk my mom into bringing me by while we're out. That way we can see each other before school starts and hang out while we shop." Excitement bubbled over in her ramblings.

"Yeah, that'd be cool," I answered.

"Okay, well, I gotta go. Andrea is here; she's spending the night with me. I'll see ya tomorrow. Oh, yeah, what time?" she pressed.

"We usually go early, like ten a.m.," I murmured.

"Great! See ya there. Bye," she said. As she hung

up the phone, I heard the echo of giggling girls in the background. My natural instinct was to guard myself. *I wonder if they're laughing at me,* I thought.

The next morning I woke up bright and early, eager for the day ahead of me. Laila was surprised to find me already awake and dressed when she awoke. She had anticipated such extreme hesitance from me that she imagined she would need to pry me from the bed herself; nevertheless, when she woke, I was sitting at the kitchen table finishing off a bowl of Rice Krispies listening to Snap, Crackle, and Pop do their thing. I was imagining they were filling me in on the eventfulness of my day, telling me all about the fun waiting on me; unfortunately, I was not certain that it would be. There was a tiny part of me that felt impending doom, and that part of me, as small as it was, was putting up a big argument with the three images on the box. Eventually, Snap, Crackle, and Pop won the argument when they insisted that Laurie was a fun and loving person.

As I looked down at my shoe and eyed the friendship pin, I knew it was true. She would never have given me that as a practical joke. True, she loved to laugh and pull pranks but never anything cruel or mean. She was such a hyper person and so full of life; she couldn't sit still for very long, so I was sure she would make me smile. It's amazing how a little noise coming from a bowl of cereal can brighten an imaginative person's day.

"Wow, up and ready? What's up with that?" Laila quizzed as she entered the kitchen.

"Being punctual," I responded in a very short and quiet manner.

"Okay, whatever. So, you still planning to let me pick out your stuff?" she pressed.

"Sure."

She rolled her eyes, turned to leave the room, and uttered under her breath, "You better not be planning to psyche me out."

"I'm not," I assured her.

Laila got dressed and ate her breakfast quickly. She was an unstoppable force when it came to shopping. All anyone had to do was say the words *shoes*, *handbags*, *fashion*, *clothes*, *make-up*, or *jewelry*; it was like pressing a hidden button on her that turned on a supercharged, energy-packed, super-cell motor. She could move at lightning speed under those circumstances, and she usually did. This morning was no different from any other under those conditions. As soon as she was ready, the phone was in her hand. Mom often commented that the phone seemed to be attached to Laila's ear.

After a few quick calls, she looked down at her black-and-white swatch watch. "Grandma should be here in five minutes, Air. She promised to be here at nine-thirty on the dot, and you know Grandma; she's always on time. I really don't think she would know what to do with herself if she were ever late. I bet she would just stay home if she couldn't be on time," she chattered away.

It was truly nice having a sister who made up for my lack of speaking. Most of the time when people commented on my quietness, it was in reference to Laila's ability to fill the room with words; therefore, they suspected I must not have much opportunity to say anything at all. There may have been a degree of truth to that philosophy on the subject, but I preferred keeping my thoughts to myself. The less I talked, the fewer opportunities there were for my wall and the wounds it sealed over to be revealed. Of course, it also kept the beautiful vine, which had burst forth from the seed hidden inside my heart, from being seen and admired, but that was the price of protection. In order to prevent further hurt, the defense mechanism that causes one to hide himself will also cost him his freedom to openly express himself. The only way to be seen and appreciated would be to risk further injury and begin tearing down the wall that not only kept everyone out, but had also locked one inside.

Grandma showed up on time as expected. We slowly and quietly made the drive to Daisy's, but on the way down to Pascagoula, Grandma began talking about things that were quite confusing to Laila and me. "So, Meredith, who's your friend?" she asked.

Laila peered deep into my eyes; her mouth dropped open, and she mouthed, "What do I do?"

"Answer her." I hesitated. "I guess."

"Her name is Aralyn," Laila murmured with apprehension.

"It's nice to meet you, Aralyn. How did you and Meredith meet, dear?" she inquired.

"Oh, we've practically known each other our whole lives. We see each other all the time," I responded warily. I looked at Laila with widened eyes and shrugged my shoulders.

"That's nice," Grandma uttered; then she went silent for the remainder of the drive.

When we arrived at Daisy's, Laila and I slipped over to the counter and asked Amy if we could use the phone to call home. Laila rigidly stood by the counter tapping her foot and waiting on Momma to answer the phone.

Burring, burring, burring, the phone rang three full times.

"Hello," Momma answered.

"Hey, Mom, Grandma is acting really funny. I think you better drive down and check her out. She just called me Meredith and asked me who my friend was. We're really freakin' out here," she squalled as tears streamed down her face.

"I'll be there soon, honey," Momma answered before quickly hanging up the phone.

"She'll be here soon, Air. Let's just shop and pretend that everything is all right," she insisted as she grabbed tissue from the counter and dried her face.

At that moment Laila's best friend, Stacy, came through the heavy glass door that opened into the small department store. Laila darted off to meet her and explain the situation; then the two glided around the store shopping for clothes and shoes. It only took a few minutes of eyeing clothes before Laila's sad countenance gleamed with excitement. She couldn't help it; shopping was her life. I was glad for her as I stood by the check-out counter and watched as she held out a royal-blue top with cut outs in the back. Her smile made me feel better. Engulfing herself in clothing had made her worry disappear.

It was about that time that Laurie came through the door. She saw the gloom weighing heavily over me and immediately sped to my side. "What's wrong?" she inquired, and before I even had a chance to answer, she was pressing, "I know something's wrong. I can see it," she assured me.

"Something is wrong with my grandma," I responded robotically.

"I'm sorry. What's wrong?" she quizzed.

"She didn't know who I was on the drive down. She thought my sister was my mother," I answered. "Laila called Mom; she's on her way." I sighed.

"Is there anything I can do? I know...How about if I get your mind off it," she said as she grabbed my arm and began pulling me through the small department store. She weaved our way through the circular racks until we came to the section she was looking for. She began rummaging through the clothes. With a slight pivot of her head, she assessed my size. "You a zero?" she asked.

"Yeah. I can still wear some sixteens though. It just depends on how they're made," I responded in a soft whisper. "What are you doing, by the way?" I questioned with a sadness weighing down my already drone voice.

"We're getting your mind off all that by shopping. It's what you came here to do, isn't it?" she smiled. Her perfect, pearly-white teeth glistened and lit up her whole countenance, and her green eyes shimmered with life. It was amazing; I could actually feel her radiance flaring (much like a solar flare) from her to me. It was a warmth that felt good and made me want to gently smile, so I did.

"I guess," I started; then making a one-eighty I locked my sight on my sister and saw that she was otherwise engaged. She was shopping away in shoes babbling on and on to Stacy. I processed that for a moment; then I remembered how easily Laila was distracted by her friends. I should've known she would be shopping with her friends and forget about me. I drew in a deep breath and then finished, "Laila seems to be shopping with her friends, so she shouldn't mind me shopping with you."

Laurie eyed the jeans she had just pulled off the rack. "Oh, would it upset her for you to shop with someone else?" She cautiously slipped them back in their proper place and dropped her bright smile.

"No, she won't mind. At this moment I don't think she even remembers begging me to allow her to help me pick out my clothes. I'm glad you're here. I'd be doing this by myself if not," I insisted.

Her bubbly smile came back in an instant. She pulled the jeans back out and went on and on talking about fashion sense. I actually laughed a few times while we shopped. Laurie had done an excellent job of getting my mind off my grandma. In my peripheral vision I noticed Laila look at me when she heard me laugh. A smile crossed her face; then she quickly turned back to her shopping.

By the time Momma arrived, I was standing at the counter waiting while Amy, the cashier who had worked for my grandparents for the last ten years, made a detailed list of the items I was receiving. She didn't ring us up like the others. My grandparents provided us with the clothing we got from Daisy's, and Amy knew the rule: make a list detailing the item description and price. She worked on commission, and my grandparents always made sure she was paid for what the sale would have been.

As Amy neatly folded and bagged my clothes, Laurie gave me a strange look. "Um, shouldn't you go get your grandma or your mom to come pay for this?" she questioned with a puzzled expression.

"Oh, we don't pay. This is my grandparents' store. They take us shopping four times a year. It's a tradition," I proclaimed.

"Wow! That's pretty cool," she exclaimed.

"Yeah, I guess it is. We never really think about it much. It's just the way it is. Momma said that when Laila was born, my grandparents insisted they be allowed to provide the clothing," I murmured in a nonchalant way while giving my shoulders a slight shrug.

When we were finished at the counter, Laurie and I stepped over toward Laila. Seeing Momma standing in the office talking to Grandma, I consulted Laila, "Do you know what's goin' on with Momma and Grandma? Is Grandma okay? Have you heard anything?" My usual word usage had been far surpassed; I couldn't help it. For some reason the questions just kept flowing. I suddenly remembered walking past the male mannequin; I crinkled my brow in confusion and blurted, "Why are you in the men's section, by the way?"

"None of your business, Nosy Rosy! I'm not sure about Momma and Grandma, Air. Everything seems to be all right. Just go on, okay. Stacy and I are still shopping." She grimaced.

I felt like a puppy seeking affection from her master only to receive a swift kick, thrusting her across the room. Laila was slowly returning to her old ways. Once again I was the little sister who annoyed her with my presence. I settled in my heart at that moment to keep a distance from her. Concerning Laila, I had just become "foot shy".

With *REJECTION* scribbled across my face, I took several steps backward until I ran into what I suspected to be the mannequin I just passed; then without warning, the male mannequin gently laid his hand on my shoulder. My eyes grew huge as my imagination got the better of me and ran off with an idea that had been implanted the prior weekend while at the Twin Cinema in Pascagoula with Laila. Daddy had dropped us off at the dollar movie to see *Mannequin* with Andrew McCarthy. He was really cute, but the frightening concept was the idea that a mannequin could come to life. As images of the acid-washed jeans and Hawaiian shirt sporting mannequin raced through my mind, my body stiffened. I squeezed my eyes shut and held my breath. As my face turned blue, I heard a gentle whisper in a familiar voice, "Are you okay?" Laurie asked as she gave my shoulder a gentle squeeze.

I was quickly sucked from my scary illusion back to reality. Discreetly exhaling, I answered, "Yeah," as I turned to face her with watery eyes.

"Hey, look. I just want you to know something. You know the song "Lean on Me" by Club Nouveau?"

I nodded my head yes.

"Well, the words are true. Sometimes we do need somebody to lean on, and I want you to know that you can lean on me," she insisted as she wrapped her arm around me and pulled me toward her, causing my body to shift and lean on hers. Holding me up, she stood firm and tall.

CHAPTER 8

NOVEMBER RAIN

Over time a nice-sized tunnel was made through the wall that surrounded me, but my insecurities kept it locked down with a humongous iron gate. In my mind and heart, I had created one key to unlock the gate, giving access to one person alone to enter through the tunnel. I had given that key to Laurie. She had earned my trust.

In the year and a half that I had known her, she had truly allowed me to lean on her in times of need, yet I had not opened up completely to her. My poetry was still hidden from all. Because she had seen me writing on the day we met, Laurie knew I scribbled my thoughts and feelings down in a special notebook in the form of poems. She had even asked if I allowed anyone to read my poetry, and when I answered, "NO," she promised to earn my trust.

After all that time, she still had not asked me if I would allow her to read my thoughts. I began to wonder if she was waiting for me to offer—believing that when I was ready, I would. I knew in my heart that once I allowed anyone into that part of my soul, there would be no turning back. It is much easier to keep someone out than it is to kick them out. If I were to allow her in and she hurt my feelings, it would be necessary to shut her out again, and I feared it would cause me to lose my one friend. I wasn't quite sure if I was ready for that or not. In my mind it was safer for me to keep certain aspects of myself a secret.

To me poetry was an outlet for my confusion and hurt. I had written about Sue, Gone with the Wind, the Dark White Knight, and The Ugly Duckling. Those were aspects of me that were very private to me as I got older. For me to allow Laurie to know that my only friend for years was imaginary was a scary concept. I feared being thought of as crazy.

When I spewed my guts to Laila about Sue, her reaction propelled me to fear allowing anyone to have that knowledge. I also shared my hurt with her, and she betrayed me. She had promised me she wouldn't tell Momma and Daddy about Sue Storm; nevertheless, she spilled the beans to our parents about my being called ugly *and* about Sue. That was where I felt the true betrayal, the breaking of her word.

My parents took Laila to my counselor, who then questioned me about my friend. She asked questions: Did I see Sue? Did I only imagine seeing Sue? Did I hear her voice, or did I speak for her? I sat quietly—never answering. She then turned to questioning me about the humiliation of being referred to as ugly by a popular boy in school. She pressed me repeatedly to talk about my feelings on the subject, but I just wanted to forget about it. I wanted to keep the wall sealed. I didn't want to let anyone else in. Finally, during my last session, I looked into her eyes and said, "Sue Storm is a comic book character. She is simply a character I watch on Saturday mornings. It's called *The Fantastic Four*. She's not real."

I knew deep down inside that Laila was trying to do the right thing by telling Mom and Dad, and Mom and Dad were only desperate to help their little girl. What had angered me so was the invasion by the counselor. I did not know her. How could anyone imagine that I would even begin to open up and talk to a complete stranger?

Laurie, on the other hand, had become my friend, and there was a part of myself that desired to share the hurt I felt with someone. She was no stranger, yet fear still gripped my heart at the idea of letting the pain out through sharing with a person. I had let the pain out on paper, and it gave me trickles of relief. Paper could not reject or alienate me, but my friend could.

On Saturday, November 4, 1989, I was getting dressed to meet Laurie at R & R Skating Rink (It was the place for all Junior High kids to go!) when I overheard Momma crying. Laila, who was part of the Lockhearts Social Club, had a belated Halloween party for the club that night. She was slipping on her bright-blue poodle skirt when we heard Momma crying.

Turning to look at me, she whispered, "I wonder what's wrong with Momma."

"Grandma," I gasped. "It must be Grandma. She's been so sick."

"Slip your shoes on, Air, so we can run find out what's goin' on," she commanded in a voice tainted with worry.

We both quickly pulled our shoes on and tied them; then we headed toward the sound of Momma's sobs. "Momma, what's wrong?" Laila begged as she wrapped her arms around her.

Momma gently laid her head on Laila's shoulder and cried; then she slowly lifted her head, grabbed the tissue, blotted her face, and dried her eyes. "Grandpa just had to take Grandma to the hospital, girls. It's okay, but I'm gonna go down there after I drop you two off, all right. I'll be there to pick both of you up on time, I promise," she assured us.

"I wanna go with you, Momma," I pleaded.

"I appreciate that, dear, but both of you already have plans for tonight. We will take you both in the morning to see her, okay?" she insisted.

"What if tomorrow morning is too late, Momma?" I pressed.

Momma's eyes grew huge; holding me tightly, she hugged me. Pressing me away, she looked me in the eyes and promised, "Tomorrow will not be too late, dear. Your grandmother is going to be all right. You will see her in the morning. Now you two go finish getting dressed." Removing her eyes from mine, she glanced at Laila. "Laila, is Brad meeting you there?"

"Yeah. His mom's gonna drop him off; his car's in the shop right now."

"Okay. Run on," Momma pushed.

I turned to look at Laila, but she was already heading back to our room. I sprinted off. As I caught up to her, I whispered, "Wait up, Laila." She stopped dead in her tracks and waited on me to stand by her side. "Do you think Grandma's really gonna be all right?" I questioned. My forehead wrinkled with worry and fear. I don't know how or why, but somehow I just knew in my heart she wasn't going to be all right.

"If it was serious, Momma would've told us, Air."

Trying to decipher the bad feeling I had in my gut over the entire situation, I demanded, "Then why was she crying?"

"She was probably just upset about the whole idea of her mom being so sick. She's been real sick for the last year and a half. Momma's had a lot on her. Daddy took on a part-time job on top of his job at the shop. He can't really help her. She's just probably overwhelmed, Air. That's all," she insisted, comforting me with a gentle side squeeze.

At that point I let it go. It made sense for Momma to be so upset; she had been taking care of Grandma for a while. We both quietly finished getting dressed for our night out. As soon as we were ready, Momma grabbed her keys, and we all headed out the door. Pulling up at the skating rink, I eyed Laurie standing in line. I grabbed my skates, kissed Momma on the cheek, and whispered, "Tell Grandma I love her, and I'll see her in the morning." Momma shook her head in agreement, and I jumped out of the car, running to get in the long line.

Colorful lights flashed all around us as we skated to our favorite Bon Jovi songs. Every time Laurie and I heard the words of, "You Give Love a Bad Name," we would pine over Jon Bon Jovi. "Oh, he is so fine," Laurie insisted.

"Yeah, he is," I agreed with a girlish giggle as we skated side by side around the rink.

"Wanna pull in for a pickle and a Coke?" Laurie asked.

"Sure."

As we skidded to a stop at the concession counter, Andrea whizzed through the game area and came to a brisk halt. She wrapped her arms around us both and smiled. "Guess what, Aralyn," she teased.

"What is it?" I hesitantly questioned, giving Laurie a quick glance expressing my worry. Andrea was always messing with me. I never knew what was coming next with her.

"Philip just told me that he likes you."

"You're lying," I declared.

"I'm serious. He asked me if I thought you'd go with him to the ninth-grade prom if he asked," she insisted with a serious tone.

"Really?" I responded. A bit of excitement filled my heart. I had never looked at Philip in that sort of way, but he was very cute. He was average height with white-blonde hair and blue eyes. He was very baby-faced.

"So, would you go if he asked?" Laurie questioned. "He's really cute." Making a gesture towards Andrea, she added, "Andrea and Milt are going, and I'm going stag if I have to." Laurie grabbed my hands and begged, "Oh, come on. Please. This way we would all be there. We would have so much fun. Please, please, please," she continued on and on.

"I guess. If he asks, I'll say yes." I hung my head to the floor in embarrassment as I answered. Fear washed over my face as awareness hit me square in the nose. "Um, you...you're no...not gonna go t...tell him right n...now are you?" I stuttered as I contemplated that realization. I could just see me standing there, red-faced, unable to breathe while Andrea skated back over to Philip to tell him that I said yes. I started feeling sick to my stomach as my mind raced with pictures of him laughing at the idea of taking me to the prom. I knew Andrea claimed it was his idea to ask me, but my insecurities kicked in high gear.

"I feel sick," I mumbled. "I...I gotta go." I held my hand firmly over my belly and dashed off toward the girls' bathroom.

By the time I made it inside, I was hyperventilating. Laurie skated in behind me. "You okay?" she asked, laying her hand on my shoulder. "I made Andrea promise me that she wouldn't say anything to him while you were around. She swore on Milt's life. That's a pretty strong swear for her," she insisted.

"I'll be all right. I just got nervous. I've never even had a boyfriend before. I was already upset when I got here tonight, so getting nervous just upset my stomach," I blubbered as tears rolled down my face.

"I knew you were acting funny. What's wrong?" Laurie demanded.

"My grandma...she's in the hospital. Momma says she's gonna be all right, but I have a bad feeling," I cried.

Laurie pulled me close and gave me a tight squeeze. "I'm sorry. Maybe she'll be all right," she whispered. "Come on. Go splash some water on your face and let's get outa this stinky bathroom. Jeez, If you weren't feeling nauseous when you came in here, I imagine you are now." She cracked a laugh. Laurie was a true comedian. She could make me laugh no matter what was going on, and, of course, I let out a slight chuckle.

The next morning I woke up bright and early. I rushed to dress myself. I made a pot of coffee for Momma and Daddy, slipped bread in the toaster, pulled out the jelly, poured everyone a glass of orange juice, and tiptoed in Momma and Daddy's room to wake them. I set the coffee down on two brown, wooden coasters on their night stands. "Daddy, wake up," I pleaded as I shook his shoulder. "I made you coffee and toast."

Daddy moaned and rolled over. "Five more minutes," he begged, so I crept around to Momma's side of the bed.

"Momma, wake up. Your coffee's gonna get cold," I insisted.

"I'm up, I'm up," she assured me as she sat up and leaned against the headboard. Her eyes were still shut as she grabbed the coffee and took her first sip. As the warmth of the coffee hit her throat, she sighed, "Um, good job," and peeled her eyes open.

Impatiently I asked, "When can we go see Grandma?"

Momma smiled; she took her free hand and ran it through my hair, resting it on the side of my face. "I know you're worried, dear. We will leave just as soon as I can get dressed, all righty?"

"Okay," I replied.

Daddy grumbled as he flung his legs off the bed. Stretching his arms and torso, he planted his feet firmly on the floor. "You made coffee?" he warily questioned as he grabbed the cup and sniffed before taking a sip. "Hmm, pretty good job, Sis."

"Thank you," I responded with my head held high. Sis was sort of a nickname for me by Daddy. He called Laila Sister and me Sis. I'm not really sure where that came from, but I always liked it anyhow.

Mom crawled out of bed, threw some clothes on, and went to the kitchen to eat the jelly toast I had made. Scurrying around the house like a chicken with its head cut off, she readied herself for a trip to the hospital. "Go tell your sister to be ready in five minutes," she commanded; with a sprint, I was off to give Laila her command.

Impatience ran through my veins like a constant irritant all the way there. I wiggled and squirmed the entire drive. When we arrived at the door to her room, Mom lightly knocked. Oddly enough, a nurse answered the door. "Mrs. Liddell," she started. Her eyes cut to Laila and me. "I'm sorry. We did everything we could. We just lost her. I was just about to call you."

Denial brewed in my mind. Finally forcing its way through my body, it rushed through like a torrent and found its way out through my mouth. "*Noooooo!*" I screamed. Pushing the nurse out of my way with the strength of a defensive linebacker, I forced my way through the door. "Wake up, Grandma," I bawled as I laid my hands on her shoulders and shook her, trying to rouse her to life. Sobs broke forth, and before I knew it, Momma and Laila were pulling me away from Grandma.

"Calm down, baby. Calm down. You can't wake her up. Shhhhhh," Momma whispered as she held me tight. "I know, I know," she breathed quietly in my ear.

I moaned and wailed for what seemed an hour. When I finally gained control over my emotions, I looked at my mother and cried, "I didn't get to tell her I love her."

Momma gently caressed my face, wiping away tears as she did so, and said, "Grandma knew you loved her, baby. I made sure to tell her, just like you asked, and she told me to make sure I let you and Laila know how much she loves you." Tears continued to flood over my face; I laid my head on Momma's shoulder and burrowed it there.

On November 7, 1989, we buried my grandmother. As I stood at the casket under the canopy, the sky turned grey. Bringing with it gentle drops of rain, a gust of cold air streamed in. As the wind forced heavier drops down around us, I laid a yellow rose on my grandmother's casket and stepped out from under the protective covering. Peering into the dark sky, I stood as goose bumps sprang up on my arms from the cold, wet weather. The bottom fell out, and the rain came down in heavy sheets, drenching me from head to toe and flattening my spiral curls to my head, but I stood quietly looking into my bleak future through the dark clouds hanging overhead.

Carrying an umbrella, Laurie walked up from behind me, shielded me from the rain, and gently laid her hand upon my shoulder. Her mother, Nan, had brought her to the graveside to lend support as I grieved. "Hey, how are you?" she asked.

I shrugged my shoulders.

"I think you should write about it. It'll help. That's how you express yourself. You need to let it out."

"Yeah, makes sense. I should," I responded in an unusually drone voice.

Laurie wrapped her arm around me. "Come on. As

your grandma would say, 'You'll catch cold,'" she said as she led me to our car.

When we arrived at the house, people piled in the living room and kitchen in droves. Laila sat with her boyfriend, so I headed to our room, pulled out my notebook, and wrote.

"Cold November Rain"

The roll of distant thunder
Causes me to shake.
A sadness grips my heart
As I shake myself awake.
I peel open my eyes
As I lie in my bed.
The sweet smell of rain,
Swirling in my head.
I stumble to the floor,
Putting one foot in front of the other.
Tiptoeing to the window,
"A cold November rain," I mutter.
Grief fills my heart
As I stare out into the day.
My grandma is gone;
Now all my days will be grey.
Sheets of rain are falling,
Filling the atmosphere with a chill.
My mind is racing;
I wish it would be still.
Visions of my grandma
Are flashing through my head.

Plain Jane

Rushing through so quickly,
Reminding me she is dead.
I clothe myself in black
And slowly walk out the door.
I wonder in my mind,
"After this life is there more?"
Placing a rose upon her casket,
A tear rolls down my cheek.
This cold November rain
Leaves my life feeling bleak.
The cold November rain
Washes over me.
Men lowering her casket
Is the last thing that I see.

~ Plain Jane ~

CHAPTER 9

WIND BENEATH MY WINGS

After my grandmother's death, I retreated to my sanctuary of books and poetry. Trying to find who I was and where I fit in the world, I poured myself into writing. Almost two months after her departure, my parents had given me a book of poetry by Robert Frost for Christmas. Since that time I had spent many hours reading and studying his works. My favorite was "Revelation." I suppose I related to that particular poem more than any other because I had hidden myself from all—even my best friend. There were many aspects of my heart she had chiseled her way into, but there were still the secret places of pain I overshadowed with either silence or feigning conversations.

The "foot shyness" I acquired with Laila led to a

superficial relationship. Although she was my sister, the relationship had never been too deep, but now it was only outer surface. I liked it that way. As long as I kept my emotions in check and away from her knowledge, we had a great trifling relationship. Philip, who had been a distant friend, had weaseled his way into closer proximity. He did it with smoothness; he simply started hanging with our group on a regular basis. He figured out ways to start casual conversations with me; eventually, he asked me if we could talk.

I'll never forget that day for as long as I live. As soon as I stepped off the bus, he joined me. Walking me to our gang's spot in front of the gymnasium, he nervously fidgeted with his hands, finally resting them on my arm to stop me. "Can I talk to you alone for a minute, Aralyn?" he asked, his voice shaky.

Bringing me to a brisk halt by the choir room, my body stiffened. Standing there as rigid as a two-by-four, memories flooded my mind in pictures. To no avail, I blinked to stop them from flashing before my eyes. The first memory jumped out in my mind with images of the Dark White Knight. I saw his beady, sinister eyes, full of hatred, glaring at me. His lip curled and his nose crinkled as if disgusted by the girl standing in front of him. I had even written a poem about him.

"The Dark White Knight"

The dark white knight
Is a boy full of fright.

Young girls he seeks out,
Sniffing them out with his snout.
He smells their fear
And the innocence they hold dear.
Upon the weaker he preys,
Leaving them burning, ablaze.
Like an angel he comes in,
But he is dark, full of sin.
Shredding his victims with words only,
Leaving them wounded, hopeless, and lonely.
Disguising himself as light,
He is, in fact, The Dark White Knight.

~ Plain Jane ~

The next memory to flash through my thoughts was of Andrea at R & R Skating Rink. Remembering what she had mentioned the night before my grandmother's death, I blushed.

"Um, yeah, sure. What's up?" I finally answered. I wondered if the time it took me to get through the painful memory was recognizable to Philip or not. To me, the memory lingered.

"Well, the ninth-grade prom is coming up in about a month. I know I should've already asked 'cause I know girls like to have plenty of time to shop, so I hope it's okay to ask now. If it's too late and you already have plans, that's okay, no hard feelings," he rambled on and on. Taking a deep breath, he apologized, "I'm sorry. I'm just really nervous, I guess. I'm trying to ask you to go with me to the prom."

Seeing the blood rush to my cheeks, he stared

directly into my eyes, awaiting his answer. Embarrassment washed through me, so I shifted my eyes to the ground. "Oh, um...thank you...for asking. I...I would enjoy that."

A huge smile crossed his face. "Really? You'll go?" He gleamed.

"Yeah, but I should probably talk to my parents first and make sure that it's okay with them before you say it's written in stone. I'll let you know for sure tomorrow, okay," I answered barely above a whisper.

"Yeah, sure." His smile dropped a bit. "Oh, hey, would you like me to carry your books for you?" he asked in a more relaxed tone.

"My books? Oh, um, I can manage, but thanks anyway," I uttered as the realization that he may actually really like me hit me like a ton of bricks. I wasn't quite prepared for that revelation. Because of my own insecurities, I had dismissed what Andrea had mentioned. *Why would any guy like me? I'm ugly,* I had said to myself time and time again after Andrea told me Philip liked me.

In a flash I became distinctly aware that Philip was a friend, a very cute friend but a friend nonetheless. For some reason I just couldn't look at him as anything else. *What am I going to do now?* I thought to myself. *Oh, gosh, I don't want him to think I like him like that. He'll end up hating me. I better call Laurie first thing this evening for advice,* I counseled myself.

The conversation within my own head was interrupted by Philip's voice, "Aralyn...Aralyn...Aralyn," he called.

Shaking myself free from the daze I found myself in, I finally answered, "What's up?"

"We're here." He signaled with a minor tilt of his head.

"Here?" I questioned, confused. Then, following the direction of his head, I eyed my class awaiting me.

"Yeah, your class. I gotta go, Aralyn. My class is all the way down on the opposite end of the first hall," he answered.

"First hall?" I responded, still zombified.

"Yeah, you know, the ninth-grade hall. Mrs. L. Thompson, the toughest English teacher on campus. Maybe you'll get her next year," he quickly explained. "Look, I really do have to go. Are you sure you're all right?" He looked at me with concerned eyes.

At that point I forced myself to snap out of my imaginary world where I occasionally slipped off to. "Yeah, I'm sorry. I just got a little dizzy for a minute there. I'll be all right. You better get to class," I insisted.

"See ya later," he stated as he darted off for the first hall.

"Later," I mumbled as I swiftly made my way to my seat at the front of the class.

Just as I had promised myself I would, I called Laurie that afternoon as soon as I walked in the front door of my house. "Laurie, I need some advice. I'm desperate for help here," I insisted.

"What's wrong?" she urgently asked, knowing I had never once in our friendship been so full of turmoil.

"Philip asked me to the prom today," I started.

"That's great! Now we can all be there. Oh, wait a minute. Why is this bothering you? What did you tell him?"

"I told him yes, as long as it's okay with my parents, of course, but I suddenly realized he likes me."

"Okay, what's wrong with him liking you? He's cute, and he's very sweet, Aralyn."

"I know, I know," I answered. "But I also realized I don't look at him like that *at all,* and I'm afraid he'll end up hating me and not want to be my friend when he finds out I don't like him that way."

"Oh, I get it. Well, you need to just be honest with him. Tell him that you'd like to go with him as long as it's just as friends," she said with full confidence.

"That's it. All I have to do is tell him I just want to go as friends?" I crinkled my forehead in worry.

"Yeah. He might be disappointed, Aralyn, but he'll be glad you told him up front rather than waiting for the night of prom. He'd be real embarrassed if he leaned in for a kiss goodnight at the front door and you told him then."

"A kiss? No, there's no way. Oh, my gosh, I didn't even think about that. Okay, I've definitely got to tell him up front because that would be very embarrassing," I blabbered.

"So, did I help?" she giggled, trying to bring a little humor into the tense, worrisome conversation.

I let out a quiet chuckle and heaved a sigh of relief. "I suppose so. Just pray for me to have the courage to actually go through with it. I could just tell him my parents won't let me date yet." Comprehension of what I had just said wrapped itself around my brain, "*Hey*! I could tell him my parents won't let me date yet. That'll avoid both situ..."

Interrupting the end of my verbalized thought, Laurie interjected, "*Aralyn,* you can*not* do that. That wouldn't be right to lie like that, and besides, I want you at the prom."

"But," I murmured.

"But nothing! No way am I gonna let you get away with that. Just be honest. I expect you to be a person of integrity," she demanded.

"Ma'am, yes, Ma'am," I spouted in response to her command.

As I exited the bus the next day, Philip met me. "Good morning," he said with a chipper smile.

I realized that, being the gentleman he was, he was waiting for me to bring the subject up. He obviously did not want me to feel pressured. "Philip, can I talk to you for a moment, please?" I requested.

His eyes grew worried, and his muscles tensed. "Sure." He hesitated. "What's up?"

"Well," I began as we stopped in the same spot as we had the previous day. "I talked to my parents, and well, you're a good friend, Philip. I just don't want to mess that up, you know? I can go, but I only want to go if we go as friends." Silence filled the air surrounding us. You could have heard a pin drop. I looked up into his blue eyes to assess his response. "Is that okay? I...I've never been on a date before. I've never even had a boyfriend, and I would feel more comfortable about the situation if we just went as friends."

A hint of discouragement revealed itself through his saddened eyes as he answered, "I understand. That's fine as long as you'll go." Then he stuck out his hand for a shake. "Friends," he whispered as he gently grabbed my hand with the friendly, common gesture.

"Friends." I smiled in return.

Five weeks passed by like a speeding bullet. With the speed in which it traveled, you would have thought that time was a person, and his name was Superman. Laila had passed down her ninth-grade prom dress to me, a fitted, sleeveless rose-colored dress with a bustled bow tapering down the back. Laila did my make-up and hair for me, so I looked like a totally different person. She pulled my hair into a very elegant French twist. I felt positive Philip wouldn't recognize me.

When Philip showed up at my front door, he slipped a beautiful, light-pink corsage on my wrist. Daddy came out to shake his hand and give him the instructions on precisely what time I had to be home.

My eyes bulged and my face flushed bright red in embarrassment as I watched Philip flinch in pain at the grip my dad released on his hand, letting Philip know that while he was much older, he was still much stronger. Mom pulled out the camera and took about a hundred pictures, causing me to blush all the more. I was afraid my face would turn pink permanently from the constant flow of blood.

As we walked out the door, I nervously intertwined my fingers together so as not to have them free for the grabbing. Philip had just gotten his driver's license in March, and his dad allowed him to drive his red Chevy S-10. Gentleman-like, he opened the passenger door for me and shut me in. Awkwardness filled the tiny cab like a weird, silent energy. I inched my way closer to the door, being certain to keep distance between us.

Feeling the need to break the tension, I finally spoke up, "I'm really sorry about my dad squeezing your hand like that."

"Oh, it's alright. It's a dad's right kinda thing. He was just making sure I knew he'd hurt me if I hurt you, that's all." He shrugged his shoulders.

"Hmmm, and you're okay with that?"

"Yeah, I have an older sister, so my dad pre-warned me about the *dad techniques.*"

"A rite of passage or something, huh," I murmured under my breath.

"Yeah, I guess so," he responded as he pulled up in the parking lot of the school and parked the truck.

The prom theme chosen for that particular year was "Wind Beneath My Wings" by Bette Midler, taken from the movie *Beaches*. To make it look as if we were dancing in the clouds, a smoke screen, floating just above the floor, was made with dry ice. Suspended by fishing line, extremely real-looking birds of all types hung from the gymnasium ceiling. We were truly soaring above the clouds that night.

Philip and I danced to a couple of songs and watched as Tabitha Purden, graced with beautiful white feathery wings by the principal, gleamed as they crowned her Queen. Steven Rossdale, crowned King, stood proudly next to her. When they played "Wind Beneath My Wings," the whole group of us (Myself, Philip, Laurie, Milt, Andrea, and Rachel) all gathered into a circle and did a group dance. This group of people had truly become my friends. They were the ones I looked up to, the ones I aspired to be like. As plain and simple as I was, they accepted me into their group. They were the rushing wind which blew all around me, lifting me up by their love and acceptance to the place where I belonged—the mountain top.

CHAPTER 10

NEVER SAY GOODBYE

Over time my friendships grew stronger, which gave my confidence a severely needed boost. Naturally, they were still outward relationships with my one small group of friends, but time had allowed a connection and bond between us all to form on the outer surface. I entered the ninth grade alone as they left me for the high school. It was a lonely year, but as Philip had predicted, I had Mrs. L. Thompson for my English teacher. In all honesty, she was the best English teacher I had been placed under. She pushed us to excel in grammar, writing, and literature. She recognized my writing abilities immediately and encouraged me to press on to higher grounds while firming up and strengthening my grammatical weaknesses.

Philip had accepted that we could only be friends

and moved on in his dating life. Rachel had approached me in February of my ninth-grade year and asked if I would be okay with her asking Philip to the Mardi Gras Ball at the high school. Informing her that there were no feelings between us, I encouraged her to ask him. They have been together ever since.

Laurie and I had grown very close. She was the only person I truly allowed in. Eventually, she carved her way into the hurt places of my heart and saw the pain as she read some of my poetry. The day I allowed her in was the day she came to tell me of her education opportunity. On the day of my sister's graduation from high school, Laurie had received an acceptance letter to the Mississippi School for Mathematics and Science; fortunately, before she had a chance to tell me the purpose of her visit, I told her there was something I wanted her to see. Looking back now, I imagine I would not have revealed so much of myself had I known of her departure in advance. Curiosity got the better of her, so she let her own thoughts go. She sat down on my brass daybed and waited patiently while I riffled though pages in my desk.

When she could hold her peace no longer, she asked, "What's goin' on? What are you looking for?"

"Just hold your horses," I commanded. I pulled a piece out here and a piece out there and laid them face down on my desk top. As I sifted through the notebook pages, I placed them in a particular order. I took my time rummaging through the pages of my poetry—I still did everything at a snail's pace. When I finished sorting through them, I had stacked five of my poems in a neat stack; then I drew in a deep breath, walked warily toward her, and handed her the small pile of papers.

"These are five of my poems," I mumbled as I handed them to her.

Taking them from my hands, she whispered, "Really?"

"Yeah. The first one is the one I was writing at the beach on the day we met," I told her. She glanced at the poem sitting on top of the pile. Nervously, I added, "It's just a trivial piece really. There's also "The Dark White Knight," "My Invisible Friend," "The Wall," and "November Rain." The last one is the one you encouraged me to write when my grandmother died."

"Thank you," she said, reaching up to hug me. "I know how difficult this is for you. I feel very honored. Can I read them now?" she inquired.

"Sure."

"Will you read them to me, or do you want me to read them quietly?" she grinned.

"You read 'em," I instantly answered.

She ruffled the papers and pulled them into view; then she began silently reading. There were only a few moments of silence as she read "Sand Castles." Looking away from the pages and into my eyes, she insisted, "This is not trivial, Aralyn. This is very good. How long did it take you to write this?"

"I don't know. About ten minutes or so, I guess," I responded.

"*Ten minutes?*" she squealed; then, she went on to

read "The Dark White Knight." Angrily, she peered into my eyes. "Who is this?" she demanded.

"I can't say," I answered, looking down at the wooden floorboards.

"Yes, you can. You can say to me. I promise I won't tell anyone. You have my word," she promised.

Wringing my hands together, I fidgeted with my fingers. I heaved a heavy sigh, sat down next to her on the bed, and answered, "His name was Thad. He's my sister's age. I think he moved or something. I haven't seen him in a couple of years."

My eyes watered as she peered deeply into them. "What did he do to you?" she asked, wrapping her arm around my shoulder.

"Nothing really. He just told me I'm ugly, that's all. It just hurt. I always knew I was plain, let's face it; I'm no Laila, but I didn't know I was ugly until that day in the fourth grade."

Allowing my head to rest on her shoulder, Laurie pulled me closer to herself. "You are not plain, and you are most definitely *not* ugly," she insisted.

We sat there quietly for a moment before she flipped through to the next couple of poems and read softly:

"My Invisible Friend"

My Invisible Friend
Came and left with a smile.
A friend 'til the end—
In glass and mirrors for a while.

Plain Jane

She came to visit me,
And by my side she stood.
Her face only I could see—
I would bring her back if I could.
She often shared
Her power with me.
Whenever I dared,
Invisible I would be.
Her power went away,
And she left in the end.
She never promised to stay,
My Invisible friend.
~ Plain Jane ~

"The Wall"

Stone upon stone, brick upon brick.
I will build it tall; I will build it thick.
A plain grey wall, I will build.
It will serve me as protector and as shield.
The taller the wall, the harder the climb.
Those who hope to plunder will be wasting their time.
Upon each stone, I will carve each name
Of all who have hurt me, of all to blame.
I'll coat it with mortar; I'll seal it with tears.
The wall will stand strong for years and years.
It will keep out all villains and murderers too.
The wall will protect me just as it should do.
Harm shall not come to me, as long as I stay,
Hidden behind the wall, the wall of grey.

I'll stand in the darkness where no light will shine.
Hiding safely behind the wall, I will be just fine.
~ Plain Jane ~

"Aralyn, you are extremely gifted," she insisted. "You should show these to the head of the English department at the school, Mr. Stanley. I betcha he'll work really hard to help you get a scholarship to a college where your gift can be embellished."

Shrugging my shoulders, I murmured, "I don't know. I'm kinda private about my writing. We've been friends for what? Almost four years, and I'm just now showing you. I don't think I could handle rejection."

"I promise you, you won't be rejected—just improved upon," she stated as she dropped her head back down to silently read the last poem in her hand. Completely hushed, she read through "November Rain." Tears trickled down her face while she pondered over the poem she encouraged me to write.

"Wow," she exclaimed. "I'm proud to know you."

With my head held high and a slight grin on my face, I responded, "Really?"

"Yes, really," she answered.

I glanced down at the edge of my bed and saw a large envelope that didn't belong to either Laila or me. When it finally registered in my mind that it belonged to Laurie, I realized she had come over for a particular reason. "So, what's in the envelope?" I quizzed, trying to hide my anxiety with a winded chuckle. Laila had been applying to colleges all over, so I had seen similar envelopes floating around the house. One day when I came home from school, there were three big envelopes on the kitchen table, each one decorated with designs in the school colors from which they were sent.

"Oh, um, I came over here to tell you about the math and science school. I applied a couple of months ago. I didn't think I'd get in, so I didn't tell you about it. Well, I was accepted!" She pounced to her feet as she lifted her hands in the air, waving them about in victory.

Feeling excitement and fear, I joined in on her victory wave. "Yes, that's so cool." Saddened by the idea of losing my friend in a year, I wrapped my arms around her in a tight bear hug. "Wow, only a year left, and you'll be gone off to this math and science college. I'm gonna miss you."

Laurie pulled away and sat down on the edge of the bed. "No, Aralyn." She drew in a deep breath and slowly let it go. "This is not a college acceptance letter."

With confusion written all over my face, I asked, "What do you mean? What kind of school is it?"

A tear welled up in her eye as she reluctantly answered my question. "It's the Mississippi School for Mathematics and Science. It's a high school. I was accepted to complete my last year of school there. They concentrate in math, science, and technology. It's the direction I want to go with my life. I'm sorry Aralyn. I know it's a shock."

"Yeah, shock. I am a little stunned right now. I guess I just wasn't expecting you to leave early. I was kinda dreading this next year, knowing it would be coming to an end, but I was also looking forward to making every moment count, you know."

"I'm gonna miss you," she whispered as she laid her head on my shoulder. "I'm kinda scared."

"When do you leave?" I asked with a jittery voice.

"My parents will drive me up to Columbus to set me up in my dorm the first week of August."

"So, we have all summer, huh?" I sighed.

"Um, well, not exactly." She hesitated. "My parents have decided to take a month-long summer vacation. My grandparents live in Washington State, so we're gonna drive up to visit. It's gonna be a slow drive; we're supposed to stop and see all sorts of things along the way. We leave the last week of June. We'll get back a week before we leave to go to MSMS, and um, I also signed up to go with my church on a mission trip to Honduras, remember?" Her forehead crinkled as she cringed.

My eyes grew huge. "Honduras? I forgot. How long will you be there?" I questioned with tears rolling down my cheeks.

"Two weeks. I'll be leaving in four days. I'll only be home for five days before we leave to go see my grandparents, but when we get back from Washington, I'll have a full seven days before I leave to go to school," she proclaimed. She tried extremely hard to be uplifting and perky, but it was to no avail. Neither of us could feel upbeat and happy about the fact that we only had sixteen days spread throughout the summer that we could see each other before she would be gone indefinitely.

"I can't believe this. Honduras, family vacation, and

superior high school, this is all a little too much for me to take right now. I don't know what to say," I blubbered through tears. "Will you be at graduation tonight?"

"Yeah, I'll be there, sitting right next to you and watching your sister walk."

"So, do you think your parents will let you go to the graduation celebration afterwards?"

She hung her head and answered, "No, I don't think so. They insisted that some of the ones who are throwing that bash are no-good drunks. Mom wants me home tonight." She rolled her eyes.

"Oh, well, Laila begged me to go with her, but I can cancel out on her and come over to your house maybe," I said.

"No way. Not that I don't want to spend time with you, Aralyn, but tonight is your sister's graduation. You should spend it with her. I'll come over tomorrow. You can go with me to shop for the clothes I'll be taking to Honduras. We'll stop along the way and pose with a few mannequins," she said, laughing as she reminded me of my most embarrassing moment.

The previous year when we went school shopping together, she stood with the mannequins and pretended to be one. She waited still as stone while people passed and stared. There was this one little elderly lady who walked up to her and went on and on to her husband about how real the mannequin looked.

My face was blood red the entire time. Laurie was always good at making me smile *and blush.* She managed to maintain a very solemn look on her face the entire time; she never blinked or cracked a smile as the elderly couple stared.

As we sat together on the edge of my bed, we both laughed and cried while we reminisced over our four years of friendship. Somehow I had come to believe it would never come to an end. I had heard the saying, "All good things must come to an end," but I never wanted our friendship to end; I never *wanted* to say goodbye.

CHAPTER 11

GRADUATION CELEBRATION

The day wore on, and Laurie reminded me she needed to head home so she could get dressed for that night's commencement service. It seemed as if the very minute she walked out the door, a massive storm came burling its way through the house. Carrying a chip on her shoulder, Laila charged through and demanded that everyone jump when she hollered. She spouted out commands like there was no tomorrow.

"Oh, my gosh, we're gonna be late to my graduation! Mother, will you tell Aralyn to pick up the pace?" she screamed as she shoved her way past me, heading toward our parent's room. When she got there, she froze in fear. "Huh," she sighed. She threw her hands up to the side of her head, grasped two hands full of hair, and tugged. "No way. This *cannot* be happening! Daddy, what are you trying to do to me?" she gasped as she looked upon a grungy man with greasy hands. A couple of smudges, resembling fingers, had been smeared across his forehead leading up to his hair, which stuck up in complete disarray. He looked like Elmer Fudd (only with hair) after Bugs Bunny had gotten the better of him; rather, after he had tried to get the better of Bugs.

"I'm not doing anything to you, dear. I happen to be doing something for you. It's called working. You do want to go to college, don't you?" he snapped off, letting out a hidden chuckle as he turned to face my mom.

"*Please* tell me you plan to take a bath before we leave," Laila begged.

"I'm goin' right now," he mumbled, making his way to the bathroom.

Momma gave Laila a glare. "Is Keith picking you up?" she asked. Keith was Laila's most recent boyfriend. After she and Brad broke up, she dated a lot of guys. Her relationships lasted three months at the most, so she had been through quite a few of 'em. *I'm playin' the field* she would tell me every time she broke up with one to date another. I liked Brad; he was smart and knew what he wanted to do with his life. Laila and Stacy had started hanging with a girl named Rhonda; she was a little on the *wild* side. She had the classic "big hair" that was still lingering from the eighties, and she wore what had to be a ton of make-up. She had a great figure and a dark tan to match it, and she was sure to show it.

Laila had overheard Mom telling her friend Lydia that she was concerned about her dating so many boys, so she hung her head in shame and said, "Um, no. We broke up."

"Good. I didn't like him anyway. So, why did he break up with you, dear?" she questioned as she gently reached her hand out for Laila's.

Laila swiftly yanked her hand from Mom's access and spouted, "He didn't. I broke up with him. I'm fine, Mom. Besides, I like someone else." She flashed a grin across her face. "So, will you tell Air to book it, *pleeeease?*" she pleaded.

Mom stuck her head out the bedroom door and hollered, "Hurry up, Ara. Your sister's gonna blow a fuse if we're not outa here on time!" Then she leaned in, gave my sister a kiss on the forehead, and whispered, "Calm down and go finish readying yourself."

Within the hour we were all ready to go. Clean as a whistle, Daddy walked out of their bedroom humming the graduation song. Laila grinned from ear to ear, and we all gathered together for a family moment—a group hug. Conviction fell on Laila as soon as we stepped out the front door and her gaze fell upon the reason Daddy was so dirty earlier. He had bought her a small red Honda Civic and fixed it up. He had been giving it a proper tune up earlier, along with a deep cleaning and waxing. There was a huge lavender, Laila's favorite color, bow strapped to the hood.

Laila's mouth dropped open, and she squealed, "Yeeeeehhhhh!" Jerking around, she threw herself in

Daddy's arms. "Thank you, thank you, thank you," she repeated, kissing his cheek between each thank you. "I'm so sorry about earlier. I can't believe you did this. I love you, Daddy."

"I love you too, Sister," he said as he squeezed her tight. "My little girl's all grown up. Now we better get going if we're gonna make it to your graduation on time," he insisted as he pulled out a Rainbow Brite key chain with her car keys hanging from it.

"Rainbow Brite? Really? Daddy, I liked her when I was ten," she said with a cynical tone as she rolled her eyes; then she burst into laughter and added, "But I don't care. I love it." Jumping up and down, she made her way to Mom, "Thank you, Mom. I love you both." Coming to a brisk halt in her ravings, she exclaimed, "Oh, I forgot my duffle bag. Remember, Air and I are spending the night at Stacy's. I promise I'll call as soon as we make it to her house from the party," she screamed as she ran back into the house to retrieve her duffle bag.

The graduation was long. Five-hundred and twelve people walked that year. Moss Point High School always allowed the top twenty-five in the class to receive their diploma first; then they started alphabetically. With the first letter of our last name being the twelfth letter, we had a lot to sit through before seeing Laila walk, but when she finally did, she gleamed. She looked exceptionally radiant that night, and Mom and Dad both glowed with pride in their elder daughter. From there, Laila was off to Perk. My grandparents had set up a college savings for Laila and me both. We found out about it when Grandma died. With that Laila was able to stay in a dorm and have her cords to Mom and Dad cut—to a certain degree, that is.

Laurie sat next to me that night as we watched those we knew walk the "plank." I say that because for many of them as soon as the diploma was slipped in their hands, they were making a leap of faith into shark infested waters. Some of those we knew were opting to go straight to work; *we're not college material* they would say, and the truth is many of them weren't. Quite a few of the girls Laila knew talked only of marriage and families. We knew several who had summer weddings planned; their desires were simply to be a wife and a mother. There were many who had planned out the next four to six years of their lives and were ready to embark on the college experience. Many roads could be and were taken that night. None of them were insignificant, but they were diverse.

We listened as the principal introduced the graduating class of 1992 and watched as they all threw their caps high into the starry night sky. There was hooting and hollering; there was even a cartwheel or two. I watched as laughing teen-agers hugged one another in congratulations while the faces of most parents were being washed with tears.

Both of my parents made their way out to Laila to hug and kiss her. She hugged them both back and cried, "I love you both so much. Stacy and I are fixin' to be heading off." Grabbing my hand, she pulled me to her. "We'll see you tomorrow." She wrapped her arm around me, pulling me to her side. "We gotta go," she whispered in my ear; then from over her shoulder, she hollered to Mom and Dad, "*Love you!*"

Trying to keep up with her pace, I asked, "Why are we in such a hurry?" I turned and waved bye to Laurie and mouthed, "I'm sorry."

Laila laughed. "Because, I need to make my moves on Justin before Angela does. Rhonda just told me that Marianne told her that Lynn told her that Angela likes Justin and is planning on telling him tonight."

"So and so told so and so told so and so and you believe it?" I questioned as we approached her graduation gift.

Rolling her eyes, she insisted, "Lynn is Angela's best friend. She didn't even know that I have a crush on Justin, so if she told Marianne, then it must be true. Marianne didn't know either, but Rhonda did. She forewarned me about Angela's plans. I have to get to that party first, and oh yeah, by the way, you have to change."

"Change?" I shouted. "What are you talking about? Besides, I don't have anything else that I could wear to a party. All I have are my pajamas and shorts and a t-shirt for tomorrow," I proclaimed.

Laila looked at me and smiled. "Oh, yeah, you do. It's at Rhonda's house. We're all going there right now to change into something sexy."

"Sexy? No way. You've got to be kidding me. Just

take me home," I demanded as I crossed my arms firmly across my chest.

Cranking the car, Laila turned to face me. "Please, Air. This is my graduation night, and you're my sister. I need you to do this for me, please. I'm begging you. I'll owe you for the rest of our lives," she begged and pleaded.

Feeling the weight of her persuasive eyes, I gave in with a huff. That night I learned that family pressure was even more powerful than peer pressure. I had always been able to stand up to peer pressure and never give in, but the begging and the pleading of my sister were more than I could bear. "Why do I need to be with you?" I questioned, still not understanding the necessity of my presence.

"Okay, the truth. There's a guy who's gonna be there who asked me if I would bring you. He's friends with Justin, and he promised to talk me up to him if I brought you." She reluctantly smiled. It was actually more of a cringe mixed with a smile.

"Who... is this guy?" I hesitated.

"He asked me not to tell you about the arrangement, so I can't tell you who he is. What I can tell you is that he is *so* gorgeous. He's very popular, too. That's actually what threw me off a little." Realizing that she had just slipped up, she bit her bottom lip. "Sorry, Air. I didn't mean that a cute guy couldn't like you, but he's a jock, and you're the smart girl. Jocks usually like girls like me—the cheerleaders! You're like the brain of the school. Let's face it; you're in the math club, the science club, the Young

Republicans club, and The Future Leaders of America club." She babbled on and on, trying desperately to dig herself out of the hole she had conveniently put herself in. She never found her way out; the hole just kept getting deeper.

I turned to gaze out the window and mumbled, "Yeah, yeah. I know. You're the pretty one, and I'm the smart one." *And being smart is obviously not better than being pretty as Dianna Berry said because boys like the pretty girls, not the smart ones,* I mused.

In her air headed way she replied, "Yeah!" As we pulled into Rhonda's driveway, she turned to face me. "But tonight you are gonna be smashing. No one will even recognize you. Also, you have to promise me something," she begged, grabbing my hands.

Looking her in the eyes, I asked, "What now?"

"First," she answered, "you have to promise that when he approaches you, that you will not let him know I told you anything about tonight." She waited for a response. I gave a gentle nod of my head. "Second," she started, "you have to go to the kitchen with me, get a wine cooler from the frig, and drink at least one."

When she saw the shock flood over my face, she quickly added, "Just one, Air. You can sip on the same one all night long. Justin will know that you are with me, and he's really cool. I really like him, Air, and if he thinks that I brought a square to the party, he'll end up with Angela. Please, please, please, please, please," she continually begged.

I sat there motionless for a moment with my mouth

hung open. "I don't want to do *any* of this, but...I will."

"Thank you," she screamed as she threw her arms around me. "I'll owe you forever," she squealed.

"Consider tonight your graduation present from me. I'll try to sneak to the bathroom to pour the wine cooler out, and you can dress me however you want, but I'm *not* gonna get with this guy. Do you understand me? I'll talk to him and be nice, but that's it," I insisted.

We got out of the car and made our way to the back of the house. Signaling to be let in, Laila tapped lightly on Rhonda's window. Rhonda's bedroom was in the very back of the house, so she easily slipped in and out without her dad's knowledge. I don't imagine he would have said a whole lot anyhow; he was a druggy. Rhonda's mother died when she was in the sixth grade from an overdose, so he had been rearing her alone. Rather, Rhonda had brought herself up even before her mother's passing. Rhonda drank heavily, and she was wild, but one thing she did not do was drugs. Fear of her ending up like her parents, kept most teen-agers from socializing with her. It wasn't that the teen-agers feared how she would turn out, but rather their parents did. That is why Laila kept her friendship with her low profile. She was sure that Mom and Dad would have forbidden her to hang out with Rhonda.

Rhonda slid the window open, and we crawled in. She opened her closet door and pulled out a black leather skirt and a crimson top and handed it to me. I gasped when I saw it. "A hooker? You want me to look like a hooker!" I exclaimed.

"No, of course not. You won't look like a hooker," Laila rolled her eyes and gave Rhonda a "ridiculous" look. "You'll look sexy," Laila assured me.

"Yeah, Air. We're gonna make you look sizzling hot," Rhonda proclaimed.

Rhonda already had her outfit on under her graduation gown, so she was given the task of dressing me while Laila took care of herself. She zipped me up in the fitted skirt. Luckily it only came slightly above the knee—unlike their outfits. The top had an opened back with thin straps crisscrossed all the way down. She tightened the spaghetti-thin straps and tied a double-knotted bow at the bottom. She took my long, spiraled hair and teased and crunched it 'til it stood on ends. She swiped a deep-red blush across my cheeks and shadowed my eyelids with sparkling blue. She used her liquid eye liner to create Egyptian looking cat-eyes; then she painted my lips a crimson red. When I looked into the mirror I would have sworn I was staring at a rock-star groupie.

"Uh." I shrugged. "It's a little much for me," I insisted.

"You look beautiful, Air," Laila gasped as she turned to gaze at Rhonda's creation. My head naturally veered in the direction of my sister.

That was all it took—one simple word. "Oh, all right. I suppose if I have to go through with this night, I might as well look *shocking!*" I spouted out just before turning back to look at myself in the mirror. I most definitely looked like a different person. There was nothing plain about the girl staring back at me through the mirror. "This mystery guy probably won't recognize me in all this anyhow," I mumbled under my breath.

It was no time before we were on the road heading to the party. Laila got dressed faster than I had ever seen her before. I knew right then she was serious about beating Angela to the party. Picking up Stacy along the way, we turned down by the small airport off Highway 613 and started toward the small community of Helena. Just before entering the area, we made a right-hand turn down a long dirt road leading back to a big white, two-story house set in the middle of a couple hundred acres.

As we approached the house, there was a sign pointing to an even smaller drive leading to the back of the property; it actually looked as if it had been made by a four-wheeler. As we drove down the hill, we saw the start of a collection of cars parked out in a grassy area. Laila parked close to the drive so as not to get blocked in because we had to call home from Stacy's house at twelve-thirty. We all got out of the car and walked down to a humongous shed decorated with lights and the school colors. As we neared the door, I drew in a deep breath and slowly let it go.

CHAPTER 12

I CAN'T GO FOR THAT

Nervously, I walked through the door behind my sister, Stacy, and Rhonda. Laila grabbed my hand and led me to the coolers. "Sorry, I didn't realize the party was in a shed; there's no kitchen, but there are plenty of coolers. I'll find you a Bartles and James peach wine cooler. They're the best. I drink 'em when I go out with Rhonda. Her dad buys 'em for her. Isn't that cool?" she blabbed on and on.

With a furrowed brow I responded, "I don't really think it is, Laila."

"Get over it, Air. You can't be a square tonight. You have to be cool. Please don't embarrass me," she insisted.

I did as I promised and took a wine cooler, holding it in my hand for a long time without drinking any. I simply walked around looking for a bathroom to dispose of it; there wasn't one to be found. "Shoot!" I mumbled.

Before long I began thinking of the loneliness I was sure to endure soon. My best friend would be gone most of the summer *and* her last year of high school. I was certain she would go to college far away as well. It was over. That was all there was to it. I was intelligent; I knew that friendships drifted apart over distance. I had every reason in the world to try to maintain our friendship through phone calls and letters, but there wasn't really anything about me that would compel Laurie to keep in touch.

As my mind became consumed with the dark cloud of loneliness and sadness, I brought the bottle to my lips. Without even realizing what I had done, I took a big swig. "Uh." I cringed and swallowed as the sweet flavor rolled over my tongue. "Huh," I huffed. "Not too bad," I said under my breath.

About that time a guy with longer hair than mine stood up on the platform on the opposite end of the shed. He had a microphone in his hand. Behind him were a set of drums and three other guys hooking up cords. "Happy graduation, everybody," he screamed into the microphone. "Most of you know me, and for those who don't, I'm Blade Parker! This is my band, Silver Blade, and we're gonna play a few songs for you tonight. On drums we have Ron Hickson. Give him a hand," he yelled as everyone began hooting and hollering. Ron played a short drum solo showing off his stuff; then Blade continued, "On the bass guitar we have Nick Wright. Give him a hand," he encouraged.

Everyone cheered Nick on as he played his bass solo. Blade grabbed the microphone again and turned to face the last guy. "And last but most definitely not least, on lead guitar we have Ray Winstrom," he sang as Ray began playing a short complex piece which echoed through the large room.

An electric energy flowed through the room as they began to play, and before I knew it, half of the wine cooler in my hand was gone. From the corner of my eyes, I saw Johnny Weatherton, a nice-looking, popular guy from school, approaching me. *This must be the guy Laila told me about,* I thought to myself. His blond hair accented his blue eyes, and his tan skin showed off his muscular physique.

When he walked up, he held his hand out and said, "Hey, I see you're about done with that. Would you like me to get you another?"

I looked down at the almost empty wine cooler in my hand and pondered that for a brief moment before responding, "Okay, why not?" I gave my shoulders a slight shrug of nonchalance.

Leaving me, he walked over to the nearest ice chest, grabbed a peach wine cooler, and made his way back toward me. "I'll hold it 'til you finish that one," he said. "So, you came here with Laila, huh?"

I gave him a confused look and replied, "Yeah, she's my sister."

Shocked, he mumbled, "Sister?" He glanced over to where Laila stood talking to Justin. Turning back to me, he added, "You two don't really look anything alike. Your name is...?" He tapped on the side of his head several times trying to make it appear as if he were thinking extremely hard. He was a little goofy that way; he had a reputation for being a bit of a clown. His blond hair fell smoothly over one eye in a skateboarder cut. He carried himself in the same manner—easy going, carefree, and radical.

"Aralyn," I answered his unasked question.

"Aralyn, that's right. Yeah, I've seen you around school and all," he said as he slipped the empty bottle from my hand. He chucked it into a nearby garbage can from where he stood. "Yeeesss," he cheered as the bottle crashed against others at the bottom of the trash bin.

"Oh, you have?" I frowned.

"Yeah, you're like really smart, aren't you?" he chuckled, opening and handing me the new bottle.

"Is there something funny about a person being smart?" I snapped just before taking a big gulp.

"No, not at all. I just figured you plan on being the first female president or something."

"Really?" I questioned with raised brows.

"Yeah, man. I see you walkin' around with all those books. You must be a pretty strong little chic to be able to carry those thick, heavy books. I figure you'll be a millionaire or something one day," he babbled on with a slight slur to his speech.

Amazed that I was actually feeling sociable, I stared at him and smiled. The song being played ended, and Blade spoke up, "We're gonna slow it down for a minute. Here's a favorite from Cutting Crew, 'I Just Died in Your Arms Tonight.'"

As the band started to play, Johnny smiled and asked, "Would you dance with me?"

I stood speechless for a brief moment. Taking another drink, I answered, "Why not?" I scanned my surroundings for some place to set my drink and followed him out to the area cleared off for dancing. He grabbed my left hand and placed it on his shoulder. Having never slow danced with anyone besides Philip, butterflies fluttered in my stomach. Johnny held my right hand in his left while placing his right hand on my waist. I nervously flinched as he did so. As we swayed to the music, I looked around the room to keep from making eye contact with him. It was at that point that I spotted Mason Davis, the quarterback of the football team, approach my sister. Mason, a tall and slender guy with dark brown hair and dreamy blue-green eyes that fell in a pouty way, was considered to be one of the most handsome boys in school. I skimmed over the room with my eyes trying to find Justin, but he was nowhere to be seen. Laila seemed to be very involved in her conversation with him. He looked a little frustrated with her. "What?" I mumbled under my breath.

Hearing me but being unsure of what I had said, Johnny asked, "What was that?"

"Oh, nothing. I'm sorry. I'm just a little nervous is all," I answered. Then I thought to myself, *I can't believe her! I'm over here doin' this for her so that she can end up with Justin. She better not be screwing that up by flirting with Mason. He's not even her age. I bet the only reason he's even here is because he's the quarterback of the football team. Laila's the only reason I'm here.* The conversation with myself was interrupted by the end of the slow-moving song and the introduction of an old Van Halen masterpiece "Jump."

"Come on," Johnny shouted as he moved to the beat.

I slipped my hand from his and screamed over the music. "I gotta go to the bathroom." As I made my way to Laila, I grabbed my drink and finished it off. I began feeling a little dizzy. Suddenly I realized the sadness that hung over me earlier was gone. I felt numb to the pain of losing my best friend.

Interrupting her intense conversation with Mason, I walked up to Laila with a little brassiness. "You better not be ruining this. I'm doin' this for you," I insisted. Laila's eyes grew huge, waves of shock and screams of shut up shot through them. "Oh, and by the way, I don't really like blonds," I added, "but I have to go to the bathroom. Is there no bathroom in this place?" I squirmed.

Laila gave Mason a curious look and replied, "Yeah, but it's up at the pool house. It's a long, dark walk, Aralyn. You shouldn't make it by yourself."

"Okay, so let's go," I demanded.

At that precise moment the band started playing "You Give Love a Bad Name," and Justin found his way back to my sister. "Hey, man," he said as he gave Mason a pat on the shoulder. "Mind if I steal this beautiful girl from you?"

Mason smiled. "Go right ahead."

"Laila," I squealed as I watched my sister skip out

to the dance floor with Justin.

Mason tapped me lightly on the shoulder. When I turned to face him, he offered in his deep voice, "I'll walk you to the pool house. I know exactly where the restroom is at."

"Oh," I gasped. "All right," I answered hesitantly.

"Wanna 'nother drink for along the way?" he asked.

"Sure," I answered as I thought of the relief I felt in the numbness.

On our way out the door, he grabbed me another wine cooler and discarded my empty bottle. When we got outside in the dark countryside with no lights except that of the moon, he looked down at me, handed me the bottle, and asked, "So, what was all that about in there?"

I took a small sip. "All what?" I furrowed my brow in confusion.

"You know, 'I'm doin' this for you. I don't like blonds.'"

As I let out a light chuckle from behind the bottle, a low whistle blew across the mouth of it. "Oh, that. Well, I was dancing with that guy Johnny as a favor to Laila. She told me on the way over that he wanted to meet me." I didn't know why, but I felt comfortable talking to Mason, maybe it was the relaxed feeling I felt from the wine coolers.

Mason stopped dead in his tracks and faced me. "She told you that *Johnny* wanted to meet you?" he spit, anger lingering in his voice.

Offended, I snapped off, "Yeah, so what's it to you?" Realizing how rude I had been, I caught myself and apologized. "I'm sorry. I don't normally do that. I think I have a little bit of a buzz. Really, normally I'm a very nice person. Honestly, I hardly even talk," I explained.

He smiled. "It's all right. I like a girl with a little fight in her."

Immediately I blushed. "Oh...Well, I don't really have any fight in me, and I also can't say my sister told me that Johnny was the one who wanted to meet me. She actually never said who it was, only that he was gorgeous. He came up and started talking to me. He mentioned my being here with Laila, so I figured it was him she was talking about. I didn't really consider him to be gorgeous, but Laila and I have different tastes regardless, so I assumed she must think he is. She made me promise not to tell him she told me in advance." My train of thought was broken briefly as I mused, *Boy, a couple of drinks sure does loosen the lips. Normally I would never talk so much.* Pulling my thoughts back in line, I continued, "Anyway, that's why I was dancin' with him."

Mason let out a deep chuckle at that. "She did, did she?...Well, I suppose I can't be too angry with her since she never told you who I was," he whispered. "I guess Johnny got lucky he mentioned your sister."

Pausing in the moonlight, I looked up into his eyes and gasped, "You?" I found myself engulfed in an emotion I had never experienced before, completely mesmerized as I peered into his lovely eyes. A distinct magnetism surrounded him, tugging and pulling me towards him. Captured in his gaze, I found myself closer in proximity to him as I whispered, "Makes more sense."

"What makes more sense?" he asked.

His question pulled me back into reality. I had not meant for my thought to be verbalized. *How did that happen? Why didn't I have control over what I said?* I argued with myself. Trying to pull myself and an answer together, I shook my head. "What makes sense is...that...Laila knows I...could care less for blonds, and you're obviously not blond," I rambled on as I squirmed, a slight chuckle slipping from my lips.

Watching me do a little dance, he insisted, "We better get you up to that restroom." Then leading me to the pool house, he reached out and grabbed my hand. A wave of electricity flowed through my hand, up my arm, and straight through my heart. The electrical current seemed to find its way back and forth; it felt strange but good. I never wanted to let go of his hand.

I was sad when we reached the pool house because I no longer had an excuse to keep my grasp on his large, warm hand. He walked me right to the door of the bathroom and took my drink to hold for me. Entering the restroom, I knew I had squirmed and danced over being stuck in an awkward position (not over my need to go), but I was extremely glad he interpreted it that way because I really did need to go.

As I washed my hands, I looked into the small mirror hanging over the tiny sink. The girl I saw in there looked like me somewhat, but there was something different about her. There was a glow on her face and brightness in her smile. That was it; I was smiling.

The small pool house contained a tall, slender bar with stools, a small refrigerator, and a grill. Exiting the restroom, I eyed Mason sitting at the bar, drinking a Miller Lite. Slouching forward with his elbow propped on the bar, the globed light hanging over him illuminated his features, casting a shadow of his masculine stature on the far wall. I inhaled a sharp breath, fixed my eyes upon him, and inched my way across the room.

I sat down on the stool next to him and looked around the room. "Whose place is this anyway? There's a lot of alcohol here being drunk by underage teens."

"Yeah. It's actually my cousin's place. He's twenty-three; he bought all the alcohol. His parents are out of the country right now, so he made me promise to have it all cleaned up."

"So, they do their grillin' in here?" I took another drink. "You know peach wine coolers aren't too bad."

"I wouldn't know. I asked your sister what you liked to drink; she told me you and her both liked 'em." He smiled. He had such a beautiful smile. His full lips stretched over his perfect teeth.

I caught myself pining over him, so I faced the bar and finished off my drink to distract myself. "Um, yeah. I really like them. You should try one."

"That's all right. I don't think the two flavors would mix," he said as he held up the can of Miller Lite. "You wanna 'nother?" He gestured and pointed to the empty bottle.

"Oh, that's a long way to walk for another drink

unless, of course, you're ready to get back to the crowd and music."

"We don't have to go anywhere," he said. He stood up, walked around to the small refrigerator, pulled out another wine cooler, popped the top, and placed it in front of me.

"Oh, okay." I took a sip.

He came back around the bar and sat down next to me. Picking up my free hand and turning it over, he gently ran his fingers over my palm as he inspected my hands. "You have really tiny hands," he whispered. He flipped my hand back over and intertwined his fingers with mine. The electrical force intensified. I wondered if he felt the same flow of energy I felt. Nervously I gulped the drink down.

Needing to get some air, I set the bottle down and breathed deep, keeping my hand wrapped firmly around it. In one brisk movement, he slipped the bottle from my grip and placed it behind his drink. "Um, that's my drink," I whimpered.

"Ssshhh," he whispered, reaching out and touching the side of my face. My heart pounded ferociously. I thought it was going to jump right out of my chest.

Oh, my gosh, I thought to myself. *I don't know what to do. What if I don't do it right?*

He ran his fingers lightly over my cheek; then he slowly inched his way closer to me. With my heart fluttering away, I closed my eyes. I had never been kissed before, and I was scared. My breathing was cut off as he sweetly laid his soft lips next to mine. When I started breathing again, I inhaled the taste of Miller

Lite from his breath. I opened my eyes to find myself staring into his. "I've been wanting to do that ever since I saw you dancing with Johnny," he whispered.

"Really?" I looked a bit puzzled.

"Yeah, I wanted to yank you away from him when I saw him place his hand on your waist in there."

"Huh," I sighed.

"I don't even dance, but I would've snatched you into my arms and danced off with you in a heartbeat," he said just before leaning into me again with another kiss. That kiss was not as gentle as the first. As he pulled himself closer to me, he grazed my thigh with one hand and grabbed the side of my neck with the other. Never having been in a situation like that before, I didn't realize what was going on in *his* head until I felt his hand slip under my skirt.

From behind his forceful kiss, I mumbled, "No. Stop. Please, Mason. Stop." I slipped my hands between us and managed to push with enough force that he realized I was trying to get away.

He removed his hands and backed off. "I'm sorry," he whispered. "I guess I got a little carried away. I thought you wanted to."

I don't know why, but a wave of guilt hit me. I felt as if I had led him on in some way. I thought about it for a quick moment, looked down at the "sexy" outfit my sister's friend had put me in, and responded, "No, I'm sorry. I didn't mean to make you think that I could or would. Look, I know you probably saw me all dressed up tonight and figured the way I was dressed meant that I would do something like that, but I don't really even know you. I mean, I like you. Don't get me wrong, but I've never even kissed a boy before tonight. I'm not this 'smart, innocent girl by day, tramp by night'. I just couldn't do something like that. I'm not like that; I plan on waiting 'til I get married. I just, I can't go for that, and another thing…just because I happen to be dressed this way, you shouldn't assume a girl is willing because of her clothes."

"Okay. I'm sorry; I pushed it too far. I wasn't trying to imply that I thought you were a tramp. Forgive me?" he asked with a pout.

"Yeah, let's just forget it all together, all right?"

"All right. Maybe we should walk back out to the shed," he said in a pleading manner; then he mumbled under his breath, "There'd be less temptation for me being surrounded by a hundred or so people."

I looked up at him and sighed. "Sounds smart." Grabbing my hand, he walked me back to the shed. Along the way we talked about football and school. I was a little tipsy, so there were several times he had to wrap his arms around me to steady me. All the way there he was a perfect gentleman, and I was dazed over the fact that the gorgeous quarterback, who could have any girl he wanted, was interested in me.

CHAPTER 13

FIRST DATE

Deservingly so, I woke up around ten a.m. the next morning with a headache. I rolled over to find Laila, Stacy, and Rhonda still crashed. Somehow we had all managed to pile up in Stacy's bed. I vaguely remembered making it to Stacy's house at precisely 12:29 a.m.

Panic struck us when we went to leave the party. Several cars parked in the small drive (rather than off to the side) and blocked us in. The lead guitar player of Silver Blade happened to be walking around outside to breathe some fresh air; he saw Laila going ballistic and came over to see if he could assist. His long, black, wavy hair hung down past his shoulders.

He scribbled down the color, make, and models of the cars blocking us. "I'll take care of it, no problem," he said with a smile; then he walked back to the shed, grabbed the microphone, and announced, "Would the owners of a blue 1990 Ford Escort, a black 1988 T-top, Pontiac Trans Am, and a white 1991 Ford Ranger please move your vehicles *now,* or they will be towed." His voice echoed through the night air.

Immediately a tall, slender red-haired boy wearing a western shirt, Wrangler jeans, cowboy boots, and a humongous belt buckle jumped up and took off. A mullet-sporting, shade-wearing (at night mind you) stocky guy slowly stood to his feet and strutted his way to his car, and a bouncy, blonde-haired cheerleader started dancing her way out to move hers. Laila folded her arms across her chest and huffed as we watched the guys amble, the cheerleader bouncing and skipping, towards us to move their vehicles. Ray had saved our butts.

From nowhere, I remembered Laurie. "I gotta get home," I mumbled while crawling out of the bed. I stumbled and fell when my feet touched the floor. "Oh, shoot," I whined. Realizing I was still fully dressed, I complained as I took off the strappy, high-heeled shoes I was forced to wear the previous night. "I better get all this junk off me before I go home. Mom and Dad will kill me, and Laurie will be disappointed in my giving in to Laila's whim for the night." *Which almost caused me*

to lose my virginity, I pondered. "I'm gonna have to tell her 'bout that one." Thinking it over, I decided it wasn't the best idea. "No. I can't do that. He really was a gentleman and all. She'll think bad of him if I tell her what happened," I whispered to myself.

I pulled myself up to standing and made my way to the bathroom. Finding Stacy's make-up remover, I scrubbed my face with that and hot water. When I finished, my face was rosy from the heat and the scrubbing, but I couldn't get all of the mascara to come off. I gave up on it all together. I scrubbed my teeth twice and mouth washed with Listerine to be sure to kill all hints of peach-smelling alcohol; then I threw on a t-shirt and a pair of shorts.

Laila finally peeled open her eyes. "What time is it, Air?" she rasped.

"Time for us to be home; that's what time it is. It's almost eleven o'clock, Laila. Laurie's coming over today. I have to get home," I insisted.

"Oh, grow up, Air. You'll probably see her every day this summer," she snarled.

Tears welled up in my eyes as I thought about how desperately I wished that were true. "No, Laila. She's gonna be gone most of the summer, and...she won't be here at all come August," I whimpered as the tears rolled down my already raw cheeks.

Laila sat up in the bed, pulled her hair back out of her face, looked directly at me, and asked, "Wha'd'ya mean she won't be here in August?"

I sniffled. "She's going to MSMS to finish out high school. She got accepted. It's a great opportunity for her."

Laila crawled out of the bed and embraced me with a bear-tight hug. "You'll be all right. I bet Andrea and Rachel will still hang with you," she assured me. "You're not gonna be totally alone; besides, I think you may have a new friend after last night." She raised her brows and smiled.

"It was probably just a one-night thing. I wasn't dressed as myself last night, and I'm not gonna change who I am for a boy," I insisted.

"Remember. He did ask about you before he saw you in that outfit, Air. You don't give yourself enough credit." She laughed as she patted my face.

"I promise I'll try to give myself more credit if you'll just get me home, please," I begged.

"Okay, okay. Let me throw some clothes on."

When we walked in the door, Momma was serving lunch to Laurie. "Hey, Laurie. Here already?" I asked. "Momma, Where's Daddy?" I inquired.

"He's taken on a part-time job over in Mobile. We probably won't be seeing much of him for a few years. He'll be working Monday through Friday at the shop, all day Saturday, and part of Sunday at a car dealership." She frowned. I could sense my mother's reluctance over the situation. She didn't like Daddy working seven days a week. A few years prior he had taken on a second job; it was very taxing on the entire family.

"Why is he doin' that?" I questioned.

"Well, your sister's college fund covers tuition, books, and her dorm, but it doesn't pay for the car, gas, and the groceries she'll need. Plus, the fund will run out after three years; if it takes her longer to get her degree, we'll have to pay for it. I offered to find a small job myself, but you know how your dad is; he likes coming home to a meal on the table. He'd rather work a second job himself than to think he wouldn't have my cooking every night."

"Oh, well, I guess it's good that I'll probably get a full scholarship, then, huh?" I blabbed. "So, what's for lunch? I'm starved!" I exclaimed, sitting down next to Laurie.

"Pancakes and sausage," Mom answered, setting a plate full in front of me. "So, did you two girls have a good time last night?" She warily looked me in the eyes.

"Pancakes? At lunch?" I shoved a chunk of buttery pancake in my mouth and swallowed. "Ummm...yeah, actually we did. I met a guy. He seems really nice. We talked a *lot*," I emphasized.

Laurie looked at me with shock written all over her opened mouth. My mom dropped the turner on the floor as she loaded her own plate and snapped, "Oh, shucks...So, *you* talked a *lot* to a boy?" She gave me that motherly concerned look and then smiled. "Oh, we all slept late, so this is a breakfast for lunch. So, who is he?" she pressed.

"His name is Mason Davis. He's the quarterback of the football team. He'll be a senior this year. He's really cute." I excitedly gave the information.

Laurie turned to face me, "Mason Davis? Really? Oh, my goodness." Making eye contact with my mother, she expressed, "He's one of the best-looking boys in school, Mrs. Liddell."

"Oh, is that right?" my mother responded with a huge grin.

Laurie leaned into me and whispered into my ear, "I need to talk to you privately, please." I nodded in response, shoveled my food in my mouth, and excused us from the table.

Laurie asked Laila if she could speak to me privately. When Laila left the room, she shut the door behind herself. I sat down on my bed awaiting the impending doom I felt lurking in the atmosphere. "Aralyn, I don't really know exactly how to say this, but...I think you need to be very careful," she warned.

"Careful about what?" I worrisomely asked.

"Mason."

"Mason? What about Mason. He was a perfect gentleman," I responded a little flustered.

"He may have been. You know I play sports. Well, when you're active in that kind of stuff, you get to know and hear things about others who are as well, and one of the things I've always heard about Mason is that he is sort of a play boy," she sighed.

"Play boy? Whadaya mean?" I questioned in fear.

"He's known to be a heart breaker. He likes to play around with a lot of girls, you know. All I'm saying is to be careful; if you're gonna date this guy, wait a long time before you let him in your heart. I don't want to see him break it."

Laurie's concern was sincere, and I believed that I had taken her advice. *I won't let him in until he proves himself,* I promised myself. I grabbed Laurie's hands, looked her sincerely in the eyes, and uttered, "You have my word that I will get to know him and trust him before I let him in. Besides, I doubt he'd be willing to scale the wall I have built around me." I laughed.

We spent the rest of the day chatting about her upcoming trips and the long, boring summer I was about to endure. When the sun was going down, Laurie announced she must be leaving. With a quick hug she darted out the door and jumped in her mom's silver Buick LeSabre. As the night came to a close, I realized Mason had not called me at all that day. *Maybe I'm really not his type after all,* I pondered.

I slipped my pajamas on and went to kiss Mom and Dad good night. When I made it back to our room, Laila started jumping up and down with her hand over the phone receiver. "Yeeeeh," she squealed.

"What's the matter with you?" I scowled.

"It's Justin. He just asked me out...on one condition," she added.

"What's that?" I rolled my eyes.

"It has to be a double-date with you and Mason." She quietly squealed again. "So, will you agree to it? He's waiting for an answer right now." She shook the phone.

"When? Where? We have to ask Mom and Dad," the words flowed forcefully.

"Next Saturday night. Dinner and a movie in

Mobile," she responded.

"What movie? Where to for dinner? You know Mom and Dad are gonna want to know all the details," I insisted.

"*Far and Away* with Tom Cruise and Nicole Kidman and dinner at the Olive Garden." Laila did a little dance of excitement.

"Okay, if Mom and Dad agree, but you know they'll want to meet them both." I reminded her.

"Yeah, yeah." She waved me off. "Okay, she'll go, but we have to ask our parents, and they will want to meet both of you as well." She gave the demands; then she hung up the phone. "Okay, bye."

She jumped up and down, grabbed my hands, and pulled me into the jump. "I can't believe it! We're going on a double date. Me and my sister," she said as she squeezed me tight, "are going on a double date with two really cute guys, by the way."

"Shouldn't we ask our parents first?" I reminded her.

"Yeah, I guess so. Come on," she commanded as she grabbed my hand and briskly led me back to our parents' room.

Mom and Dad agreed to the double date fairly quickly. Mom showed a sort of excitement that was missing from Dad's countenance. I figured it was the typical "daddy not wanting to let his little girl grow up" gloom.

The first part of the week went by in a flash for me. I spent every moment I could with Laurie. Most of it was spent shopping for clothes to take to Honduras and at her house helping her pack them. When Tuesday morning rolled around, Laurie's parents woke us up at four-thirty a.m.

"All right sleepy heads, time to get up," Mrs. Nan whispered behind several gentle tugs. "We have to leave in thirty minutes, girls," she insisted.

Laurie and I both rolled sluggishly out of the bed. We dilly dallied around with brushing our teeth and hair, threw on jeans and t-shirts, and laced up our tennis shoes. We quickly scoffed down a bowl of cereal and a glass of juice and headed out the door. We made it to the Mobile airport in an hour. Mrs. Nan was a very safe driver. Laurie checked her luggage and waited patiently for them to board her plane. We both sat quietly while we waited. I don't know why, but there seemed to be no words to say. When they called for her flight to board, she hugged her mom and kissed her on the cheek; then she threw her arms around me and whispered, "You're the best friend I've ever had. I love you, and I'm gonna miss you." As she boarded the plan, Mrs. Nan wrapped her arm around me, and we both cried.

The rest of the week passed by slowly for Laila and me; actually, the entire week lagged for Laila, but for myself the latter part of the week was dismal. I was so overcome with gloom that I could not seem to lift myself out of it. I wanted to be excited about my first real date, but I missed Laurie and knew that an end to that part of my life was on the horizon.

As the time ticked away, Laila kept trying to cheer me up. "You know, if you're down and drab like tonight, Mason will not ever want to take you out again. You've gotta snap out of it. She'll be back in a couple of weeks," she snarled. Seeing the sadness reflecting in my eyes, she drew in a deep breath and sat next to me on the bed. "I'm sorry, Air. I guess I just don't understand. I have a lot of friends, and we're all going to different colleges. I probably won't ever see any of them again, and I know that."

She pulled my hair back from my face and situated it behind my ear. I turned to gaze at her and responded, "Maybe that's the difference, Laila. You have a lot of friends. You always have. I mean, I know Stacy is your best friend, but you hang out with a lot of girls." I paused and closed my eyes as tears rolled down my face. "Laurie is my only friend. Andrea and Rachel are her friends, not mine. Can you comprehend what it's like to have only one friend?" I cried.

"No, I guess I can't," she answered, "but I can tell you that having a boyfriend can be just as good in a different kind of way...Look, go get your bath, and I'll fix you up nice—not slutty—I promise. You'll look like yourself, only prettier. You can let Mason get to know who you are, not the "groupie" he met last weekend, all right?"

"Okay," I answered. I stood up, went to the closet,

and pulled out a pretty dress, something feminine, romantic, and modest like me. It was rosy pink, printed with small, delicate flowers. I laid it on the bed and gave my sister an insistent look. She gave a sigh and a nod of hesitant agreement.

Laila made good on her promise to me. When Mason and Justin arrived, I looked like a character from a romance novel—make-up does wonders! I didn't really recognize myself when I looked in the mirror. She took my spiral permed hair and pulled it in a French-twist with a few strands falling smoothly around my face. My make-up, which covered my hideous freckles, looked natural. She painted my eyes with shades of mauve to match my dress and lightly lined my upper eyelids. She lined my lips and glazed them with a soft mocha. The dress fit me nicely. My figure was nice, outside of my small chest. I had heard that that sort of thing mattered to guys, so I was sure that I wouldn't be found attractive in that manner.

Mom came out of the bedroom to greet and meet the guys as expected, but Dad was nowhere to be found. I had been anticipating the "firm" hand shake that my father gave all suitors. "Mom, where's Dad?" I asked as Laila grabbed her purse.

"Oh, he's still at work, dear," she answered; then looking up at the boys, she uttered, "I'm so sorry my husband couldn't be here to meet you two. He's never not been here before when either of the girls have been picked up by a boy. He'll be sorry he missed it, but I'm sure both of you will appreciate being able to move your hand." She chuckled.

Mason smiled and turned to me and whispered, "What did she mean by that?"

"Oh, my dad likes to give a real tight squeeze when he shakes a guy's hand, just to let 'em know that he'll hurt 'em if they hurt one of us," I answered nonchalantly.

Mason cringed. "Oh, glad not to meet your father, I guess."

"All right boys, have my girls home by midnight. Not one minute later," Mom demanded.

"Yes, ma'am," they answered in unison just before opening the door and allowing us to walk out before them.

They were both perfect gentlemen—opening the car doors for us and shutting them as well. I sat in the front next to Mason, who was driving his very own red Firebird, while Justin and my sister sat in the back. Mason kept both hands on the wheel and the music loud, so there wasn't really any opportunity to talk. I was sort of glad about that. I was still extremely nervous.

The energy that flowed between us the previous weekend emerged again, so I was pretty certain it wasn't related to the consumption of alcohol. The day after that experience, I had wondered if wine coolers could have contributed to the feeling of electricity running through my body. I was a very intelligent girl; I had taken Chemistry I and was signed up for Chemistry II. Intellectually I knew our bodies were made up of different chemicals that reacted with one another, and I had always heard people talk about couples having "chemistry." While we drove to Mobile, I mused over the idea of chemistry—*two people containing certain chemicals in certain levels which react with one another causing a physical reaction (possibly a flow of electricity) to take place in them both; could it be a reality?*

Mason's voice awoke me from my meditation. "Aralyn, hey, we're here." He snapped his fingers several times in front of my face.

I shook myself out of my daze and responded, "Oh, um, sorry 'bout that. Sometimes I daydream a little." I cringed, hoping he wouldn't be insulted or turned off by that piece of trivia about me.

"It's all right. I get caught up in a good song too," he uttered. He got out of the car and opened the door for me. Taking my hand, he walked close by me to the entrance of the restaurant.

Dinner was very romantic; Laila and I both ordered veal parmigiana. It was delicious. We actually had plenty of opportunity to talk. The restaurant was crowded but not overly loud. Mason shared his dream of getting a football scholarship to Mississippi State. There he wanted to study engineering. It was nice to hear that he had plans for his life; he wasn't just blowing around in the wind without a destination. He was pursuing something, and I respected that. Mason did most of the talking, but occasionally he would pry information from me. I was honoring my word to Laurie and keeping my guard up.

The movie was wonderful. I thought Nicole Kidman was so beautiful. I overheard Justin whisper something to Mason about her being sexy while Laila pined over Tom Cruise; she craved his movies ever since she saw *Risky Business.*

When we walked back out to the car after the show, Mason opened the door and let me in. He walked back around, let himself in, leaned toward me, and whispered, "Is it okay if I do this before I get you back home?"

Cutting off my words, a lump formed in my throat, so I simply nodded my head as he reached out with his hand and pulled my face closer to his; then he gently caressed my lips with his. The fragrance of his breath was sweet and cool like wintergreen. The tingling in my lips lingered even after he pulled himself away from me and cranked the car.

Laila let out a soft grunt; I turned to look into her widened eyes and watched a half smile creep across one side of her face. "Watch it, Mason. That's my little sister," she warned. Mason angled his rear-view mirror to see her and smiled.

When we pulled up at the house, they both walked us to the door. Justin laid one hot and heavy on my sister, but Mason leaned in and gave me a gentle kiss on the cheek. "I'll call you," he said as I opened the door.

I grabbed Laila's arm and pulled her away from the leech trying to suck her face off, or so it appeared to me anyway. When I shut the door, I fell back against it and grabbed my heart. "My first date," I whispered.

CHAPTER 14

LOST IN YOUR EYES

After our first date it was several days before he called me, but on Wednesday, June 17, my phone rang. Justin had come over to see Laila, so she didn't jump and run to the phone as usual. My heart pounded in anticipation; I answered the phone, "Hello."

"Aralyn," the voice on the other end of the line said.

"Speaking," I acknowledged.

"It's Mason. Look, I need to apologize in advance," he mumbled.

Not wanting to appear upset by the fact that three full days had passed without a phone call, I asked, "For what?"

He let out a deep sigh and answered, "For not calling before now. I have a summer job working construction, and I haven't been getting off until late in the evenings. You know how long the sun stays out in the summer." He nervously chuckled. "I've just been beat by the time I've gotten home. I've gone straight to the shower, grabbed a bite, and crashed."

"You have to work on *Sundays*?" I tried to sound concerned about that fact rather than suspicious.

"Yeah, as long as it's sunny, Mr. Lee has us out there. He says, 'off days are rainy days,'" he imitated his boss's rough voice.

I laughed at his failed attempt to sound like Mr. Lee. Most of the folks in town knew him, so I knew he was way off in his impersonation. He was from an old family who had a long history in the area. After my laugh, which released the small amount of tension and frustration I had been feeling over not being called, I spoke up, "So, today it's raining, and you decided you would call." I stated it as a matter of fact rather than a question.

Not sure exactly how to take me, he responded, "Yyyeeaah, are you...mad at me?"

"Of course not. I understand the need to get plenty of rest, especially when you're working out in the hot sun all day; it drains you," I answered intellectually.

"Good. So, are you up for some company?" he asked reluctantly.

"Sure. Come on over. Justin is here too. So about how long will it be before you get here?" I inquired.

"Give me thirty minutes, and I'll be right over."

"Sounds good. See ya in a minute. Bye." I hung up the phone. "Oh my gosh!" Panicking, my eyes bulged. "*Laila!*" I screamed as I ran out on the back porch to find her. "Hey, Justin," I squealed as I grabbed my sister's arm. "I'm sorry to have to do this, but I need to steal my sister for a few minutes. You stay right here; she'll be back in a few minutes," I insisted, tugging on Laila's arm. "Come on, Laila. Quick!" Justin stared at me in an odd way. It threw me off for a minute. *Why is he looking at me like that,* I briefly thought to myself. I didn't have time to concern myself with analyzing looks, so I quickly shoved the thought from my mind.

"What's goin' on, Air?" she demanded an answer; then she looked me over and raised her brows in question.

What is up with these two? Why are they looking at me funny? I reflected momentarily. *Aralyn, you don't have time for this. Stop trying to pick apart every look you get,* I commanded myself. I pulled her close to me and whispered through my teeth, "I need your help. Mason is on his way over, and I'm not dressed." At that moment I looked down at myself and realized I was still in my pajamas. I had gotten up that morning and gone straight to my desk to write. I had been so consumed in my poetry that I lost track of reality and the fact that I was still wearing my hot pink pajamas. Awareness flooded over my face; first it ran blood-red in embarrassment; then it washed out to a pale, sickly white in humiliation.

Laila cringed; grabbing my arm, she turned to Justin. "I'll be back in a few. I need to help my sister with something." She pulled my unresponsive, shocked body with all the force she could muster. "Pick it up, Aralyn," she snapped.

"I think I'm gonna be sick," I mumbled.

"No, you're not," she insisted as she dragged me through the back door. "You're gonna go right in here," shoving me in the bathroom, "and wash your face while I pick you out something to wear. I'll be right back," she promised.

She came back with a cute summer outfit. While I slipped my clothes on, she brushed my hair and braided it; then she sat me down and put a light layer of make-up on me. "We want you to look pretty but natural. It's okay to dress up fancy for a hot date and wear a lot of make-up, but guys like a girl with natural beauty. So...we need to let him see that you are pretty on an average day." She instructed me in the affairs of love, romance, and beauty.

Laila made me pretty (or so she said) and went out on the back porch with Justin. Within a few minutes a firm knock resounded from the front door. I took a deep breath and answered the door. "Hey," I said with a smile.

"Hey." He smiled back.

"Come on in," I nervously insisted, simply being around Mason made me smile despite my nervousness. My mother came out to see who was at the door and commanded that we either stay in the living room or go on the back porch. "You wanna go out back with Justin and Laila?" I asked.

"Um, nah. I'd rather stay in here and talk to you. If I go out there, he'll wanna start in on football. I came to visit you, not him. He's one of my best friends; I see him all the time."

I blushed. "Oh, okay."

We sat down on the couch, and he proceeded to ask me all about what I had been doing over the last several days. I told him all about my uneventful days. Remembering Laurie's warning, I kept my poetry a secret at that point in our relationship, but I couldn't keep myself from feeling a connection to him. There was just something alluring about him. He seemed to be very sincere in wanting to get to know me.

He stayed most of the day. We watched a couple of television shows together: "Wheel of Fortune" (both of us playing along), "Matlock," and "The Oprah Winfrey" show. As supper time neared, he grabbed my hand. Turning to face me, he mentioned, "There's this party Saturday night in Gulfport. The band Silver Blade is gonna be playing there. The lead guitar player, Ray, is a friend of mine. He invited me to come. They're gonna be playing some of their own stuff. I think he wrote some of it himself. Anyway, I was wondering if you would like to go? Just you and me."

"Just us?" I choked, nervously. "Can I say in advance, what you saw at the graduation celebration, that wasn't me. *None of it,*" I insisted sternly.

"I get it." He nodded. "So, will you go if I promise not to expect you to wear that outfit?" He smiled and wiggled his brows playfully. "And I promise not to get you drunk and not to try anything?"

"I'll have to ask my parents first; I've never been on a single date before—not really, anyway, but yes. If my parents will allow it, I'll go." I smiled.

Saturday rolled around sooner than expected; I was nervous and unprepared. Laila was going on a date with Justin, but they were going to a miniature golf course in Mobile. I wanted to be myself, but the real me would have been laughed out of the party; I ended up resorting to a pair of faded jeans and a Queensryche t-shirt. My choice of clothing was the first thing Mason commented on when he arrived.

"Queensryche?" He raised his brow and a half smile crossed one side of his face.

"Yeah?" I responded, perplexed.

"Hmm," he cleared his throat and chuckled at the same time. "I just didn't figure you for the type to listen to heavy music," he explained.

"I appreciate a diverse range of music. I look for true talent and ability amongst all styles. There's a lot out there that I don't consider gifted, but have you heard Geoff Tait's voice? He's remarkable. His octave range is amazing."

"Oh, well, sorry. I guess I shouldn't've stereotyped you. I just had you pegged as a Celine Dion, Mariah Carey, and Whitney Houston girl."

"All very talented as well, but you have to realize that even if their style is more my taste, Laila is my sister." I laughed.

"That would explain your exposure," he said, giving that irresistible half-smile.

My father was home that time and came out to

greet Mason. Of course, he was sure to give his *firm* hand shake. I have to admit I felt a sense of pleasure in seeing Mason flinch. It wasn't because of the mild pain he felt, but rather, the elation of knowing I had a defender. Daddy was still my superhero.

When we pulled up at the party, Mason opened my door for me. Shutting it behind me, he grasped my hand and led me inside. "I'm gonna take you to meet Ray; he's the lead guitar player I told you about," he uttered.

"He's one of your friends?" I questioned.

I found it slightly odd because most of the people in our school fell within certain groups. Most of the time, those imaginary lines separating the different classes of people were not crossed. Ray was a head banger, and he had the long hair to go along with it. He just didn't seem to fit as one of Mason's friends, but then again I didn't fit in Mason's class either. Mason was the jock, and I was the nerd.

"Yeah. Ray's my next-door neighbor. We were best friends when we were in elementary school, but you know how that goes; you grow up and take on different interests. We're still friends, but we don't hang together, you know?" he explained.

"Oh," was all I replied.

Holding my hand, Mason approached Ray, who was squatting down and hooking up wires to an amplifier. "Hey, man," Mason called.

Ray pivoted his head; a smile broke out across his face, and he responded, "Whuz up, man?" He swung his arm around; their hands collided in some weird guy handshake male-bonding thing.

"Ray, this is Aralyn." He introduced me.

"Yeah, right. You were at the graduation celebration, weren't you?" He squinted in thought.

"Yeah, I was," I answered. I remembered meeting him that night; he had rescued us in a way by making sure we were unblocked. He didn't seem to recollect any more than my presence at the party, so I didn't bring up his life-saving act.

We walked around the enormous house; I stood silently and smiled while Mason talked to different ones. I don't think he even knew anyone at the party; he just had a way of making conversation. The guest of honor, a girl named Brook, was celebrating her twenty-first birthday. The owner of the home was her wealthy fiancé, Darrell. We were only there because of the invite from Ray, but no one seemed to notice or care either way.

We danced, and I kept my promise to myself that I would not drink. Mason also kept his word by not even offering to get me a drink outside of a Coca-Cola. He slipped two beers in himself, but he kept it light since it was a long way home.

When he drove up in my drive-way, he leaned over, bringing his face so close to mine I felt his breath brush over my cheeks. Laying his hand on the side of my face, he gently placed his lips next to mine. He slowly pulled away and whispered, "I really like you a lot, Aralyn. Can I ask you something?"

A knot formed in the pit of my stomach as I braced myself for his question. "Uh, yeah, sure," I managed to mumble.

"Do you consider me to be your boyfriend?"

Shocked, I gulped, pushing against the lump rising into my throat from the pit of my belly, and stammered, "What? I...haven't really...Um, Is this a...trick question. I mean...we've been out and all...but you haven't...I like you, but I don't...I don't want to assume anything."

"So, your answer is that I haven't asked you to be my girlfriend?" He raised his brow.

"Yeah. You haven't," I insisted softly.

"You've probably heard that I've dated a lot of girls and never settled down to just one, haven't you?"

"Yeah, actually I have heard that, but I don't judge people based on what I hear; I examine the evidence for myself."

"It's true...what you've heard; I have gone out with a lot of girls. I did have one real girlfriend several years ago, but she moved off to West Virginia. She was my first, and she ended up sleeping around after she moved off, so I decided not to do the girlfriend thing again," he revealed his reasons.

Stunned that he seemed to be exposing a hidden place in his heart, I stared intently in his eyes. He allowed me to see him for who he was, being honest and transparent about his ways and why he chose not to settle down with one girl.

"So, who was she?" I asked.

"Her name was Samantha. We dated for a year," he answered.

"Did you love her?"

"Yeah, I think I did, on some level." Looking at his steering wheel, he sat silently for a moment; then he faced me and asked, "Have you ever loved anyone?"

"No," I quickly answered. "I've honestly never had a boyfriend. I went to ninth-grade prom with a friend, but I didn't see him that way."

"Do you see me that way?" he asked.

I turned beet-red and stared at the floorboard. I never responded.

He touched my chin with his hand and guided my head back to facing him and asked, "So, if I asked you to be my girlfriend, would you say yes?" His eyes pierced through mine like he was looking into my soul.

"Yes," I murmured.

"So, will you then? Be my girlfriend, I mean."

Lost in his eyes, I felt a surge of electricity rush through my body. I couldn't believe that moment was actually taking place. *I must be dreamin'*, I thought to myself. *He's so gorgeous, and I'm just a Plain Jane. He's the quarterback of the football team, and I'm a nerd. He's popular, and I'm invisible,* I mused.

Needing to convince myself I wasn't trapped in some sort of realistic dream, I pinched myself. "Ouch," I mumbled under my breath.

"What was that? I couldn't tell what your answer was," he said.

"Yes. It was yes," I answered.

A bright smile flitted across his face; he snatched

me in his arms. Fiercely kissing me, he whispered, "Please don't ever do what she did."

Mason's summer job with Mr. Lee, a local contractor who hired teenagers during the summer, kept him busy. His boss was known for personally getting out there, working with them, and teaching them the ropes of construction. He specialized in roofing, but he was a jack-of-all-trades. Mason worked most days over the course of the summer, but we had our summer nights to spend together, getting to know one another. There were also those rainy days that he would show up on my front porch rather than going home. Considering the fact that we lived on the Gulf Coast where hurricane season brought thunder storms, tropical depressions, tropical storms, and every so often a hurricane, there were quite a few days he showed up on my doorstep, and every night after becoming *his girl*, I found myself lost in his eyes.

CHAPTER 15

PARADISE CITY

As promised, Laurie came home on the twenty-third; it was early in the afternoon when she arrived, so I spent the rest of the day and that night with her. Since they were going to have their daughter for a solid month, her parents allowed me to steal her for the following three days. She spent those three hot, sunny days at my house; we did our usual leisure activities: went to the I.G. Levy Park in Pascagoula and played racquetball and tennis (Laurie was athletic; I wasn't, so she took it easy on me), spent a day at the beach in Biloxi, went shopping and to the movies in Mobile, and spent time talking and crying.

Because the days were cloudless, Mason never stopped by. Each night I received a brief phone call to see how my day had been and to tell me of his grueling day. I had told him all about Laurie and her finishing high school away, so he kept the details of his days short and sweet so as not to intrude on my few days with her before her summer vacation.

On the twenty-seventh, I drove Laurie home in Laila's car. I hugged Mrs. Nan and Laurie's little brother Timothy goodbye and shook Mr. Carl's hand. Laurie hugged me tight and promised, "I'll send ya a postcard from every major area we hit, I promise."

"I'll read 'em a dozen times," I assured her. With tears in my eyes, I watched as they drove off in their silver Buick LeSabre.

The remainder of summer flew by at the speed of lightning. On rainy days Mason and I spent the day together, and on sunny days he came over at night. Even though he worked when the sun was shining, I still managed to see him briefly at lunch time. Laila would allow me to borrow her car and take him lunch; the construction site changed a few times over the course of the summer. Weekends were spent going to dinner and a movie or going to listen to Ray play at a party. We spent every free moment we had together.

Every three to four days a postcard found its way to my home. Branson, Missouri, Chicago, Illinois, Yellowstone National Park, and Mount Rushmore were just a few of the ones I received. Four weeks passed in a flash, and before I knew it, a light knock echoed from my bedroom door. Time had slipped away from me, so I didn't realize what day it actually was. Mason's schedule had changed slightly; he now spent his days at the football field preparing for the upcoming season. He was still at my house every afternoon, so all I recognized, once I pulled my thoughts away from my poetry, was that it was Saturday, and he hadn't made it over yet.

Our routine had become so ingrained in me that I knew he stood on the other side of my door knocking and waiting patiently for me to answer, so I slid my chair away from my desk, shoved my latest poems in my drawer, and dashed to the door. Opening the door, I complained, "Where've you been?" Shocked, I stood staring at Laurie.

"Tennessee, Missouri, Chicago, North Dakota, Washington State, California, Texas. I sent you postcards; you know where I've been." Laurie smiled.

"Oh, my gosh!" I screamed, throwing my arms around her. "You're home."

"Yeah, I wrote you on the last postcard that I'd be at your house on the twenty-fifth around two o'clock. Didn't you get it?" she questioned.

"Of course, I did," I insisted. "I'm sorry. It just slipped my mind what day it was. Mason's usually here by now. I thought you were him," I explained.

"Oh, Mason, huh? So, you two getting along good?" she asked with reservation in her voice.

"Great. He's very sweet. We spend every day together. He asked me to be his girlfriend. See," I trilled, proudly showing her his class ring on my hand.

"Really? Wow, I guess I had him pegged wrong."

"Yeah. I kept my promise to you though. In the

beginning I was cautious about letting him in."

"In the beginning?" She pierced through me with her eyes.

"Of course, I promised I would, but we're very close now. He's told me a lot about himself and his feelings. I don't know; I feel good when I'm with him. I think I'm actually in love," I sighed. "But I haven't told him that," I quickly interjected.

"Good." She breathed a breath of relief and sat down on the edge of my bed. "Don't tell him that until he's confessed that to you. Guys'll use information like that to get what they want," she insisted.

"I don't think Mason would, but I'm not saying anything. Besides, it would be so humiliating if I said that and he didn't say it back."

Laurie wrapped her arms around me and hugged me. "Just be careful, okay?" she whispered in my ear.

Mason understood; he came by for a few minutes every evening, but he gave me time with Laurie. Laurie and I were inseparable for seven full days; then August 2 came upon us, a difficult day for us both. I drove to Laurie's house to see her off and watched as my best friend, my only friend, drove down the road. I held back the tears for as long as I could, but as her car moved out of sight, I could hold them back no longer.

Trembling, I climbed in my mom's car and drove home weeping. When I pulled up in my driveway, I eyed a shiny red Firebird parked in the shade.

Surprise washed over me, and a flicker of joy rushed to my heart. I shut off the car, opened the glove compartment, pulled out a small box of tissues, and frantically tried to dry my eyes.

I looked in the rear view mirror and sighed. "It's no use; my eyes are red and my face is blotchy. What is he doing here anyway? He's supposed to be at football practice," I complained to my reflection.

Giving up on hiding my embarrassing appearance, I got out of the car and walked to the house. Upon entering the house, I eyed him sitting on the couch, watching "Matlock," one of our favorite shows to watch together. When he looked up and saw me standing in the doorway, he jumped up and dashed to my side. "Hey," he whispered, caressing the side of my face. "Don't cry." Catching my tears, he gently ran his thumb under my left eye; then he pulled me close to his chest and held me. The warmth of his body felt comforting, and without realizing it, I began to sob. He tightened his grip on me and softly whispered, "Sssshhhh."

The roar of an engine rumbled up the drive. Prying us apart, he quickly jumped back. I had returned his embrace and didn't realize the vise-grip my arms had formed around him until fear of my dad walking in on the picture of us standing in an embrace gripped him, causing him to swiftly pull away. He pulled back the curtains and peeked to see if it was the impending doom he had imagined. "Your dad's home," he mumbled in his deep, sultry voice.

"My dad?" I whimpered.

"Yeah. Sorry 'bout that." He snickered with widened eyes.

Dad came in and shook Mason's hand. He gave him a wary look of distrust. Noticing my reddened eyes, he remembered the importance of the day. "Oh, how are ya, Ara? Laurie left today, didn't she?"

"Yeah. I'm okay. Well, I'll be okay anyway," I said.

Daddy excused himself from the room and went outside to his small shop, but I heard a small echo ring through the house as he shut the back door, "Don't trust that boy."

Mason and I spent the remainder of the day cuddling on the couch watching television. When the sun went down, I remembered that he should have been elsewhere; he should have been at football practice, but instead he had taken the day off to spend with me. I could only imagine his motive was his knowledge that it would be a difficult day for me and that I might need him. I thought about the implication of that, *He must at least care for me even if he's not in love with me.*

August the nineteenth brought the first day of school with it. It was a new year for me in many ways; I was friendless, but I had a boyfriend. I would be eating lunch by myself if Mason didn't have the same lunch as I did. All of those thoughts made me very nervous, plus the fact that Mason was popular. I feared being rejected by his friends, and if I were rejected by them, would Mason end up rejecting me as well?

A bombardment of thoughts flooded my mind as I crawled out of bed that morning. Loneliness had been an integral part of my being, but I was lonelier than usual that day; Laila was gone. She had left two days prior to situate herself in her new dorm and meet her new roommate. As I dressed myself, old feelings of inadequacy seeped from my mind and ran over my body like hot oil. The thoughts and feelings left a burning sensation and a residue in their wake; I began to tremble uncontrollably. I suddenly slipped back in time to that awful day in school—the day I was told I was ugly.

I watched the memory unfold like an old home movie. I saw myself talking to Sue. "Sue," I whispered, leaning over the vanity and peering into the mirror.

"Sue? Who's Sue?" a deep, familiar voice asked with a chuckle.

I jerked myself back to reality. "Oh, Mason, what are you doing here?"

"Came to pick you up for school. Are you avoiding my question? Who's Sue?" A half-smile crossed his face. His smile always made my heart melt.

"Sue? I'm sorry; I was just in a daze. I was remembering something that happened in school a long time ago. Sue was just someone who was there, that's all. I didn't realize I said her name out loud," I explained.

"You just about ready? Don't wanna be late on the first day of school."

"Yeah, just give me five minutes. Can you wait in

the living room, please?" I pled for some privacy.

"Sure thing," he whispered. Before he walked off, he leaned over and kissed me on the cheek. "Wouldn't want to mess your lipstick up," he mumbled; then he walked away.

Pulling up to the school, we parked across the street from the gymnasium and walked to the Atrium of the building, situated by the cafeteria; that's where all homerooms were posted. Ms. Michelson in building **A** and was my homeroom teacher and Mr. Lowe, who was in building **C**, was Mason's. Staring at the paper hanging on the wall, I mumbled, "I hope we get to see each other throughout the day."

Mason smiled. "We will. Meet me here after homeroom, no matter where your first period class is at, and we'll check out each other's schedule," he insisted.

"Okay."

He walked me to my homeroom class and quickly made his way back to his class. Homeroom was a short class that allowed for roll call and handing out important information such as progress reports and report cards. As Ms. Michelson called our names, we were given our schedules. Overall, my schedule was pretty good. I had all AP classes, so they were mostly located in building **A**. All science classes were located on the science hall in building **B**.

I had Mr. Stanley, the AP English and Literature teacher, during first period. His class was in room **A** 29 on the second floor. For second period I had Mrs. Lang, the AP History teacher, in room **A** 07 on the first floor. Third period was back to Mr. Stanley's class for Poetry and Creative Writing; it was a new class offered to only a few who were handpicked by the tenth-grade English teachers. The longest period of the day, fourth period, was in the science hall for me. I had Mr. Stringer for Chemistry II. Along with that class came second lunch. *I hope Mason has second lunch,* I mused as I read through my schedule.

Fifth period was in building **B** on the math hall. Mrs. Nettles was my AP Trigonometry teacher; she was brilliant. I jumped for joy (in my imagination) when I saw that I had her. Sixth period found me back in building **A**, but this time, I was in the principal's office as an aide.

As promised, I met Mason back in the Atrium. My locker was there, so I locked away my math and science books. Mason's first class ended up being in building **A** on the second floor, so he gave his word to come by my class and see me when he made it to the building. His second class took him to the **T** building for typing. It was all the way on the other side of the entire school. He would have to run to make it there, so I could walk him out to the Atrium before heading back into building **A**. I wouldn't see him again until lunch. Our classes were just too far apart, but we did both get second lunch. Both of our math classes were fifth period, so we could spend time together after lunch. Unfortunately, his last class of the day would take him in the opposite direction once again. I would be forced to ride the bus home every day because his afternoons would be spent in the field house with the rest of the football team.

As we walked to our first period class, he wrote down my schedule, and I wrote down his. When he dropped me off at Mr. Stanley's room, he eyed Ray. "Hey man. You have Mr. Stanley, huh," he stated.

"Yeah," Ray replied.

"Wow, dude, I didn't know you were so smart." He laughed as he slapped Ray across the shoulder in a joking manner.

Ray laughed back. "Yeah, don't tell anybody, man."

I picked a desk at the front of the class and set my books down. Mason grabbed my hand and uttered, "I'll meet you outside your class when it's over. I'll have to move pretty quickly."

"I'll keep up," I promised.

Mason turned to leave the room, laid his hand on Ray's shoulder, and mumbled, "Don't let anybody mess with her." Ray simply nodded his head in agreement.

Ray sat directly behind me. I assumed he was keeping his end of the deal in some sort of code amongst guy friends. He sat quietly, never uttering a word.

Shutting the door behind himself, Mr. Stanley entered the room. "Once the door is shut, the door is shut," he commanded. "Unless you have an excuse in your hand, you will not be allowed to enter my classroom. This class is set up for those who mean business and plan to attend college. My expectations of you will exceed that of other classes. You will write more as well as read more than you ever have. I expect your full attention while I am speaking," he stated as he explained the rules and regulations of the classroom environment. He shuffled through some papers and began passing them out. "Pass these back, please. It is your reading list for the year. You will give book reports, written and oral, write essays and critical analyses, as well as write a research paper," he instructed.

Several of the teenagers squirmed in their seats; dread washed over many of their faces, but elation washed over mine. I could do this. This was exciting to me. This would be a class I looked forward to each day. As I pondered all the reading that lay ahead of me throughout the year, I realized the amount of reading I did on a daily basis had severely declined since I had been dating Mason. *You'll have to buckle down, Aralyn,* I commanded myself.

Second period was boring, as history so often can be. My eighth-grade history teacher had made the class exciting and fun, but so many history teachers were just about the memorization of dates. It seemed that Mrs. Lang was one of those. I walked by myself back upstairs to Mr. Stanley's room again. He was a young teacher, probably twenty-six or so, and he was a nice-looking man, tall and slender with light-brown hair to match his caramel eyes.

I was surprised to walk in the class and see Ray. I sat in the same desk as before, as did he. Turning around in my desk to face him, I asked, "Your teacher recommended you for this class?" I didn't mean to be condescending, but apparently I did a good job of sounding that way.

He snickered. "Yeah, I know. I don't look like the intelligent type with the long hair and all, besides the fact that I play lead guitar in a rock band." He helped me out by laughing and making light of the situation.

"Sorry, didn't mean to sound that way," I apologized. "It's funny how stereotyping rubs off on everybody." I laughed in embarrassment.

"It's all right. I get it all the time. So, you like to write?" he asked.

"Yeah, poetry mostly. How 'bout you?"

"I write songs, so poetry as well," he answered just as Mr. Stanley shut the door. I turned around in my seat quickly. I had never broken a school rule not one day in my life, and I wasn't about to start in the class I had been anxious for.

As Mr. Stanley covered the same rules as he had earlier, I drifted into a daydream. My life was seemingly perfect. I had never expected it to be so. I was sitting in a class that was sure to cultivate my writing abilities, I had a dreamy boyfriend who was one of the star football players, and I was in love with him. Although he had only said the words himself once when he was drunk and trying to get me to sleep with him, I was certain that he did actually love me on some level.

The fears, anxieties, and loneliness I had felt earlier in the day, as well as most of my whole life, couldn't touch me at that moment. My life was paradise city, the most wonderful place on earth. I wasn't sure what happened in the loom of the Fates to change my life, but I was certain something had shifted in my favor. One of the Fates must have picked up a different color of thread, a thread that was weaving happiness within my life. For me, the class I was in and my boyfriend made life better than I could have ever imagined.

CHAPTER 16

SIXTEEN CANDLES

In the midst of the chaos of Laurie leaving for her elite high school and Laila moving into a dorm and starting college, my birthday had been swept under the rug. It wasn't totally overlooked; on the actual day itself, Mom made my favorite chocolate-on-chocolate cake, but no party had been thrown for me. I felt *more than* slightly bummed over the whole thing because it was my sweet sixteen, and for a girl the sweet-sixteen birthday party is supposed to be the most special of all.

Mom and Dad had gone all out for Laila's; she had a semi-formal party at the Escatawpa Community Center. She wore a beautiful wreath of delicate, pastel flowers in her hair. She was the only one in a formal dress, a white chiffon gown which was later used for her senior year in the Rose Ball. The Lockhearts Social Club put the Rose Ball on every year. Laila had been invited to be a part of the club. The seniors always wore white; they were the only ones allowed to do so. Laila, adorned with a crown, was graced with the title of queen during her senior year ball, and she was offended that Mom and Dad insisted she wear the same dress. They had spent a fortune on it and felt it was worth more than one use.

On my birthday Laurie and I had been at the beach. We came home so I could shower and prepare for the special event. At the time I had no idea there would be no surprise special event. I cleaned myself up and picked out my best Sunday dress. It wasn't solid white, but it was beautiful with tiny lilac flowers embossed on the a-line skirt. The solid-white bodice fit perfectly, and across the shoulders lilac-colored sheer wrapped around and formed a knot in front where a rose bud sat.

I walked in the living room expecting to see my grandpa, my parents, my sister, and a few aunts and uncles, but the room was empty. I released my excitement through a saddened heave, slumped my shoulders, and walked through to the kitchen. When I walked through the archway, I saw Mom standing with a homemade cake, and sitting on top were the numbers one and six. Behind Mom stood Dad, Laurie, and Laila. When Laila saw me all dressed up, she giggled. I wasn't really sure what it meant at the time, but I knew it was directed at me.

Immediately after blowing out the candles on my homemade cake, Laila clapped and said, "Happy Birthday, Air." She walked around Mom and approached me. When she hugged me, she cattily remarked, "Why are you so dressed up? It's just us."

Pain shot through me like the words were knives stabbing me in the gut. It felt so real and forceful that I threw my hands over my belly to stop the joy and happiness I had found over the last several years from bleeding all out. Then the gangrenous infection from past hurts began to fester. The Wall had been penetrated by invaders. The bitterness, mingled with indignant rage, burst past the borders of The Wall and spewed forth from my mouth. "It's my *sweet sixteen*, Laila. *You* had a beautiful formal dress bought for you, and *you* had a big, fancy party thrown for you, and *you* were upset that you had to wear the same dress!" Behind the gush of words, a bitter waterfall of tears emerged.

Shocked that I had reacted in such a way, I ran to my room. Mom took off behind me. Dad laid into Laila about her inappropriate and hurtful remark, and Laurie stepped back, speechless. Slamming my door behind me, I threw myself across my bed and wept. Mom quietly opened and shut the door. She tiptoed to my bedside and knelt down. Caressing my face, she whispered, "I'm sorry, Aralyn. Dad and I have had to put so much money out to send Laila off to school that we couldn't really afford to throw a big bash for you. I should've sat you down and talked to you about it."

Muffled by the pillow, I responded, "I thought Grandma had a fund set up?"

Mom sighed. "She did, but there are still a lot of other expenses. Her graduation itself was expensive, and your dad bought her that car, so she would have a way to get to college and back home occasionally. We've had to buy her things she will need for her dorm. It's an accumulation of a lot of things, dear, but no matter what our excuse is for not having more for you, Laila should not have said what she did. In fact, we should have all dressed up for you. I'm sorry. Will you please forgive me?"

I rolled my head around to face my mom. She reached out her hand and dried my tears. Sniffling, I whispered, "I forgive you, but I just want to be alone for a while, okay?"

"All right," Mom whispered just before kissing my forehead and leaving the room.

Mom left me alone; within a few minutes, Laurie poked her head in the door and announced her departure, and before I knew it, I was asleep. An hour or so later Laila woke me with a gentle tap on my shoulder. "Air, Air, wake up, Air. Mason's on the phone."

Grunting, I rubbed my eyes and sat up. "Tell him I'll be there in a sec," I grumbled. Laila dashed off to deliver my message while I yawned and stretched. Making my way to the living room, I grabbed the cordless phone and stepped out on the front porch. "Hello," I answered, my voice still raspy.

"Hey, how's your day been? You sound tired," he uttered.

"I just woke up from a little nap. I guess it was little; what time is it?" I questioned.

"Six-thirty," he answered. "So, you haven't answered my other question."

"Not so good actually."

I told him about my day and the horrible experience of it all. Neither of us had ever thought to ask about birthdays, so he didn't realize it was my sweet sixteen.

Promising to help make up for it, he apologized for not knowing and for the bad day I had. "I'll take you out to eat somewhere special next weekend, okay?" He gave his word.

When the weekend of promise rolled around, we ended up at a party where his friend Ray and the band Silver Blade were playing; he had forgotten his promise of a romantic dinner. Still depressed over Laurie having left the prior weekend, I never brought it up. I had no desire to rub his nose in forgetting his promise. Riddled with pain, I remembered how the wine coolers aided me in forgetting my hurts the night I met Mason, so I decided to drink a few that night, hoping the numbness would return. Before I knew it, I had consumed four and was starting my fifth. I was not walking a straight line; that's for sure!

That was the night I considered breaking up with Mason. I started feeling sick, so Wyn, the man having the party, offered to let me lie down in one of the spare bedrooms. Mason walked me upstairs and checked to make sure the room was not already occupied. I lay down, and he crawled in the bed beside me. Pulling my hair away from my neck, he softly kissed on my throat. He ran his hand down the side of my body and brought it back up my thigh; then he whispered in my ear, "Please, Aralyn."

Turning to face him, I insisted, "Mason, no. I don't want it to be like this. When I do, I want it to be special. I don't want to remember my first time as being drunk at a party. I want it to be with the person I'm going to spend the rest of my life with."

He continued to beg and to plead. After he told me he loved me, I still refused, and he finally gave up. Frustrated, he left me in the room by myself and went to rejoin the party. Lying in the dark with the room swirling and spinning around me, I thought about the three little words he had said. I knew he was drunk and trying to convince me to have sex, but I also knew I really did love him. I loved him so much that it hurt to think I might end up losing him over the sex issue. I didn't want to give in, yet I did desire him.

Eventually I felt better, so I slipped into the bathroom to touch up my face and hair before rejoining the group downstairs. When I walked down the stairs, I heard loud laughter coming from the den. Knowing we had been in there earlier, I went to check it out. I walked in on Mason, Wyn, a girl named Jennifer, a guy they called C.J., and Blade inhaling some sort of drug. I didn't know what it was, and I didn't care. I stood speechless with my mouth hung open until Blade elbowed Mason, prompting him to turn and look. When Mason glanced across the room and into my eyes, I took off. Yanking on the front door, I swung it open, slammed it shut, and darted toward his car. I crumpled to the ground behind the red Firebird and wept.

I could hear Mason's heavy footsteps over the driveway as he chased after me, and I heard his voice as he hollered my name. Furious, I kept silent. Drugs were never a part of the deal. He wasn't supposed to do that kind of stuff, and I didn't want people involved in my life who did. As I sat crying, I knew I should break up with him, but I wasn't sure how to be strong enough.

When Mason found me, he sat on the ground next to me. After a couple of silent minutes, he spoke up. "Aralyn, I didn't mean for you to see that."

I snapped my head around and shot darts of anger at him through my eyes. "What do you mean by that? You just planned on hiding the fact that you do drugs from me?" I hollered.

"Look, I've fooled around with stuff for a while now. It has nothing to do with you. I know you don't do that kind of stuff, and I would never ask you to. I don't even do it often," he promised. He grabbed my hand.

Yanking it away from him, I snarled, "I don't like it; I don't want that kind of stuff in my life *at all*."

Reaching out for my hand once more, he begged, "Aralyn, please forgive me. You're more important than that stuff."

Lifting my head, I peered into his beautiful eyes, and my heart melted. At that moment I knew I could never go through with it. I couldn't imagine my life without him, so with a soft kiss I relayed the message of forgiveness. "Will you promise to stop?"

He sighed, "Promise."

Two weeks before we were to be let out of school for Christmas break, Mr. Stanley passed out the assignment that sparked the memory of those events. We were to write a poem reflecting one of our lost dreams. As I reminisced over the events of my sixteenth birthday, the following weekend slipped right in. The two were seared together in my mind.

I pulled out my notebook and wrote:

"Sixteen Candles"

My lost dream
Would be my sweet sixteen.
Wearing a dress of white
On a starry Friday night.
In the background a lake,
And a dazzling cake
Made with three layers of white
Trimmed with rosebuds, pink and bright.
On my head a wreath rests
Made of white baby's breath.
Made a princess for the day

I watch as sixteen candles burn away.
Blowing them out, I make a wish
That Prince Charming would give me a kiss.
~ Plain Jane ~

Mr. Stanley slipped out of the room without saying a word. Our class was very well behaved, so if he needed to, he often ran down to the office for a few minutes during our period. Of course, he always left us working on an assignment, so our time was occupied.

Ray tapped on my shoulder and whispered, "Are you having a problem with this one?"

"Nah, uh," I answered; then I asked, "Why? Are you?"

"Yeah. What are you doing yours on?" he inquired.

"My sweet sixteen," I answered. Ray and I had been sitting next to one another in two classes for three months, so we often talked. He divulged several of his songs to me and I my poetry to him. A love for words was a bond that the two of us shared.

"Your sweet sixteen is a lost dream?" he asked, confused.

"Yeah, it's a long story. It was basically shoved to the side—not exactly a girls dream." I brushed off the subject.

"Sweet Sixteen is a rite of passage for a girl. What happened?" he pressed.

I disclosed the events surrounding my sweet sixteen, leaving out the plea for sex and the drug use, of course; however, I filled him in on my sister's special day and her aggravation over having to wear the same dress, the things she said to me, my best friend moving away, and Mason forgetting to keep his word.

"Whoa, he didn't?" he exclaimed. "You deserve better than him."

Jolted by that proclamation, I hung my head. "You shouldn't say things like that," I declared.

"Well, it's true; he's said it himself."

"Really?"

"Yep, the night of that party at Wyn's, as a matter of fact. Mason fools around with some stuff." I looked up at him in disbelief. "He told me you caught him that night. That's when he said it."

Removing eye contact, I uttered, "Yeah, I don't like that kind of stuff. You don't mess with it, do you?"

"No way. I like my brain cells. Don't get me wrong, I've dabbled with some stuff before, but I found out real quick that it's not for me. I plan on going to college and making something of myself. I don't want to waste my life and let it go down the drain. I've seen too many people get hooked and screw their lives up," he explained. "So, can I read your poem?" he asked.

Without even thinking twice, I passed it back to him. It was a simple movement with no reflex to withdraw. He read my poem to himself; then he looked at me and smiled. "It's good. A lake, huh?"

"Yeah, it's my dream. Actually my dream is to have an outside wedding in front of a lake, but sweet sixteen is close enough." I sighed.

The sound of heavy footsteps caught my attention; I snatched my paper back and turned around in my desk just before Mr. Stanley came charging in the room fuming mad about something, so everyone froze in fear and stared at his blood-red face. Blowing off some steam, he marched to his desk and mumbled quite a few things under his breath. We never knew what had cranked his tractor that day, and we surely never asked.

CHAPTER 17

MORE THAN WORDS

The following months ticked away; Friday nights were always spent watching Mason take the team to victory at a football field somewhere, and much like St. Nick, Christmas came and went in a dash. Laurie came home for a couple of days. I only saw her for a short time because her parents wanted to spend time with her, which was only natural, but there seemed to be some sort of invisible shield separating us. She and I both had done a fair amount of changing, and I imagined it was those changes that created the shield of awkwardness. I spent Christmas Day with my parents and sister, but Mason came over that evening.

We stepped out on the back porch to exchange gifts with a little privacy. He gave me a necklace with a heart-shaped charm that read *special*. A bright smile crossed my face when I unraveled the paper and opened the box. It was a completely unexpected surprise. When he slipped it around my neck, I turned and stretched to wrap my arms around his neck; then I pressed my lips against his in a passionate kiss.

Adrenaline and excitement rushed through my veins, and before I knew it, he was pushing me away from him. "Better calm down there, Aralyn, or you won't be able to hold me accountable for what ends up happening." He laughed.

"I'm sorry. I don't know what got into me," I explained. He just shook his head and smiled.

"If we weren't at your house with your parents right inside the back door, I probably wouldn't have stopped you," he whispered and touched the tip of my nose.

My eyes bugged open, and with both hands I shoved him in the chest. "I can't believe you just said that," I squealed. "What if my mom or dad would've walked out of the door at that precise moment? You would've never known; your back's to the door."

"Then you would've been really embarrassed, and I would be on my way to the hospital," he answered with a chuckle. Swiftly changing the subject and his attention, he grabbed his gift off the rocking chair and opened it. Pulling out a brown leather jacket, he leaned over and kissed me gently on the lips and mumbled, "Thank you. I love it. How did you afford it?"

"Baby sitting for Mr. and Mrs. Sampson," I answered with a smile.

It wasn't long before the night came to an end, and he was preparing to go home. He slipped on the jacket

I had gotten him. Holding my hand, he walked me around the side of the house. Butterflies fluttered away in my belly as he stretched his hand, lifted my chin, and lightly pressed his lips against mine. Just as my heart rate increased and my breathing became rapid, he climbed in his red car and drove off. With my hand clutching my chest, I stood where his car had just sat and watched as the red tail lights disappeared in the distance, the darkness eventually swallowing them whole.

Dad had still been working his part-time job, and he and Mom rarely saw one another. They argued a lot about all the time he spent at the car dealership. "It's helping to pay for Laila's college. Don't forget your other daughter has to go to college too!" He would always yell back at Mom when she mentioned him taking a day or two off.

Laila and I both noticed the tension between them Christmas Day, and when Mason left, she brought it up to me. "They're gonna end up divorced, Air," she grumbled.

"No, they're not. Don't say things like that. Dad'll eventually get tired of working seven days a week and quit. That's all Mom wants," I responded. I refused to accept that a divorce was even a possibility. My parents had always had a great relationship. Sure, they argued, but intellectually I knew that no two people saw *everything* eye to eye.

That night Laila cried, and I sat in stubborn denial. Before she left to go back to Perk, we had our worst fight ever. The day before she was to leave, Mom stopped me outside. Grabbing me by the arm, she pulled me away from Mason's car. "What's up with that?" I blurted out thinking it was Laila. When I looked into the eyes of my mother, I quickly spit out, "I'm sorry, Momma; I thought Laila grabbed me."

Mother's eyes looked fierce. "I wanna talk to Mason before he drives off," she demanded.

Mason jumped back out of the car. "You need something Mrs. Meredith?" he inquired.

"I most certainly do; I need you to keep your hands off my daughter; that's what I need," she commanded in a stern teacher-like voice.

Mason's eyes just about popped out of his head. "I...don't understand, Mrs. Meredith. Did I do something?" he asked, confused. "Because I've never laid a hand on Aralyn. I would never hurt a girl, much less her. I don't agree with boys using their physical strength against a girl, Mrs. Meredith. I assure you if anyone ever did hurt her, I'd be the first one there to put 'em in their place," he assured her.

"This is not about you hitting Aralyn, Mason." Mom threw her hand on her hip and continued, "Laila informed me that you have only one purpose for dating my daughter; she said that Aralyn's a trophy to you because of her innocence. I *know* you know what I mean, and if you think I'm gonna let you get away with robbing my daughter of that, well, you've got another thing coming, young man," Mom shouted. The louder she raised her voice, the closer her finger got to his face. It was the most humiliating moment of my life.

My eyes grew huge, and my face flushed scarlet.

"*Mother!*" I exclaimed. Throwing my hands in my hair, I shrilled, "It's not like that!"

Mason shut the car door and approached my mom with his head held high. "Mrs. Meredith, I don't know why Laila said a thing like that, but if *that* was what I wanted from your daughter, I would've convinced her to go through with it long before now."

Mom took a deep breath, turned to face me, and asked, "Have you?"

"No, Ma'am. I swear. We haven't," I insisted.

She let out a contented sigh. "Okay, but if I find out..."

Mason didn't wait for her to complete her thought. "You won't; I promise. I care about your daughter. I wouldn't hurt her."

I felt a sense of satisfaction make its way to the surface of my heart. While it was the most humiliating moment of my life, it felt good to hear him say those words. Even though his words lightened my initial response, I was enraged with Laila. I vowed right then that someway, somehow, I was going to pay her back for that.

I saw Mason off and stormed back into the house to let Laila have it. "Who do you think you are?" I screamed as I swung our bedroom door open. My eyes boiled over, yearning to release tears of rage!

She squirmed her way out of bed and jumped into defensive mode. "Why are you screaming at me? I haven't done anything to you, Air."

"Oh, you haven't?" I threw back. "You're telling me that you didn't tell Momma that Mason was only after

186

one thing with me?" My bottom lip trembled as my emotions got the better of me. I had to work hard to keep back those tears.

"I was trying to help you, Air. I know that's what he's after," she hissed.

"Huh," I sighed. "And how is it that you *know* that? Do you have some sort of magical power that allows you to read the minds and interpret the motives of teen-age guys?" I sarcastically questioned with my arms folded tightly across my chest.

"No," Laila huffed and sat back down on the bed. "Look, Air. I know the kind of guy he is. He's the quarterback of the football team; he's popular, Air. Look at you; you're not his type. He's always gone out with the cheerleaders and pretty girls. Everybody knows that he's after one thing when he takes a girl out. I'm not trying to be mean; I just want you to be aware."

Pivoting my body, I faced the long mirror that hung on the closet door. Speechless, I stared at the plain reflection for an infinitesimal moment. What she was saying to me was true; I wasn't his type. All the other girls he had dated were gorgeous, and there were many of them as well. Laila was exposing what I feared—he couldn't possibly be interested in me for anything else.

Snapping out of the split-second thought, I reminded myself and Laila of the time we had spent together. "We've been together for six months now. Don't you think that he would've given up by now?" I rationalized. "What kind of guy hangs around for that long just to get that? I know that I'm not beautiful like you, Laila. I know that there is no reason for a guy like Mason to be attracted to a *nerd* like me, but he is. I don't know why. Maybe he's just another Gilbert Blythe: handsome, popular, and over shallow girls, so he falls for Anne, the red-haired, freckled-faced," I pointed to my blotches, "and intelligent young woman. Gilbert respected Anne, and maybe, just maybe Mason respects me on some sort of level that *you* can't comprehend because you're too pretty and too shallow!" I spewed.

Feeling the force of those last few words, Laila sighed and gave in. "Maybe you're right, Air; I hope you are. Please don't be mad at me forever," she begged.

I rolled my eyes. "I'll think about it," I spit. Grabbing my pillow and a blanket, I stomped off to the living room to sleep on the couch.

The next day Laila went back to Perk. She came home every couple of months for the weekend, but things were never the same between us again. There was always an invisible wall shoved right in the center of us. Neither of us could see it, but we could both feel its force; it felt as if the wall was formed from a large magnet, and lying inside each of our hearts were opposing magnets, which were pushed away from one another as the wall repelled the magnetic charge within them both.

In a twinkling moment the Junior/Senior Prom was upon us. The theme chosen for that year was "Once in a Lifetime." With Laila and Laurie both gone, my list of shopping partners was short. As suspected, Andrea and Rachel barely recognized my existence. They would speak in passing at school, but they never called or came by.

Earlier in the year, while Mason was at football practice, I was forced to ride the bus home. Sheena lived four houses down from me, so I saw her every day on the bus ride home. She was my age; she moved to our little town just one year prior. She was originally from Houston, so she was used to big city life. We began talking on the bus, and before I knew it, a friendship had formed. It was a superficial relationship but a friendship nonetheless. She spent the night with me on a couple of occasions. We would sit up watching "MTV" while munching down on pizza. Of course, her spending the night was usually after a party Mason and I had attended. If Silver Blade were going to be performing, I would invite her along; it was always nice to have another female to converse with.

I ended up being what I called a *social drinker*. If we were at a party socializing with others who were drinking, I would sip on a few wine coolers. It was only occasionally and never much, so I saw no harm. Mason would always make sure I had my favorite, peach-flavored Bartles and James. I had tasted enough beer on Mason's breath when we kissed to know I did not have the acquired taste that he had.

One night at a party in Pascagoula close to the

beach, talk of the prom came up, and Sheena asked me if I would go shopping with her. Instead of my going with her, she ended up going with me. Her mom was called into work that day (being a single parent made it imperative that she go), so Mom let me borrow her car. We merged onto Interstate 10 and drove to Ocean Springs, headed to a big warehouse-type dress shop called Formals Galore. One could usually find a beautiful dress at a decent price.

I ended up finding a royal-blue princess dress with a full skirt and puff sleeves. The bodice was covered with sequins and light-blue rhinestones. It looked like a dress that came straight out of a fairytale. Sheena found a burgundy dress with spaghetti straps. The satin dress was fitted until just above the knees where it flared out with burgundy tulle. It was gorgeous, and something she could definitely pull off—she had an hourglass figure. Daniel Lamont had asked her to the prom. They were a perfect match; he was a partier, and so was she.

The night of prom was supposed to be one of the most special moments of my life. I anticipated a night of memory making that would forever be engrained in my heart and mind. I dreamed of dancing across the floor in the arms of the most handsome man there and hearing the words *I love you* seconds before a tender kiss. I imagined myself being swept into his strong arms and held so close that I could feel the beating of his heart; then as I listened to the intense pounding, I would sense it as my heart beat synchronized to his.

Things don't often turn out as we suspect they will, and all too often those special moments end up being marred as our expectations crash into the deep, dark waters of regret.

On May 1, 1993, Mason pulled up at precisely five-thirty p.m. He had made reservations at the La Font in Pascagoula for dinner. He pinned a beautiful white corsage to my dress, and I pinned a boutonniere to the lapel of his black tux. He looked more handsome than he ever had; he wore a royal-blue vest under his black jacket with tails. Mom took several pictures of us in front of the fireplace and a few in front of his shiny red car. I kissed Mom and Dad goodbye, and we drove off.

Mason had thought of everything. He secretly ordered our meals while I went to the restroom to wash my hands. When they set our platters in front of us, I gasped, "Lobster?"

He smiled and answered, "You said that you've never had it and always wanted to try it, and I wanted to do something special for you. I wanted to be able to give something to you that you've always wanted." My eyes glistened with tears, but I managed to hold them back. It was turning out to be the most romantic night of my life—just what I had fantasized.

After arriving at the prom, we were joined by Ray, Sheena, Daniel, and several of Mason's buddies and their dates. Mason and his buddies slipped off to procure several glasses of punch while Sheena and I admired each other's attire. Showing off her elegant dress and hairdo, she spun around. I tried to do the model spin but failed miserably at pulling it off. It wasn't the spin I had the problem with; it was the lack of confidence. Despite my beautiful dress, I didn't feel pretty—especially not in the presence of supermodel gorgeous Cassie Bennett, one of Mason's exes.

Cassie, Donna, Linda, and Prissy formed a tight-knit circle excluding the two of us. They were the senior cheerleaders, and regardless of who my boyfriend may have been, they wouldn't stoop to associating with either Sheena or me. Sheena was the newer girl living in lower-income government housing. Although her house was four houses down from mine, hers sat on the corner, so it was technically on a different road. That road happened to be full of duplexes for lower incomes. Her mother was widowed early in her marriage; she worked two jobs to make ends meet. Sheena and I were so excited about our perfect, magical night that we both allowed the intentional shun to roll off our backs.

When our dates came back with our punch, we giggled and sipped while watching certain class clowns perform on the dance floor. The song "Look Away" by Chicago came on, and I turned to Mason. "Can we dance, please? I love this song," I pleaded. Dancing was something I did a lot of, though usually in private, and I loved it.

He cringed at the thought of having to dance; then he tapped Ray on the shoulder and asked, "Hey, man, will you dance with my girl?"

A look of shock flashed across my face. I couldn't

believe he was pawning me off on his childhood friend, but I was glad at least that it was someone I had grown close to. Ray glanced at me and saw my embarrassment and shock; then he mumbled to Mason, "Sure, man."

Holding out his hand, he walked toward me and with a bow he asked, "Will you do me the honor, Ms. Aralyn, of joining me for a dance?" He sounded like a guy from a Jane Austen novel.

A nervous smile flitted across my pink flushed face. Looking down at the floor, I answered, "It would be an honor, Mr. Winstrom." A delicate giggle caught me unaware as I wrapped my arm in his.

I felt uncomfortable as we moved around the dance floor in circles, but I was enjoying myself. Ray turned out to be an amazing dancer. Without looking at his face, I asked, "Have you taken dance or something?"

"Nah, my mom, she loves to dance; she taught me. She's had me dancing with her ever since I was old enough to learn the moves."

"You have all kinds of hidden talents," I mumbled.

He spun me around, and when he brought me back, he looked into my eyes and whispered, "As do you."

For a brief moment I saw something through his eyes. It was almost as if a magical window had appeared in his deep-brown eyes, and I could see straight through and into his heart. My breathing stopped as I was trapped in his gaze. Gasping for a breath, I uttered, "Song's over," and pulled away. "What was that? I hope Mason didn't see it," I mumbled under my breath as I made my way across the convention center to his side.

When I approached Mason, he was laughing with several of his football buddies: Terrance, William, and Jackson. Slowing down, I hesitantly moved toward him. Laughing, he looked up and saw me from the corner of his eye. He reached his arm out and pulled me to his side, wrapping his arms firmly around me. I stood quietly while he joked around with his friends.

The night moved on, and it came time to announce the king and queen of the prom. As the principal took the microphone, Mason dropped his hands from my waist and whispered in my ear, "I'll be right back." He walked toward Sheena and signaled for her to meet him. I assumed he was discussing another surprise for me or something of that nature. She leaned in and listened as he shared his secret with her. Smiling, she nodded yes before returning to Daniel's side.

Mrs. Moore, the principal, announced, "This year's Queen is Cassie Bennett." The head cheerleader, Cassie, gracefully strode to the front of the crowd to receive her crown. She held her head high, a bright smile glistening across her gorgeous face. Her eyes brightened as Mrs. Moore called Mason forth as King. Just before walking to the stage to receive his crown, Mason leaned over and spoke to Ray. As Mrs. Moore placed the crowns upon their heads, she announced, "Now the king and queen will share their traditional dance."

The D.J. played the song "Once in a Lifetime," another Chicago favorite. Mason reluctantly grasped

Cassie's hand and led her to the dance floor. Ray tapped me on the shoulder and announced, "I've been instructed to dance with you for a minute and then cut in on Mason and Cassie."

"Oh," I gasped. "All right." I nervously wrapped my arm around his and followed him to the floor. He spun me out and pulled me quickly back in his grasp. Spinning his way toward Mason, he apologized, "I'm sorry if I offended you earlier. You seemed anxious to get away from me."

"You didn't do anything, Ray. I'm just not used to dancing with guys; that's all." I blew the subject off.

He narrowed his eyes in disbelief. "So, you're used to dancing with girls then?" He smiled.

I hung my head and laughed. He had accomplished his goal to make light of the situation and brushed off the awkwardness. Before I knew it, he spun me around and asked to cut in on Mason and Cassie. Mason relinquished his rights to dance with the queen and took me in his arms. I noticed a firm scowl on Cassie's face as Mason held me close.

As we danced to the remainder of the song, he gazed into my eyes. My heart melted as I stared back into his dreamy blue-green eyes. He laid his forehead gently next to mine as he whispered, "Aralyn, I love you." My heart stopped in the middle of a beat. Every inch of my body tingled with excitement. It was the fulfillment of my fantasy.

Entranced in the moment, I whispered back, "I love you, too."

He gave me his irresistible half-smile and breathed,

"Come on."

Intertwining his hand with mine, he led me through the side door. Approaching his car, I asked, "Mason, where are we going?"

"Somewhere special," he answered. Reaching in the back of his car, he pulled back a small blanket, revealing an ice chest, and opened it. "Here, drink this," he uttered as he handed me my usual brand of alcohol.

I was surprised when we crossed the state line into Alabama. We drove all the way into Mobile. When we pulled up to the hotel, I turned to him and insisted, "I'm supposed to go home with Sheena. She'll be wondering where I'm at. Her mom's not getting home until early in the morning, and she doesn't like to stay alone."

"I've already taken care of it. You'll be there before her mom makes it back," he promised.

Realizing what was special about this place and what would be expected of me shortly, I started feeling sick to my stomach. The night had been so perfect and romantic; I should've known when he told me he wanted to give me something I had always wanted, that he'd require something he wanted in return. I didn't want to go through with it, but I didn't want to ruin the romance of the night either. When he went into the lobby, I quickly guzzled down my second wine cooler.

Registering as a guest of one, he checked in at the front desk; then he parked the car and slipped me in through the back door. A knot formed in the pit of my belly, and the closer we got to the room, the tighter it got. I didn't know how to get out of what was about to take place. I knew I loved him, but I had always wanted that moment to happen on my wedding night.

He unlocked the door and turned on the light. He set the cooler down on the floor and grabbed me another drink. I fidgeted with my hands and wrung them together so tight that my knuckles turned white. Without uttering a word, I sat on the end of the bed. Knowing my nervousness and modesty, he turned out the lights and sat next to me. He handed me the drink and kissed me on the forehead. Unable to even sip, I froze in fear. Sensing my uncertainty, he wrapped his arms around my stiff body and pressed his lips to mine. "You said you wanted it to be special, so I thought *what's more special than making love for the first time on prom night to the king of the prom,* who happens to be your boyfriend who loves you," he mumbled while he ran his fingers over my lips. "You do love me, don't you?" he asked.

I sighed. "Of course, I do. I'm just not sure I can go through with this."

He ran his hand over my cheek. "Love needs to be more than words. I need you to show me that you love me." Caressing my neck, he mumbled, "You're just nervous; that's all. Just finish that drink; it'll help you relax and calm down. You're as stiff as a board, Aralyn."

We both drank another drink while we sat on the edge of the bed. In order to help me relax, he made casual conversation with me. When I had finished my fourth drink, he threw the empty bottle in the trash and laid me back on the bed. Lying next to me, he whispered, "I promise I'll be careful. I'll try not to hurt you." Then he gently kissed my lips.

His kisses remained gentle, but my fear never went away. After it was over, I lay there under the covers and faced the wall. Mason wrapped his arm around me. Pulling me around to kiss me good night, he saw the tears streaming down my face. "You're crying," he gasped. "I didn't hurt you, did I?"

The buildup of emotion suddenly came bursting out. "You'll never respect me again," I cried.

He sighed, "Of course, I will."

"No, you won't, and I'll never respect myself again either." The tears rushed over my cheeks.

Mason grabbed some tissue from the nightstand and dried my face. "I don't take this lightly, Aralyn. I know you gave me something special to you. I promise I won't lose respect for you." Tenderly he kissed away the new tears that formed and rolled down my face.

CHAPTER 18

CRUEL SUMMER

Bright and early the next morning, Mason dropped me off at Sheena's. Her mother was due home by 8:00 a.m., so we cut it close by pulling in her drive at 7:45. Gloom dripped over me throughout the entire drive from Mobile to Escatawpa, filling the car with an odd silence. I read the blurry road signs through watery eyes. I felt such shame for what I had done that I knew he had to be feeling some residue of my shame. Although I felt melancholy, the overwhelming fear of getting caught pushed adrenaline through my veins at an accelerated rate when I looked at the clock on his dash. I may not have been proud of what I had done, but I most definitely wasn't looking forward to getting busted.

"She said she'd leave her window unlocked for you," he uttered.

I gave him a quick kiss on the cheek and jumped from the car. I slipped around back and lifted her window. About two seconds after I threw on pajamas and pulled the covers over my head, I heard the front door shut. My heart pounded deep within my chest when the bedroom door creaked open. Mrs. Lambert poked her head in to make sure we were sleeping. From a tiny hole in the comforter, I watched her stand in the doorway and smile. She was probably imagining a wonderful, starry night only made in fairytales. Her weary eyes shifted and fell on the two formal dresses flung across the white wicker chair in the corner.

We both slept 'til noon. When I finally peeled my eyes opened, I groaned. "Oh, gosh, Sheena, I have to get home. My dad'll be home from work soon," I explained.

Sheena moaned, "All right. See ya later," and pulled the covers back over her head.

I gathered my things and shut the bedroom door behind me. In order to keep from waking Mrs. Lambert, I tiptoed my way out the front door. With my dress hung over my left arm, I walked down the road to my house. The heaviness of regret rose around me like a flash flood—quick and unrelenting. As it rapidly rose, I sloshed my way through it; the deeper it got, the more difficult it became to take each step. A strong current rippled its way through the water and pushed against me. With each step I took, I kept hearing the words which echoed through the riptide, *How could you do it? You can never get it back? You've ruined your reputation.* Combined with the weightiness of regret, the immensity of the choice I had made to sleep with Mason engulfed my every thought and every fiber. I could never go back. I couldn't close my eyes and wish it away. My virginity was gone, and there was no way to retrieve it.

When I was close enough to see through the trees, I noticed my dad's blue truck sitting in the driveway. Approaching the front door, I could hear hollering from within the house. "I'm doin' all this for you and the kids, Meredith. You want a nicer car? You want a nicer home? Well, I can't provide all that on a mechanics pay," Dad howled.

Hearing Mom scream back, I quietly turned the knob and pushed open the door. "I never said I wanted any of those things, Robert," she cried; as she broke into sobs, she whimpered, "I just want you home; that's all." Holding the knob tightly in my hand, I shut the door and silently walked to my room. Without being spotted or heard, I made my way to my empty room and threw myself across the bed. Tears of anger over my parents' fighting welled up behind my lids; they mixed with the tears of regret and broke forth from the dam that held them in. All of my emotions that had been locked away behind The Wall suddenly came bursting forth. As the waters of emotions washed over the stones which built the fortress, they tossed and crashed like great rapids, and I was swept away into a river of grief. My emotions were flung about with great ferocity by the turbulence of confusion, anger, and regret. All I could see were the whitecaps forcefully making their way down the river and pulling me along; I could see no calm in the near future.

The last day of school fell on the twenty-eighth of May, and by that time I had found my way to relaxed waters and a safe little beach on the side of the river of grief. One of the ways I did so was to write a poem about it, so for my last installment of poetry in Mr. Stanley's third-period class, I wrote a new poem.

"River of Grief"

A river of grief
Came and snatched me away,
All I could do was
Take a deep breath and pray.
As the rapids tossed me
Against the cold, hard stones,
They each let out their own cry,
Their own moan.
Each stone left its mark
As it cried out to my heart,
"I was molded by you;
In your life I play a part."
I was drowning in memories
Of all the hurts of the past
When upon a sandy shore

I finally crashed.
The river had consumed me
And left me for dead;
Then I woke up from a dream,
Crying in bed.
I determined that grief
Was a dangerous river,
And of my heart
It could have only one tiny sliver.
I resolved in myself
I could never swim back through;
If I attempted or tried,
I would always be blue.
The river of grief
May have snatched me away,
But I learned through it all
How to live each day.

~ Plain Jane ~

As my pen scribbled the last word, Ray poked his head over my shoulder. "You're writing on the last day? Mr. Stanley said it could be a free one," he murmured.

"Yeah, I know. It was something I needed to write. I'm not even gonna turn it in," I responded.

"Aralyn, can I ask you something?"

"What's that?" I inquired as I turned to face him.

"Are you okay? You haven't been the same since the night of the prom." His eyes shifted away from mine; fidgeting with his hands, he continued, "You're not like upset that Mason made you dance with me, are you?"

I sighed. "No, Ray."

Looking me in the eyes, he smiled momentarily; then his countenance went solemn. "I feel like I need to apologize to you."

"For what?" I squirmed a little in my seat as I remembered that night and what I saw in his eyes.

Looking back to his desk, he answered, "Well, I know you caught me looking at you that night." He nervously shifted in his desk. "I was just taken off guard. I mean, you and I have gotten to be pretty good friends, and Mason asked me to dance with you—you are an amazing dancer by the way. You looked so beautiful that night. The combination of it all just caught me off guard. I didn't mean to cross a line. You're not mad at me, are you?" He wiggled and squirmed.

"Of course, I'm not mad at you, Ray. I think we both felt a little awkward dancing together because we are such good friends. To tell you the truth, you're the best friend I have. Sheena is a good gal pal, but we don't really share our feelings, and I've never even shown not one piece of my poetry to Mason. He's my boyfriend, and I love him, but that's just a part of me I can't bring myself to expose to him. You're the only one I've shared that part of myself with, outside of Mr. Stanley," I chuckled, "and my best friend Laurie who I've only seen three times this entire year." I hung my head as the truth surfaced in my heart. "Truth be known, she's no longer my best friend. She was when she was here; I'm so sad that she's not anymore, but it was inevitable. On an intellectual level I knew it would happen."

Ray sat silently as I droned on about my lost friendship. I passed him back the sheet of paper containing my poem. He read it. When he finished, he looked up at me; once again his eyes were a window, and I saw straight through to his heart and knew he understood what it meant.

That afternoon when Mason pulled in my drive, I saw Laila's car parked in the shade. She sat with her knees to her chest on the front porch. Gloom filled the atmosphere around her. I raced to her side not knowing what to think. Mason followed close behind. She glared at him and shifted her watery eyes to me. "Daddy's gone, Air. I came home from Stacy's house about an hour ago and found Momma crying. The house is a wreck. Clothes are tossed about and boxes are *everywhere*." She let out a weak laugh. "There's even a couple of tools lying on the floor. I guess he figured mom could use 'em." She threw her hand over her mouth and held back a sob.

It was a cruel way for summer to start. Without even saying goodbye, my dad had split. He was gone. At that moment I thought life couldn't get any worse. I was certain that the tearing apart of a family was the worst possible thing that could happen in one's life. What I did not realize at the time was the truth revealed in the statement, "When it rains, it pours." It wouldn't be long before I experienced the flood of destruction the Fates seemed to find in my destiny. I imagined the thread being woven throughout that portion of my life to be an extremely deep, dark blue, like the waters within the depths of the ocean.

My hands violently shook. I tried to speak, but no words came forth. All that would come out were whimpers. "Huh...," I cried tearless cries. Mason wrapped his arms around me, and I fell into him. He simply stood there and held me. I gained some form of control over the shock I was in and pulled away from his chest. I looked at Laila and asked, "Where's Momma?"

"She's in her room, Air. I don't think you should go in there; it's not pretty."

"A family being ripped apart never is," I spewed in anger. Walking toward my mother's room, my mind raced, *My daddy, my hero, how could he abandon his family like that? Why? What did we do? What did I do? I was his little princess. How could he just leave? What is this gonna do to Momma?*

When I opened the door to my momma's bedroom, I eyed her lying on her bed, her milky-white complexion stained with blotches of red. Her arms wrapped around her chest and pressed something against her. I approached her side and laid my hand on the side of her face. I brushed the tear soaked hair away from her cheek and looked to see what she held. When I tried to grab it, she grasped it tightly, shrugged away from me, and murmured, "No."

Recognizing the frame that encased a small 5x7 of my parents on their wedding day, I whispered, "I'm here, Momma. Please let me help you." I crawled into the bed next to her and wrapped my arms around her. Momma turned to face me, laid her head on my shoulder, and bawled like a baby.

When she had cried out all of her tears, she drifted off to sleep. I looked up and saw Laila standing at the door. Crawling out of bed, I sniffled, "Did Mason go home?"

"No, he's in the living room."

I edged my way into the living room. Leaning into the entryway, my eyes zoomed in on Mason sitting on the edge of the couch. When I walked into the room, he jumped up and darted toward me. "You okay?" he whispered in my ear as he wrapped his firm, muscular arms around me.

Tears streamed down my face; instead of speaking, I looked up at him and shook my head "No." We stood motionless for a while; then he traced his fingers over my jaw line, kissed my forehead, and whispered in my ear, "You should sit," as he led me to the couch.

Laila had retreated to our room as soon as Mason sped to my side. Prancing back through the room, she huffed, "You should go home, Mason. This is a family situation, and I need my sister. None of this involves you."

Hearing her catty remark, Mason jerked his head up. "Nuh, uh. No way. I'm not goin' anywhere. If this involves Aralyn, it involves me. She needs me, and I'm not leaving," he spit back.

She threw her hands on her hips and ranted, "You'll have to go home eventually. It'll be bedtime before long, and it's not like you can just sleep in her bed with her."

While never moving from my side, he cut his eyes toward her. "I said I'm not leaving. I'll sleep right here on the couch if I have to. I'm not leaving her, Laila; I mean it."

"Laila's right, Mason. My mom needs us. If she came in here in the middle of the night and stumbled upon you, she'd freak big time. You can go on home; I'm just gonna go to bed," I explained.

Grabbing my chin, he lifted my head and peered into my eyes with an intense and genuine look of concern. "I'm not leaving you, Aralyn."

"What if my dad comes back and finds you here?" I questioned.

"*If* that happens, then I'll deal with it. You let me worry about that. All I care about right now is that you're okay."

Laila stomped her foot and shrilled, "Aargg. I guess I'll go call Stacy and get her to come over and comfort me!" She stomped back to our room, picked up the phone, and dialed Stacy's number.

Within fifteen minutes Stacy came charging in the door. "Oh, my gosh, I can't believe this! Where is she?" she rambled.

Sitting on Mason's lap with my head lying on his shoulder, I mumbled, "She's in our room; go on back." Stacy plowed her way through our bedroom door.

That night was one of the sweetest and most memorable times with Mason. He truly expressed concern and love for me. He turned the radio on; softly playing in the background was "Silent Lucidity." Lying down on the couch together and listening to the words, I fell asleep in his arms. I drifted off into my dreams as I listened to the music and rhythm of his every heartbeat. He kept his arms securely wrapped around me. Wiggling and squirming, I cried off and on throughout the night. Every time I made the slightest whimper, he pulled me close, caressed my face, kissed me tenderly, and whispered, "It's okay. I'm right here." Every tear that flowed from my eyes, he dried. He never once tried to take advantage of the opportunity; that night he was simply there to comfort me.

The following weekend Mason drove to Starkville, Mississippi, for a recruitment meeting with the football coach at Mississippi State. He had been accepted by the college and hoped to make the team; it was his dream to play for the Bulldogs. Who was I to stand in the way of it? I was not looking forward to a long distance relationship, but I felt certain we would survive the distance. He promised he would drive home every other weekend, and I promised to drive up as often as I could. Of course, I had no car at the time, but I was determined to see him as often as possible even if it meant having to take a bus to get there. The minute he got home, my phone rang. "Hey, Babe. I'm taking you to Gulf Shores this coming weekend," he pronounced.

"Gulf Shores? No, way. My mom won't go for that," I squealed.

"She won't know you're there with me. Ray just told me that him and Daniel are going, and Daniel's taking Sheena. You can say you're going with her. The two of you can drive over there together and meet us."

"And how exactly will Sheena drive over there?" I questioned sarcastically.

"Simple. I'll let you borrow my car to have a girlie weekend, and I'll ride over with Ray and Daniel."

"Oh," I sighed. "You've thought this through then." Warily I questioned, "Will we all be in a room together?"

"Nah, we'll be in a three-bedroom condo together!" he said. A light chuckle, full of implications, slipped through his lips.

"Hmm, I guess. I don't know though. I haven't left the house since my dad left, and my mom...she's still in another world. The doctor gave her some sort of tranquilizer to help keep her calm. I don't know if I can leave her; she needs me," I rambled on releasing my welled up emotions.

"That's exactly why you have to go away with me. Laila can tend to your mom for the weekend. She's had plenty of breaks lately; now it's your turn for one," he insisted.

I conceded. Before we hung up the phone, he stopped me, "Aralyn," he said.

"Yes," I answered.

"I love you. I hope you know that."

"I know you do, and I love you, too. I don't know what I'd do without you right now. I missed you this past weekend. Come over as soon as you can, okay?"

"I will," he uttered just before hanging up the phone.

Mom still hadn't acknowledged our presence; she knew we were there and that we were taking care of her, feeding her, bathing her, and helping her to the bathroom when she needed it, but she was still disoriented from the medication the doctor had prescribed her. Dr. Loxley had even mentioned hospitalization, but he wanted to give her an opportunity to snap out of it. I knew she wouldn't even comprehend my story, so I told Laila the truth. I asked her not to tell Mom unless she sobered up and asked for me, and in that case, she was instructed to tell the lie Mason had conjured up. I figured that in her state of mind, it was safer for her if my absence was not brought up unless she herself recognized it.

Laila agreed to take care of Mom for the weekend and to cover for me if the need arose, so early on Friday morning Ray followed Mason over in his car. Mason passed me his keys; kissing me on the cheek, he instructed, "Drive careful."

I smiled. "Worried about me scratching your car?"

"No, worried about it scratching you."

I drove to pick up Sheena; she met me outside. Hollering her goodbyes to her mother over her shoulder, she dashed toward the car. She threw her bags in the back seat, and we were off. It was a two-hour drive to Gulf Shores. We stayed right behind

Ray's car all the way there. We pulled up at the condo around 11:00 a.m. Mason grabbed my bag, and Daniel grabbed Sheena's. Like gentlemen the two of them carried our bags up both flights of stairs.

The condo belonged to Ray's grandparents, which gave him full rights to choosing the largest bedroom to be his own, but he chose the smallest of the three and left us to flip for the biggest one. *It was the simplest way to solve the issue* he insisted. Daniel and Sheena won the toss-up fair and square; Sheena was ecstatic and immediately went to unpack her things.

As soon as we were all unpacked, we piled up in Ray's car and drove to the nearest IHOP to eat; then we headed to the beach. Dousing ourselves with tanning accelerator, we lay out on oversized beach towels while the guys went into the water. Admiring their physiques, we sat up and watched them as the waves crashed against them. Occasionally flipping over, we laughed and talked for hours while the guys goofed off in the Gulf of Mexico.

When the sun started to set, we gathered our things and drove to a burger shack. We munched down on burgers and fries and then drove back to the condo. Our plans were to spend the next day at the beach as well, but plans are often interrupted by unexpected tragedies that life often throws one's way. Most of the time, they hit us right in the blind spot—much like my father's abandonment.

When I awoke the next morning, I felt awkward and feverish. I swiped my forehead and found beads of sweat popping up all over. I crawled out of the bed and made my way to the hall bathroom. I stared for a long time at the hideous, pallid face glaring back at me. I fit the descriptive saying, "You look like death warmed over." One minute I was freezing, and the next I was burning up. Bracing myself against the doorframe, I stumbled back into the room; Mason sat up in bed, peeled his eyes opened, and groaned, "What's wrong? You're as white as a ghost."

"I don't feel very well. I think I may have a virus or something."

"Why don't you come lie back down?" he asked, pulling back the covers.

I took about five steps toward the bed when a sharp pain shot through my belly. "Aaahhhh," I belted as I grabbed my stomach; then without warning the pain intensified. It felt as if something had gripped my insides and begun twisting and pulling. I doubled over and hit the floor.

CHAPTER 19

LOVE BITES

Not knowing what had caused my collapse, Mason bounced from the bed to my side. "Aralyn! Aralyn!" he screamed as he frantically moved his hands from my head to my face and to my shoulders. Being unsure of what else to do as I lay wailing in pain, he wiggled his arms under my body and picked me up; standing to his feet, he quickly paced through the condo screaming, "Ray! Ray! Where's the hospital?"

Sheena came charging from her room; when she saw me lying limply in his arms, she screamed and dropped her glass of juice. "What's wrong with her, Mason?" she screeched over the sound of shattering glass. Orange juice splattered all over her silk pajamas.

"I don't know; she just collapsed. I need to get her to the hospital, *now!*" he yelled.

All I could manage to do was moan, "Ooohhh, it hurts, Mason."

"Ssshh, you'll be all right. I'm gonna get you to the hospital," he assured me.

Ray bolted through his door. "Go to my car; I'll drive you. I know how to get there," he bellowed.

Mason carried me down both flights of stairs. When we arrived at the hospital, the nurse led him back to a small, cold room. Laying me on the bed, he stepped out of the way while the nurse took my vitals. As she left the room, he stepped to my side and grasped my hand while we waited for a doctor to tend to me or for the nurse to return. I stayed curled up in a ball of pain. Finally, a short, overweight, balding man wearing thick glasses, green scrubs, and a white overcoat entered the room.

He shook Mason's hand. "I'm Dr. Marsh." Shifting his eyes in my direction, he asked, "And you are," he looked at the file and my wrist band, "Ms. Liddell."

"Yes, sir," I answered through gritted teeth.

He asked what had happened, made me lie flat on my back, and began feeling around on my belly. "I'm going to have to ask you a few questions, Ms. Liddell, and I need you to be honest with me," he said in a stern, firm voice.

I crinkled my forehead in pain. "Yes, sir," I responded.

"I need to know if you are sexually active." He gazed at my face seeking the truth.

I hung my head in shame, and without looking him in the eyes, I mumbled, "Yes, sir." I began to sob.

"Have you been using protection? Is it possible that you're pregnant?" he asked the questions back to back.

When that last word fell from his lips, I suddenly realized I had *not* had my menstrual cycle. Fear washed over me; lifting my head, I peered into Mason's wide eyes. I saw realization and shock echo through them. With a trembling lip, I answered, "No, we...we haven't. I never thought to...I...I am late. Am I pregnant?" I looked into the doctor's eyes searching for reassurance that I wasn't pregnant, secretly hoping his questions were routine and held no weight or real meaning.

Dr. Marsh glanced at me and answered, "I'm going to have to do an exam and run a test."

Reassurance drained from my countenance. "Okay," I cried.

He asked Mason to leave the room, but I went ballistic! "No, he can't leave me. I'm scared. Please don't make him," I begged.

Dr. Marsh glared at Mason. "Would you be the father?"

"Yes, sir," he replied.

"All right then. You can stay, but don't move from her side." He sounded like the father who just found out that his teen-age daughter was pregnant, and he planned to make the guilty young man stand up and be a man and take responsibility for his actions.

He sent me to the restroom to pee in a cup, had the lab come draw blood, and then he returned and did *his* exam; Mason dried the tears of physical and emotional pain that flowed like a river over my cheeks. The doctor left as soon as he completed his exam. Silence filled the small, cold room. I sensed Mason didn't know what to say to me, so he just sat quietly holding my hand and caressing my face. I was an intelligent young woman, but even the brightest of us all can fall prey to the idea that we are invincible. I had fallen for the trap that said, "It can't happen to me." I had never considered taking any precautions the night of the prom; being seduced was not part of my plan.

The following weekend Mason and I were together again. How could I have possibly told him no at that point? We had already been together once; therefore, I couldn't say I wanted to keep my virginity and respect. I had already lost both of them. Although he swore he still respected me, I had lost all respect for myself, and that made it more difficult to say "No," so I reluctantly gave in again.

Unexpectedly alone that weekend, he naturally wanted to take advantage of the opportunity. We had not anticipated being alone, so Mason had not considered protection either. The thought of pregnancy had never crossed my mind. I was *so* consumed with preparing for finals at school that I overlooked the fact I was late; then with the stress of my families' desertion by my father, I simply forgot, not being used to thinking on those terms. Mason, being a guy, never thought to bring the subject up; my modesty kept me from divulging information about my monthly cycle to him. I kept him in the dark about when I was or when I wasn't, so when I collapsed on the floor, I thought I must have been dying, and he was simply frightened.

When the doctor returned, a nurse followed him. She opened a set of drawers and sifted through, pulling medical utensils and paper sheets out.

Doctor Marsh approached my bedside. "Ms. Liddell, you are pregnant, but—" He hesitated before continuing, "but you have had a miscarriage. We are going to have to do a procedure to make sure your body is cleaned out properly so an infection does not occur," he explained in a very clear, precise way.

I shook my head in compliance as tears rushed over my face. The nurse inserted an IV into my hand and injected a dose of medication through it. Within a short time, the lights dimmed. Mason squeezed my hand and leaned his head to my ear. "I love you," he whispered, his voice muffled from the medication. Groggy, I couldn't protest when the nurse escorted him from the room. Aware of my surroundings but not coherent enough to know precisely everything taking place, fear shuddered through my body. Alone, with the exception of the doctor and nurse, I closed my eyes and imagined Mason holding my hand.

Doctor Marsh performed the procedure and released me from the hospital several hours later. Ray drove us back to the condo; awkward silence flooded his small vehicle. I caught him glance at us through the rear-view mirror, his eyes full of compassion. I wondered if Mason had told him what had happened or if he had figured it out for himself.

When we walked through the door of the condo, Daniel and Sheena bombarded us with questions.

"What happened? Are you okay? What did the doctor say?" the questions flowed.

I looked into Sheena's eyes and glanced toward Daniel. I felt such shame that I couldn't speak when I opened my mouth. Then I heard the words, "Doc said food poisoning. She'll be okay," Ray explained.

Thank God, Mason must not've told him the truth, I sighed somewhere inside.

I spent the rest of the weekend in bed. Mason stayed by my side the entire time. Once he asked me if I wanted to talk about it, but I just cried and said no.

On Monday morning we drove home. I had lost my baby on June 12, 1993; it was a pregnancy I was not prepared for, but a baby I would have wanted and loved nonetheless. I didn't know for sure if Mason would have been able to love the baby or continue loving me, but I believed he would.

My summer was taking a fast spiral down into the depths of pain, regret, and abandonment. Although I never knew I was carrying Mason's child, I felt like something was missing; something was horribly wrong, and I could not put my finger on it. Over the following two weeks, I found myself crying uncontrollably while holding my stomach. I woke up every night to tear-soaked sheets. I withdrew from communicating with everyone—even Mason. I did not withdraw from him completely, but when we got home, I shut myself in my room for two days; I didn't even speak to him during that time.

When Laila questioned him about what had happened to cause me to shut down, he lied. He suggested it was most likely the stress of everything going on with him preparing to go off to college, with Laurie not returning for the summer, and with our father's betrayal and abandonment.

When I did start talking to Mason, things were different in both him and in me. We didn't know what to say to one another. On Friday, June 25, I borrowed Laila's car to go see him. I pulled in his drive and caught him about to leave. He had just cranked his car when he spotted me in the rear-view mirror.

Stepping out of his car, he leaned against it and mumbled, "I was just coming over to talk to you."

I heard the tone of his voice. Eyeing the way he stared at the concrete and shuffled his feet on the drive, I knew in my heart something was seriously wrong. "What's going on?" I asked.

"I need to talk to you, but I want to do it in private," he mumbled barely above a whisper, kicking at a loose rock.

"Okay, where?" The pounding in my heart echoed through my ears as my blood pressure rose.

"Climb in; let's go for a ride." He pointed to the passenger side of his car.

I drew in a deep breath and opened the door. He backed out of the driveway and took off down the road. He drove out to Helena and turned down an old road that led to a small lake. All the way there he never spoke a word. A strange silence, one I had never experienced between us, filled the car. As I stared at the lake, pictures and images of my fantasy wedding bombarded my mind. In all the times I had envisioned that moment and day, I had never actually seen my Prince Charming. I wondered if part of my dream could be coming true. *Is he going to propose?* I thought.

My heart raced; I reached over and touched the back of his hand. Gently laying his free hand on top of mine, he faced me and stuttered, "I...I need to tell you something." Fear gripped my heart. His eyes pierced through me, riddled with guilt and dread rather than the smoldering, passionate look I had imagined. I couldn't speak; I simply nodded. "Aralyn, I did something I'm not proud of," he murmured. He waited for me to respond for a brief moment and then continued, "Do you remember the weekend I went to Starkville for football recruitment?"

I managed to utter, "The week after my father left." My voice cracked.

He looked down at the floorboard. "Yeah," he whispered. Inhaling a deep breath, he continued, "Well, it turns out that Samantha was there, and..."

"Samantha," I interrupted with a gasp.

"Yeah. She goes there. I didn't know that when I went up there," he assured me.

"She goes there?" I questioned, confused.

"Um, she's a year older than me," he explained.

"Oh," I sighed.

"Well, I was invited to this party, and she was there. I had a lot to drink; she approached me." He stopped and inhaled another deep breath. "Well, one thing led to another, and we slept together. I felt so horrible about it. I didn't want you to ever know. I thought I could just forget about it and go on, but with everything that has happened lately, I just couldn't hide it anymore."

"You...you slept...with...her?" I stammered. My chest closed in on me. I understood the meaning of the words, but I couldn't believe they had just come out of his mouth. The tightness in my chest increased, and my breathing grew short and shallow. I began fiercely panting as my lungs tried desperately to fill themselves with life-giving oxygen. Dying to hang on to the one constant left in my life, I looked into his eyes and frantically declared, "I forgive you. I'm not saying that it doesn't hurt, but I forgive you. I love you, Mason."

Mason narrowed his eyes in pain. "You forgive me?" He sounded shocked and disappointed in my response.

"Yes. I forgive you."

"How could you?"

"I know I don't really know what I'm doing in that area. I'm inexperienced, and she was your first..." I tried to rationalize my response.

Looking down at my hands as they gripped his in desperation, he whispered, "Aralyn, I brought you here to confess the truth to you and to break things off." He sighed. "With everything that's happened, I just think that if I loved you like I should, it wouldn't've happened. Aralyn, I'm going to college in a month. You came close to having a baby. I just don't think I can deal with all that right now."

Frantically shaking my head *no*, I felt a clenched claw force its way through my chest. The ice-cold fingers encased my heart causing it to instantly stopped beating as the blood being pushed through it froze. The arteries and veins that connected to it broke away as the claw ripped my heart from my chest. In my mind I saw it crumble into a million tiny shards of dead tissue.

There was no Sue there to put me back together; she had left me when I was a little girl. My best friend had forgotten me while away at a top-of-the-line school. She had made another friend and was going to spend the summer on her ranch in Colorado. She had sent me a short letter telling me how excited she was about the trip. She expressed a sorrow over not seeing me, but she was sure I would be tied up with my boyfriend. My sister only cared about her friends and getting back to college, and my mother lived in a constant state of shock. My father, my daddy, the man who assured me I was his princess, had forsaken us all, and now the guy I loved, the guy I had given my heart and soul to, the guy whom I had given the most precious gift I could ever give, was discarding me.

"You're all I have left, Mason. How can you do this to me? I don't understand. What have I done to deserve this?" I bawled.

He looked me in the eyes and answered, "You haven't done anything to deserve this, Aralyn." He stared into my watery eyes and wrapped his arms around me. Pulling me to his chest, he pleaded, "Please don't do this to me, Aralyn. This is hard enough as it is."

Lying against his chest, I felt the warmth of his body and heard the pounding of his heart. I took a deep breath breathing in his scent, desperate to hang on to him; I never wanted to let him go. As I listened to the drumming of his heart, he ran his fingers through my hair. Impulsively I kissed his chest. Moving closer to him, I lightly pressed my lips against his neck; if I was going to lose him forever, I wanted to taste his lips one more time. I wanted to absorb all of him that I could.

I made my way to his ear and whispered, "Will you kiss me goodbye?"

Sighing, he gave in and pressed his lips tenderly to mine. As the kiss lingered, I thought about my lakeside fantasy, and I knew it would never come to pass. Every lake I ever saw from that day forward would only remind me that love bites, sinking its teeth into your heart, and leaves you scarred and bleeding.

Mason and I stayed by the lake for more than an hour. Ironically he held me as he ripped my heart out. Consoling me as I sobbed, he dried my tears. He whispered that he loved me as he held me in his arms and kissed me on the forehead. After I had shed all the tears I could, he drove me back to Laila's car. He made sure I was all right to drive before he allowed me to get behind the wheel, and he followed me home to make sure I made it safe.

Even in breaking my heart, he was a gentleman. I couldn't even attempt to be angry at him for hurting me. When I looked in his eyes, I saw pain. I didn't understand it, but he seemed to be hurting himself. The one thing I did understand, he had forever changed my life. I loved him, and I did not see how I could ever stop. I would always long for him, long for his touch and his warmth. The truth of the matter was that my heart had been taken from me by him long before that night. It belonged to him, and I could never get it back; I would never be free.

CHAPTER 20

THE FLAME

Six days later while I sat at my desk writing, I heard a knock on the door. Still in my pajamas, although it was nearing 5:00 p.m., I pushed myself away from my desk and slowly made my way to see who it was. I had been doing a good deal of that—never getting dressed. When I opened the door, my eyes bulged in shock to see Mason standing there dressed like he was prepared to go out on the town.

He stood there fidgeting and asked, "Can I come in?"

"Sure," I said. I held the door open for him; he walked through the door and stood in the middle of the living room like he felt out of place. I shut the door behind him. Gesturing to the couch with an extended hand, I asked, "You wanna sit down?"

"Yeah, sure," he mumbled. As soon as he sat down, he began shaking his legs like a hyperactive child. "Have y'all heard from your dad?" he asked.

I sat on the opposite end of the couch and folded my hands in my lap. "No, we haven't, but Uncle Brian has. He said that Dad said he couldn't face us, that's all. It's a lame excuse if you ask me. I think we deserve an explanation at least," I insisted.

"Yeah, you do. So, how's your mom?" he asked.

"She's a little better. She can take care of herself better, but she still stays in her room. I'm expecting her friend over in a bit to take her to her house for a few days."

Mason's casual friendliness felt like salt being rubbed in my opened wounds. I appreciated his concern for my family's wellbeing, but the small talk was just too much for me at that point, so I looked up at him and asked, "Why are you here, Mason?" I had already shut and sealed the door in the wall which I had opened to him, so my tone was very short and cold.

"I was wondering if...if you'd like to go to dinner with me?" He stumbled over his words.

Perplexed I knit my brow and asked, "Dinner?" I knew I sounded stunned, and strangely as much as it hurt to be in his presence, I didn't want to lose any opportunity to be near him, so I quickly interjected, "Where?" I immediately felt the sealant I had used around the framing of the door begin to soften.

"Some place nice, some place quiet," he answered.

I scanned over my appearance, eyeing and tugging

on my ragged sleepwear. "It'll take me a little while to get dressed."

"That's okay. I'll wait," he mumbled.

I went to my room and picked out a nice pair of pants and a matching blouse. I slipped them on and went to the bathroom to brush and fix my hair. Horrified by the reflection in the mirror, I washed my face and applied a light layer of make-up. I did not want to have lines running down my cheeks if I ended up crying again, so I skipped over applying mascara. It *had* only been six days, and the wounds were still fresh and sensitive.

When we got in the car, he looked at me and asked, "You okay?"

With bewildered eyes I answered, "Yeah, why?"

"Just wondering." Once we turned off my road, he glanced my way and asked, "Are you hungry?"

I thought about that for a fleeting moment. In reality huge knots twisted inside my stomach. His presence confused me. It felt like the nervous butterflies of a first kiss or the first proclamation of love. I wasn't sure if my stomach would actually be able to handle food at the moment, so I finally answered, "Um, not really." I cringed slightly, not wanting to offend him or to give him a reason to turn the car around and take me back home. I was treading on dangerous ground; I was vulnerable. With every second that passed, I could feel the mortar melting. As it melted it dripped its way down the framing of the closed door.

"Good," he responded. "I don't think I could eat if I

wanted to right now."

I sat in the awkward silence for a minute and asked, "Where are we going then?"

"Somewhere quiet. I'm not really sure; I guess I'll know when we get there," he rambled, aimlessly driving down the road. He turned on Hwy 613 and drove over the high-rise bridge into Moss Point. A wave of relief hit me when he turned in the opposite direction of our last drive together; I was so frightened that he might drive back out to the lake where our relationship had ended. The spirit and life in me had been completely drained since that night, and I was afraid that if we drove out there I might end up seeing my own ghost. It would be a scary thing to *think* you were living and breathing only to find the shell that your soul dwelled in was empty. *Is it possible?* I mused. *Could my soul be out there floating around the lake, and I'm only imagining that I'm still alive?*

Thanks to Mrs. L. Thompson, my ninth-grade English teacher, I had read *Wuthering Heights*. The haunting love story left a resounding assurance in my mind. I was certain the love that Cathy had for Heathcliff was so ardent that her soul could not let go of this life or him. As I read it, I pondered the question, *Does she still believe that she's alive?*

Mason drove slower than usual, which caused the lingering silence to thicken in the air making it difficult to breathe. It was a Thursday night; normally during the school year that would mean most teenagers were home, but it was summer, so the roads were packed with young people heading to Market Street and the

Point. For many teenagers those were the places to party and see your friends. I held my breath as I saw the Pascagoula city limits approaching. Several cars full of people we knew had already passed us; I knew where they were headed, and I knew that it would not be quiet. I released all the air stored in my lungs in one long sigh when we turned off the highway onto Jefferson Street. We were not heading to be with the crowds of people, but I still had no idea where we were going.

We made a few more turns, and I started to recognize the path that led to the I.G. Levy Park, but when we turned off Chicot Street, I was lost again. He ended up pulling around to the back side of the park. I did not realize there *was* a back side until that moment. It was nice and quiet, but there was a small lake there. I held my breath again. He got out of the car and came over and opened my door. I wasn't expecting him to do so, but he was being a gentleman. He held his hand out for mine; my heart beat so loudly it rang in my ears, muffling my own thoughts and preventing me from thinking straight. I felt certain he had to be able to hear it pounding away. Hesitantly I reached out and took his outstretched hand. The warmth of his skin radiated to mine. I blinked my eyes shut and concentrated every thought on his firm yet soft hand. He intertwined his fingers with mine and led me to a bench in front of the small lake.

I slipped my hand from his and sat on the far end of the bench. As difficult as it was to pull away from him, I knew it was necessary. The pitch around the door of my heart grew softer and more pliable; the door could crack open at any moment. The warmth of his hand seemed to accelerate the melting process of the mortar making it weak. "What is it with you and lakes?" I asked.

Realizing the significance of the lake for me, he asked, "Oh, sorry. Does it bother you?" Keeping distance between us, he sat down.

"A little," I answered honestly.

"We can go somewhere else if you like. I just like the peacefulness of the water; that's all."

"No, it's fine." I complied to his wish for a surrounding which brought a sense of peace.

The night was clear; the stars shined brightly in their constellations. Looking up into them, he asked, "Do you think we're alone?"

I peered into the vast universe. "I don't know. I'd like to think that we are. It'd be nice to know that we're a special creation. It always feels good to think that you're special."

He looked down at me as I gazed into the night sky, slid closer to me, stretched his arm forth, and intertwined his hand with mine. With his free hand, He angled my face toward his. "Aralyn, I've been thinking a lot over the past six days. I've been thinking about my future and what I want with my life, and I know that I want you in it."

"What?" was all I could manage to utter.

"Aralyn, I love you, and I want you to be a part of my life, not just now but forever. I want to spend the rest of my life with you," he whispered.

"What are you saying?" I asked.

Realizing he just sounded as if he was giving a proposal, he squirmed a little. "I'm not proposing, not right now anyway; I just know I want you to be a part of my life. I haven't been able to eat or sleep this past week. I've missed you. Would you take me back?" he pled.

Tears welled up in my eyes, all the mortar disintegrated, the door swung wide open, and I started to cry. *Could this really be happening? He really loves me; he really wants to spend the rest of his life with me.* He pulled out a handkerchief and wiped the tears away. "Yes," I cried. "Yes, I'll take you back."

He smiled his beautiful smile and kissed me. With our faces close to one another, we gazed into each other's eyes. I smiled; then grabbing the handkerchief, I chuckled, "A handkerchief?"

"Huh, yeah, I thought I might need it. Borrowed it from my dad," he said, laughing; he caressed my face and whispered, "I love you. I'm sorry I hurt you." Then he sat back and explained, "I think I just freaked out over the baby issue. I've never felt this way about anyone, and that frightened me. I knew that I would've dropped college and everything I want for my future in order to take care of you and our child. When I realized that, I lost my mind for a minute. A selfish part of me rose up and demanded that I not let anything get in the way of my plans." Leaning closer to me, he whispered, "I'm so sorry, Aralyn. You're the first person I've ever truly been in love with, and I want you to be the last as well."

Tenderly pressing his lips against mine, he kissed me. In that kiss I could feel his love flow like a warm healing oil; it trickled its way down to my heart and filled the void residing there. Through his kiss the pieces of my heart found their way back home. The tiny shards molded back together as he wrapped his arms tightly around my body; then as we made love, the hole in my chest, left by the ice-cold claw that yanked out and crushed my heart, was miraculously healed. A warm flame infiltrated the cold, empty space in my chest. I felt whole again, as if I had never been harmed.

We spent every waking hour together during the month of July, and things were as they had been. We watched our favorite television shows together and went to hear Ray play at a couple of parties; I still sipped on my occasional wine cooler, a social drinker who only drank at parties. Mason drank more frequently. I never caught him doing drugs after that night the previous summer, but I never asked if he did either. I was too frightened to hear an answer that would disappoint me. Outside of that, that part of my life was wonderful.

Laurie sent me one postcard from Colorado; that's all. It read, "Having a great time! Sorry to hear about your dad, Love ya! Laurie." That was it; I had not said a word about my father to her, so I figured one of her parents must've. Her life had gone on, and our friendship was altered in the process. I had anticipated that result, and that's why I feared her going off to school. It hurt to lose my best friend. I felt as if she had just forgotten all about me. I vowed I would never let another friend get that close again.

My mother was doing. That's the only way to describe it. She functioned, but that was about it. Her emotions were seared. I convinced myself the medications the doctor had her on was the source of her void. Part of me was glad for her obvious disillusionment with life; that was the side of me that knew she would be getting a hospital bill in soon. The details of my trip to the hospital in Gulf Shores would be displayed for her to read. *Maybe if she's strung out on medication, she won't pay any attention to the diagnosis*, I tried to convince myself.

My dad finally called me on the twentieth of July; he apologized for not calling sooner and admitted he was afraid of my response. He said he was sorry for letting me down and admitted he had fallen in love with another woman, a woman he had worked with at the car dealership. Apparently the affair must've been going on for some time; she had given him an ultimatum, and he chose her over his family. I didn't respond to him in anger that day; I simply cried.

Laila stayed at her friends' homes while in town. She figured Dad would no longer assist her with her living expenses, so she applied for a part-time job close to campus. She got one at a bookstore of all places. It wasn't her cup of tea, but she was set to start the weekend after school kicked back in.

On August 4, Mason left to attend college. I dreaded facing that day. It was difficult because I would be alone. Despite the fact I had my friends Sheena and Ray, I knew, in reality, I would be facing *my* world alone. Sheena had never made it past The Wall around my heart, and Ray had only been allowed through to the creative side; of course, there were often other parts of my heart exposed through my writing, but I had never actually let him in those areas. I found him physically attractive, but more than that, I saw beautiful things in him when I occasionally peered in his eyes, so instinctively, a guard shot up around me in his presence. Ray possessed gifts and qualities Mason did not have, and I adored them. The night of prom, when I realized he inhabited those characteristics, I thought I saw the same admiration gazing back at me through his deep-brown eyes. He was Mason's friend. A line had to be drawn in the sand, a line neither of us could ever cross.

Standing in Mason's front yard, I kissed him goodbye. "Aralyn, I have to go. It's a long drive. I'll see you next weekend, I promise," he whispered.

"Call me when you get there," I demanded, hesitantly pulling away from him.

"I'll call you every day, I promise," he said.

I stood in his driveway and cried as I watched him leave. I squeezed my eyes shut and wrapped my arms around my chest. Suddenly an onslaught of insecurities flooded my mind; *would he get there and change his mind? Would he see Samantha again? Would he sleep with her again? He broke up with me once. What if he did it again? Would my heart survive another wound? Would it ever be able to heal if it were ripped out again?* I fussed at my own thoughts and told myself I had to believe I was there with him in his heart. The bombardment in my mind silently slipped away as I pondered trust. There was no way to answer any of the questions infiltrating my head. All I knew at that moment was I had to trust the guy I loved.

CHAPTER 21

I HEARD A RUMOR

I stood, eyes closed, and soaked in the realization that Mason was gone. The wind blew around me, fanning my hair across my face. I felt a soft touch on my shoulder and heard a familiar voice, "Aralyn?"

The voice was not Mason's, but I so longed for it to be him that I answered, "Mason?" before even opening my eyes.

"Nah, it's me, Ray. You okay?" he asked.

I opened my eyes and shook myself free from my trance-like state. "Oh, Ray. Sorry. Yeah, I'm all right. I was just seeing Mason off is all. It's kinda hard, you know?"

"Um, Aralyn, that's why I came over. I heard his car leave thirty minutes ago. I looked out the window to see who it was and saw you standing out here. I just came out to check the mail; when I saw you still standing over here, I thought something must be wrong. You've been standing in that spot for thirty minutes. Are you sure you're all right?"

"Oh, wow, I didn't realize. I could've sworn I had only been standing here a few minutes."

"You sure you're okay?" He raised his brow in uncertainty.

"Yeah, I'm sure," I answered, still dazed.

"Why don't you come in and drink a glass of tea or something?" he suggested.

Pulling my hair from my face, I slipped it behind my ear and sighed, "Ummm...that's okay. I'll head on home."

"I insist," he said, grabbing my arm and pulling me toward his house. Knowing I probably did need something to wet my whistle, I submitted. His house was smaller than Mason's, but it was nice. We both sat at the kitchen table while I drank a glass of tea. He made casual conversation about school and his expectations for the coming year. It would be our senior year, the most anticipated and most exciting year of one's high-school career. I was preparing myself to graduate at the top of the class; then it was off to the University of South Alabama to study English. Eventually I looked at the clock and realized I needed to get home, so I said my goodbyes; he walked me to my mom's car.

Outside of my brief conversations with Mason in the

evenings, the following seven days were grueling. Sheena and I shopped for school clothes together; it was my usual trip to Daisy's with a short trip to Mobile thrown in. Sheena insisted on going to a particular store in the Bel Air Mall, so we drove over for a look.

The first day of school started with a bang. I was on a roll; I had all the classes I wanted. Mr. Stanley had asked me at the end of the previous year if I was interested in being an aide during his creative writing class. He knew I would do a good job assisting him in proofreading the papers. I accepted his offer and had him for the last period of the day. I had my pal Ray in one class and Sheena in two of them, so I did have the opportunity to socialize. Ray was always sure to inform me of his next gig and pass me his most recent lyrics. He kept trying to convince me that I should pull all of my poetry together as a collective work and write a story to go along with them. I wasn't so sure about that. The idea of publishing my life, my poetry was my life, for all to read was not appealing to me.

My mother went to work for her Daddy at Daisy's. She managed the store for him, but it wasn't enough to make ends meet, so she had gotten a weekend job at a florist in the area. She had always loved fooling around with flower arrangements and such. Dad had not been consistent in sending any support. Apparently his new gal pal required a great deal of indulgences. There was only a year left on the mortgage of our house, so Uncle Brian paid it off to help Mom out. He was ashamed of what his brother had done to his family. He had a little money put to the side and insisted he be allowed to secure our homestead (a huge blessing for Mom), but there were still electric bills to pay, utility bills to pay, phone bills to pay, car insurance to pay, and groceries to buy. Dad had only sent fifty dollars here, a hundred there, and he did not even start that until after his phone call to me.

Since Mom had a job, I was forced to ride the bus to and from school. I dreaded the bus ride, but I was proud of the fact that my mother was functioning well enough to work. Although she was able to get up and go to work, emotionally she was still shut off to the world. I tried on several occasions to talk to her about the situation, but she would never respond; she literally ignored me. Eventually I gave up and settled for coexisting in the same house with the empty body that once encased the life and vitality of my mom, Meredith. One thing about it all: I really had no one to answer to, and for a seventeen-year-old girl whose life had been inundated with the cruelty of the Fates with their black threads, that was not a good thing. With no one to answer to, a teenager will often go astray.

As promised, Mason drove in on the fourteenth of August early that morning. We spent the entire day and all of Sunday together until time for him to pull out and head back to Starkville. I was so glad to see him, but it was hard to say goodbye when he left. To numb the pain of missing him so much and the loneliness of no longer having a best friend, I went to several parties with Sheena. I always made sure I had several of my favorite drinks. It felt good to be around others and deaden the emotions, but no matter how numb I became while at the party, when I woke up the next morning, the loneliness had returned.

A couple of weeks later, I noticed a difference in the sound of Mason's voice. He called to tell me he wouldn't be able to make it down that weekend because of the game, but I sensed there was something more to the story; then he simply quit calling. I became frantic; I called him every afternoon and every evening, but his roommate Tom always answered and said he wasn't in. I couldn't sleep or eat. After several sleepless nights, hysteria set in. I lost all desire to attend school, so I curled in my bed under my covers and ignored the alarm clock telling me it was time to get dressed. After missing three days of school in a row, the phone rang. Thinking only of Mason being on the other end of the line, I dashed to the living room. "Hello," I said, desperation in my voice.

"Aralyn?" he guessed.

"Mason?"

"No, it's Ray."

"Oh, hi, Ray. I'm sorry, I haven't had much sleep. You sounded like Mason for a minute there. I guess I'm going a little delirious."

"I was just calling to check on you; you haven't been at school in three days. Are you all right?" he asked, genuine concern echoing in his voice.

"Oh..., yeah, um, I'm a little sick is all. I haven't felt too good. I'll be okay. Don't worry about me. I appreciate your call," I answered in broken sentences.

"Do you think you'll make it tomorrow?" he questioned.

"I'll try," was all I said. "I need to go; I think I hear something." Without saying goodbye or waiting for his response, I hung up the phone.

I needed to do something to stop the throbbing in my chest and the words that kept speaking in my head, so I called the one person I knew who could get me alcohol; I called Rhonda. All she would need to do was go in her frig. I begged her not to reveal my phone call to my sister, and she agreed to keep it a secret. I sat in the middle of my bedroom floor, pulled my knees to my chest, and rocked back and forth while I waited for my relief. Within thirty minutes Rhonda's knock pounded on the door. When I opened the door and saw nothing in her arms or hands, I grasped two handfuls of hair and freaked; she shushed me and led me to my room.

"I left it by your bedroom window. When I leave, you can open it, and I'll pass it through, but you've got to tell me what's going on. My dad keeps two or three cases at a time, so he'll probably never even notice the disappearance of that case, but if I do get caught, I wanna know what for." She looked me directly in the eyes and demanded, "This better be good."

I opened my mouth to try to explain my inner turmoil, but when I did, no words came out—only travailing cries.

"Does this have anything to do with Mason?" she snapped, and when she did, I collapsed to the bed moaning. All I could do was shake my head *yes*. She looked at my pitiful state and took off. "Open the window," she spewed her instructions as she darted through my bedroom door.

I opened the window, and she passed the alcohol through. She came back in and locked my bedroom door behind her. Popping the top, she handed me a can and said, "Here, you definitely need this. What did that jerk do to you?"

"He's not a jerk," I spit; anger twisted my tone and peered through my narrowed eyes.

She shook her head an infinitesimal amount. "If he's got you this messed up, he most definitely is, but I'll drop it. Just drink. You'll forget all about him after a few."

Seeing that the can read Miller Lite, I hesitantly took it. My hands shook violently as I wrapped them around the cold can. I slowly brought the can to my face; the strong, potent smell wafted through my nostrils. I had never cared for the fragrance or the taste of beer, but as I breathed in the scent, I could see Mason's lips in my mind, and as I drank in its flavor, I could feel his kisses. Making sure to savor the taste of his kisses, I slowly drank the first one, but I guzzled the following three. Once the buzz kicked in, they went down smoothly.

The next afternoon a light knock on the front door drew my attention. Still in a drunken stupor with my hair matted to my head from not being brushed, I stumbled from my room dressed in sloppy clothes that did not match to answer the door. I glanced in a small mirror hanging in the living room, ran my fingers through the knots in my hair, and eyed the mascara smeared over my face from rubbing my tear-soaked eyes. Licking my fingertips, I removed as much as possible before opening the door. My head swirled as I flicked my eyes wide to see Ray rubbing his hand across his forehead.

"Ray?" I belched.

"Aralyn, are you drunk?" he asked with narrowed eyes.

"Um, I think so." I hiccupped.

Pushing his way past me, he interrogated me. "What's going on with you? Four days, Aralyn, you've missed four days of school in a row. Have you looked at yourself in a mirror? You look like walking death. I'm serious. Have you eaten at all because you look like you just returned from an audition for a part in Michael Jackson's "Thriller" video? This is not you; you've got dark circles under your eyes, and your face is sallow. You are a beautiful young woman with a bright future ahead of you. Why are you drunk in the middle of the day?" He plopped down on the couch and awaited his answers.

244

I plonked down next to him, laid my head on his shoulder, and cried, "It's been a week. I haven't heard from him in a week. I'm going crazy. I can't think straight. I can't even breathe; it feels like something is crushing my lungs, and the harder I try to breathe, the tighter it squeezes."

"Ah, man. I'm sorry, Aralyn. I didn't know. Have you called him?" he whispered.

"Yes, but his roommate always answers and says he's not in. I think he might be back with Samantha," I bawled.

"Samantha? She goes there?" Puzzled, he crinkled his brow.

"Yeah, he cheated on me with her back in May. It was only a week after my dad left. I can't believe he did that. I mean, I can see my not being enough, you know. I'm not pretty; I don't have the kind of figure guys are usually interested in, and I'm not popular at all. I can see why he would rather be with her, but I...I...I thought he loved me. How can you cheat on someone you love? I know he was drunk, and I understand temptation, but did he not even think of me at all? Why didn't he see a picture of my face and think about what I was going through at the time?" I released so many of the feelings and thoughts that had raced through my mind trying to drive me insane.

Ray sighed. Pulling me closer to him, he gently laid his hand on the side of my face and whispered, "You'll be okay. I promise." I sat there and cried as he held me. He never said another word; he just sat there quietly and allowed me to cry it all out.

Ray started showing up on my front steps every morning in plenty of time to make sure I was dressed and ready for school. If I was still in the bed, he dragged me out, so under his daily commands I attended school. I went to my classes, but I couldn't seem to make myself pay any attention to the words that came out of the mouths of my teachers. All of the sounds seemed to be muffled by the aching in my chest. I was positive I could hear the blood swish through my veins. On Friday, September 17, as soon as I walked in my front door, the phone rang. Awaiting Sheena's call about where we would spend the evening partying, I answered the phone, "Hey, Sheena."

"Aralyn?" My heart jumped at the sound of the familiar, deep voice, the voice I longed to hear. Just hearing him say my name caused a great flood of emotions to wash over me. The elation of love had every fiber of my being feeling once again. My whole body had been numb for so long that it felt like pins and needles covered me.

"Mason!" I couldn't hold back the excitement from my voice. Immediately I realized I should have sounded nonchalant, but it was an instinct.

"Aralyn, I'm calling to make this formal. I'm gonna need my class ring back. If you want, you can mail it to me, or you can give it to Ray, and I'll get it from him the next time I drive down," he said, his tone short and devoid of any emotion. He said it like there had never been anything between us at all.

"What?" was all I could say.

"Just give it to Ray," he demanded; then he hung up the phone.

My knees gave way, and I collapsed to the floor. A deep, travailing cry broke forth, and once it started, I couldn't seem to shut it off. I lay there wailing until my mother came home from work. Naturally she freaked out and didn't know what to do; she called Sheena and asked for help. Sheena came over, and the two of them managed to carry me, dead weight and all, to my bed.

I spent the weekend in the bed. When Monday morning rolled around, Ray showed up as usual. Knowing he wouldn't let me get away with not going to school, I dressed myself. When we climbed in his car, I slipped Mason's ring off my finger and placed it in his hand. "He...asked me to...give this to you." My voice broke.

Ray peered into my eyes. I knew that if he could see into my soul, the way I could see into his, he was seeing an empty soul. He just looked at me and closed his hand around the ring. I could tell he didn't know what to say, so he chose to say nothing. The funny thing is just his presence helped.

The following weekend, I called Rhonda, desperate to numb the aching in my hollow chest. She came over and convinced me to go to a party with her. Instead of Miller Lite she brought a bottle of vodka. She stopped at a convenience store and bought two quart-size bottles of orange juice. "Here, drink this down some so I can add the vodka," she instructed.

Before I took a sip, I asked, "What does it taste like? Is it nasty?"

"You won't hardly taste a thing," she laughed. "That's why this stuff is so great. It's not like whiskey or scotch. You'd be spittin' those back out."

I did as she suggested, and she was right; the vodka barely had a taste to it. We pulled up to a large house in Moss Point; the guy throwing the party had graduated with Rhonda and Laila, so most of the people were older than me. Rhonda and I both finished off our spiked orange juices and searched the party for something else to drink. Mack, the guy whose house we had invaded, found some more orange juice for us, so we refilled our plastic bottles.

I had only taken one sip of the refilled drink when my head started swimming. Liquor turned out to be much more potent than beer or wine coolers, and I felt the effects of it. Rustic, handsome Mack approached me. He shifted his weight and leaned his chest toward me. Lifting his right arm, he traced the back of his fingers down my arm. Grabbing my hand, he intertwined his fingers with mine, pressed his mouth closer to my ear, and asked, "So, are you seeing anyone?"

"No," I slurred, "I'm not actually." I smiled at him with my eyes as a strange surge of confidence rushed through my body.

"Good," he replied. His sandy-blond hair tufted around his face, accenting his deep-green eyes.

We stood there and talked for a while. I finished my drink, barely able to stand, and decided I couldn't handle any more. Mack squared his thick, broad shoulders and drew closer to me, smiling, and excused himself. I had never been attracted to blonds, but in my book, for a blond he was a hunk. It felt nice to have the attention of an attractive guy. He left me standing in the den by a large fish tank. I leaned over and peered through the glass at the colorful fish swimming around in their aquatic world.

Feeling a tug on my arm, I spun around. "Rhonda, is it time to go?" I pouted, glancing around the room and eyeing a steady stream of people leaving.

"Not for you, it's not." She smiled.

"Whadaya mean?" I overran my words.

"Mack just asked me if I thought you'd stay here tonight."

"What? Are you serious?"

"Yep. I think you should; it'd make you feel better," she insisted.

"How would *that* make me feel better?" I asked, knitting my brow as I tripped over my feet without even walking.

Rhonda held out her arms for support and answered, "Think about it; Mack played football with Mason; they're friends. One sure-fire way to make a guy realize he loves you is to make him jealous. If you slept with Mack, it would definitely get back to Mason.

It would pay him back for cheating on you, and he'd turn green with jealousy and beg you to go back to him."

"Really?" My heart leapt with a thud.

It's amazing how stupid things seem to make sense to a person when their brain cells are swimming in alcohol. For some reason, I'm not sure if it was naivety or drunkenness or a perfect combination of the two, I believed that it just might work, so I made a decision to stay and go through with it.

When I woke up the next morning, I wasn't sure where I was at or how I had gotten there. I only knew that I rolled over to see a guy lying next to me, and seeing neither one of us had clothes on, common sense and reasonable deduction said we had slept together. I quickly came to one conclusion, if this helped me get Mason back, it wasn't worth it. The ache in my chest only felt worse. I didn't feel like I had paid Mason back for cheating on me by sleeping with one of his friends; I felt like I had degraded and cheapened myself.

The guilt and shame weighed upon me, and I couldn't bear its load. I knew of only one way to escape its torment—drowning it with alcohol. Every morning, as soon as I awoke, voices bombarded me telling me how stupid I had been, how ugly I was, and how no one could ever possibly love me now, not after what I'd done, so every morning before Ray picked me up for school, I took a couple of shots of vodka, attempting to silence their screams.

Although the buzz always wore off by sixth period, Mr. Stanley knew something was wrong, so he checked up on me. He approached my teachers and inquired about my status; then on October 28, he called me to his desk at the end of class. Being his aide, I assumed he had an errand for me to run, but instead he asked me to hang around after school because he wanted to talk to me. Mona Hampton overheard his request.

When the last bell of the day rang, I hung around to find out what Mr. Stanley wanted to speak to me about. I happened to notice Mona slowly edging her way to the door with a curious look spread across her face. As soon as she slipped out, Mr. Stanley shut the door. He sat me down and told me he knew I was barely passing all of my classes. Quizzing me, He asked about what was going on in my life to cause such a drastic change in my grades. I quietly stood with my head hung low, never answering any of his questions.

"Aralyn, you are a brilliant young poet who can really make something of herself," he said, encouraging me.

With tears in my eyes, I looked up at him and replied, "Nobody cares about poets, Mr. Stanley."

"I do," he insisted. "But if you don't get your act together, I'm afraid you're going to mess up your opportunities."

After at least ten minutes of prodding me for an explanation for my failing grades, he lectured me for an additional thirty minutes on the importance of a college education in the work force. When he was finished, he permitted me to leave. I left the room knowing I *had* messed up my life. I shut the door and looked up to see Mona standing at the end of the hall; the shame weighed so heavy on me that I quickly shifted my eyes to keep her from seeing through to my failures, but what she saw in that was something totally different.

The following day I woke up with a determination to change the path I was on. I set my mind to focus on my schooling. Since it was a Friday, I resolved within myself not to go out partying with Rhonda or Sheena that night. "You're gonna have to shape up, Aralyn," I told myself as I looked in the mirror and primped my hair.

Ray picked me up as usual and walked me to my first class. As we walked through the hall, girls whispered amongst one another. Occasionally one would break out in a snicker. Guys looked me up and down like they were checking out my body or something; then a girl named Abigail walked right up to me and asked, "So, how'd you do it?"

Perplexed, I asked, "Do what?"

She laughed, "Oh, come on, for a teacher he's hot. How'd you get him to sleep with you?"

"*What? What* are you talking about?" I belted.

"Everybody's been talking about it since last night. The whole school already knows; don't act like little

Miss Innocent. Mona saw it with her own eyes."

At the name *Mona* the light bulb in my brain turned on. What Mona had suspected when I couldn't look her in the eyes was guilt, not the guilt I felt (the guilt of being a failure) but the guilt of sleeping with a teacher. I couldn't breathe. I felt trapped in a small room with the walls closing in on me. I jerked my head from side to side searching for an escape route to no avail.

Once again words were unleashed as weapons into my life, but this time there was no lone assailant clothed in white with tiny horns hidden beneath a thick head of hair; this time almost the entire student body had gathered to unleash my demise—words that came together and formed a heinous rumor!

CHAPTER 22

COMFORTABLY NUMB

My breathing became shallow and rapid as my lungs caved in on me. The hall started spinning, and the faces of my accusers became distorted like they were standing in front of mirrors in a fun house. Sinister laughter echoed in my mind. Attempting to stop the visions and the voices, I squeezed my eyes shut and covered my ears with the palms of my hands. Gasping for air, I screamed, "*Stop!*" Unable to move, I stood frozen until I felt a warm hand touch my shoulder. Instinctively, I winced and pulled away, shuddering.

Black dots swam before my eyes; my knees buckled, and I collapsed. Ray caught me before I hit the floor. He draped my arm around his shoulder and lifted me to standing. "Come on, Aralyn. I'll take you home," he promised.

Supporting my weight, Ray led me to his car and drove me home. Outside of rapid, shallow breaths, I sat motionless in the passenger seat with my arms wrapped around my torso, desperate to hold myself together. He parked in my driveway, helped me to my room, and laid me in my bed. He stayed with me for several hours. Slumping to the floor, he leaned his head back against my bed and hummed his latest creation, a beautiful melody, yet he sang no words.

I retreated and hid behind the wall which I had built so long ago, but that time there were no tears left to shed. All that existed for me was the cold, empty, lonely dungeon I had created to protect myself, and growing within it was a beautiful flowering vine that had grown over the inside surface of the wall, covering it with its delicate, intricate beauty. The tears of past pains had watered the vine which blossomed with fragile white blooms, and despite the agony which my heart had endured, the gifts inside of me were brought forth through them. My poetry had flourished as a result of the words which were meant to demean and destroy me. Unfortunately all the beauty lay hidden behind the wall.

The ground turned to stone, and the wall seeped with thick, green ooze. Emerging from all the wounds of the past, the putrescent decay dribbled its way down to the stony surface. The rock on which it settled opened up, welcoming the bitter hatred. As the vine absorbed the infection of the wounds, the stalk transformed into a brown and brittle tare. I watched as the innocence and purity of the white petals withered, and the life and the vitality in the leaves fell. The stems shriveled, falling limp as the last petal dropped and drowned in the dense liquid which now covered the surface of the stone. Feelings of anger, hatred, bitterness, and despair swam about in the gooey poison.

The following Monday morning my alarm sounded. I pulled the covers over my head, ignoring the constant beeping. Thunderous pounding echoed from the front door. I rolled to face the wall and slapped my palms over my ears. Moments after the noisy banging went away, several quick, light taps resounded from my bedroom door. Groaning, I curled in a ball and refused to respond.

The door creaked open with a screech. "Aralyn, Aralyn," Ray's voice whispered. I rolled over and pulled the covers down enough to peer across the room. He stood straight and tall, folded his arms across his chest, and commanded, "Get up. I'm not leaving here until you do. You need to be in school."

I slipped the covers back over my head and groaned. He knelt next to me and whispered, "Look, I know it's gonna be hard to be there, but if you *don't* show your face, it'll make you seem guilty, and hey, you've got me. I'll be right there, and if anybody says anything in front of me, you can pick 'em up off the floor after I put 'em there." He chuckled, trying to make light of the situation.

With a loud sigh I submitted. I knew the only way to deal with the situation was to face the mocking and ridiculing with my head held high. I was not guilty of the crime; I wasn't going down without a fight. We pulled up at the school and watched as heads turned when they saw me step out of Ray's car. I imagined they suspected I would not return because of guilt. Most of them looked shocked to see me, but there were those who gave sinister looks implying a desire to torture; they seemed to feed on the idea of my torment and pain. Revealing razor-sharp teeth intent on tearing their prey to shreds, their devious grins glowed with every wince I made.

Walking me all the way to class, Ray stayed close to my side. He even arranged to leave each class a few minutes early so he could make it to my class before I walked into the hall with the ravenous wolves. He was my strong tower that day, my defender.

Fourth period had just gotten started when Mr. Wells stepped into the room. He interrupted the class by announcing, "Ms. Robinson, I need Aralyn Liddell to come with me." He pointed his finger toward me and signaled for me to approach him. Trembling, I followed him to his office. When I walked in, a tall, slender black woman stared at me with a grim look on her face. She wore a business suit; what she did, I did not know, but she looked very professional whatever it was.

She escorted me into a small room. There she introduced herself. "Aralyn, I'm Ms. Dexter." She held her hand for me to shake. Nervous, I complied and shook her hand. Her stone-cold face contorted, and with a fearful grimace, she gestured for me to have a seat. "Ms. Liddell, I'm here at the request of the school board to talk to you. We are investigating an allegation against Mr. Stanley and yourself."

"Investigating? I don't understand," I murmured. Fear took over my body; I could literally feel it running through my veins. It pulsed through with such force it threw my body into fight or flight. I had to clench the arms of the chair I sat in to keep myself from fleeing. My natural instinct screamed at me to avoid all confrontations with flight, but the logical side of my brain kicked in just in time and warned me of the consequences of that impulse. Inhaling a sharp breath, I steadied myself.

Ms. Dexter raised her brow. "Yes, this past Friday ten different teachers in the school reported overhearing several students speaking of an affair taking place between you and Mr. Stanley. I am giving you the opportunity to tell your side of the story before we pass any judgment or make any decision."

Aggravation replaced fear. With narrowed eyes, I shot darts across the desk, and raising my voice, I blurted, "Judgment? I haven't done *anything*."

"Then, please oblige me with *your* account of what took place."

I shook my head in confusion. "I don't really know what happened; I mean, I know what *happened* I just don't understand how all of this has come about. Look, all I know is that I'm Mr. Stanley's aide during sixth period. He knows me; I had him in two classes last year. I haven't been doing so good in school, and he knew something was wrong with me. He did some checking up on me with my other teachers and found out that I'm barely passing. Thursday he asked me to hang around after class. When the bell rang, I did what he asked and waited for everyone else to leave. Mona Hampton was the last one out the door. Mr. Stanley told me he knew about my grades, that's all. He asked me what was going on; he wanted to know what happened to me," I explained.

"You two were *alone* in the classroom after school had been dismissed for the day?" she pressed me for an answer; a subtle hint of speculation mingled in her words. Her tone of voice and the way she emphasized the word *alone* left me with the feeling she either wanted us to be guilty or wanted it to look as if we were.

"Yes, ma'am. It was a private conversation. He knew I wouldn't talk about it if another student were present."

"So, you two were not involved in a physical relationship that day?" she asked.

"*Of course not!*" I hollered as I stood to my feet and slammed my palms down on the desk.

"You need to calm down and sit down, young lady," she instructed, rising to her feet.

I took a deep breath and tried to relax, but the anger already built up inside the wall bubbled and roiled. I was sure it was about to boil over. I gripped the arm rails of the chair and slowly sat back down. She followed suit, never removing contact with my eyes.

"So, can you explain to me why Mona insists she heard *and* saw you two having an affair?"

Gritting my teeth, I spit, "No, I can*not* tell you why she would lie in such a way, but she did. I would never do such a thing!"

She grilled me for another forty minutes. The day turned out to be a long, grueling one. My head swam with the unremitting questions for days after the event. Mr. Stanley, myself, and Mona had all three been interrogated. The accusation made by Mona was a severe one; if found to be an outright lie, she could have faced charges, but the investigators came to the conclusion that it was inconclusive. They said there was no solid evidence either way. Secretly I wondered if that were because of the fact that Mona happened to be related to a high-ranking local politician. All he had to do was talk to a few people and have it swept under the rug. It would be bad press for *him* if his niece were found guilty of such a scandal.

Mr. Stanley was reprimanded for being alone with me in the classroom with the door shut. He admitted it wasn't the wisest decision he had ever made, but firmly declared he had only done so out of concern for me. He proclaimed he knew me well enough to know I would not misinterpret the situation but admitted he had not thought about how it might appear to others. At the end of the day (so to speak), he resigned.

The ending of his letter of resignation read,

"Although I boldly proclaim my innocence, I believe it is in my best interest to resign. I have already lost the trust and respect of my students; I do not foresee the potential to regain either. Because of the investigation's inconclusiveness, my presence here would always be coupled with whispers. I fear for the student involved that, should I remain, she would have to live amongst the continual, harassing accusations from her peers. As a school system I admonish you to do what is right by her and protect her future.

Sincerely,

Caleb Stanley."

Ray worked in the office as an aide to Mr. Wells; seeing the letter lying open on his desk, he waited for his opportunity. When Mr. Wells left his office to attend a meeting with a parent in the conference room, Ray sneaked in and made a photocopy of the letter. He gave it to me when we pulled up at my house after school. Tears spilled over as I read it. He was a teacher who truly cared about what happened to his students, and because of the stupidity and cruelty of a teen-ager with a razor-sharp tongue, he would no longer have the chance to pervade the minds of the students with his wisdom and intellect.

I appreciated Mr. Stanley's concern for me, but it didn't matter whether he stayed or whether he left, either way the damage was done. The whispers and looks continued; Ray made sure I attended daily, but I sank deeper and deeper into the cold, black depths of despair.

My world had become a dark, gruesome place. Because of my friend Ray, I woke up, and I dressed myself, and I put one foot in front of the other, and I breathed in the air around me, but I was a walking corpse. I could never find my way to the surface of the waters that had rained down on my world and flooded the dungeon I had created for myself when I built The Wall. Surrounded by words and wounds, I frantically swam through the poisonous emotions of dread, pain, despair, anxiety, worthlessness, loneliness, fear, anger, and hatred. Hysterically kicking and paddling my way through the blackness, I searched for the surface. My lungs longed to inhale oxygen. The weight of it all crushed them; in desperation I took a breath. Sucking the poison into my lungs, I drowned.

My body continued to float around and go through the motions, limp and lifeless. The innocent, intelligent young Aralyn had died. Who I was at that point, I wasn't sure, but I knew I was not the same. My hurts had turned me bitter.

When life spirals into a deep, black hole, one often

questions the things they were brought up to believe. I had been taught that God loved me. In the darkness of my mind, I wondered how a God who loved me could allow the hurt and pain that had been poured on me. Those questions came out through my poetry. One night as I sat on the back porch watching fireflies swarm around, I wrote:

"Fireflies"

Fireflies are scurrying
All around
While the dark shadows
Have me bound.
Are they here to vindicate me?
Are they here to set me free?
I see them flying
Around in my mind;
Even though in the darkness
I am blind.
I envision them as angels
Sent by God to break my chains,
But maybe they're just demons
Engulfed by flames.
To me they have to be
one of the two.
The question is
What are they to you?
I watch them flying,
And I realize

Plain Jane

To anyone else
They're just fireflies.
~ Plain Jane ~

After finishing "Fireflies" I ambled back into my room, put my notebook away, and pulled out the picture of Mason and me from prom night. Staring at it for a long time, anger rose to the surface of my heart. That was the night that started it all. "Had I not given into you that night, if you hadn't persuaded me that you loved me and we would always be together, I wouldn't be like this right now. It's all your fault. You're to blame!" I screamed at the picture just before throwing it across the room; then I pulled my notebook back out and wrote:

"Dark Heart"

I stand and watch as you walk away from me.
Tears start to flow as I fall to my knees.
A knife has just ripped open my chest.
My heart is exposed; you have left it a mess.
It's tangled and twisted as blackness creeps in.
It cries out in pain as it's overtaken by sin.
Corruption and distortion are now in its vice.
Its twisted thoughts refuse to play nice.
My heart insists that you are to blame.
It curses you now to live forever in shame.
~ Plain Jane ~

Outside of poetry, alcohol was my only escape.

Once my blood-alcohol level hit a certain point, I felt as if I could breathe again; I could even laugh, but that level kept rising, and the need to consume more and more in order to get to that place, increased. One night in January at a party, Cliff Taylor offered me pain pills. Already plastered, I took them without hesitation. As I threw back my head to swallow, I pondered the idea, *If they numb a person to physical pain, I wonder if they can do a better job of numbing someone to emotional pain?* Within thirty minutes the effects of the pain medication kicked in, and before long I found myself comfortably numb. While in the deadened, unfeeling state, I decided to live out my remaining days in that emotionless state of mind.

CHAPTER 23

WITHOUT YOU

Numbness became my goal in life. For the next month, no matter where I was, I was high. Sheena and I still hung out, but she would not have anything to do with popping any pills. Ray? He stood by my side every day, but disappointment in me and my decisions reflected in his eyes. Peering into the eyes that once held admiration for me, I cringed. Daily disappointment in myself covered me like black soot—no matter how hard I tried to scrub it away, but to have the person who had turned out to be my very best friend disappointed in me was more difficult to bear. I quit looking him in the eyes. Many days I convinced him I was sick and refused to get out of bed. He would eventually give up with a sigh on those days.

On February 25 I woke up feeling all right. For some reason unbeknownst to me, I sensed I could face the day without being overwhelmed emotionally, but when I got to school, my positive outlook changed rapidly. While in the restroom, another senior came up to me and asked, "Why aren't they gonna let you graduate?"

Glaring back at her through the mirror, I froze in shock. I couldn't comprehend why she would ask such a thing. I knew I had messed my life up, but to not be allowed to walk across that field with some form of dignity left was more than I could bear. My eyes watered and I managed to utter, "I."

She belted. "Sorry! I thought you knew," she squealed as the heavy door closed behind her.

My world tumbled out of control; it had been falling in a downward spiral for eight solid months, and it was not slowing down. Awareness of it all hit me in that moment. Oh, I knew it was bad before that moment, but my eyes had just been opened, and in the mirror I saw the hideous image of me. The storyboard of my life I had conjured as a young girl, the one with the cracked mirror causing a distorted view, shattered in front of me. As I gazed upon the wounded reflection in the fracture-free mirror, I saw a frightened little girl searching for her invisible friend.

I closed my eyes and cried out, "Sue, I need you; I need you to come back. I need to be invisible again. It hurts, Sue. It hurts so much. I don't want to hurt anymore. I'm so alone; please come back to me. Look what I've done to my life, Sue. I've screwed it up; I'm a failure. I'm an outcast! They're not gonna let me graduate, Sue. It's my fault; I know it is, but I can't seem to focus anymore. I hate life; I hate myself. Sue, I've become everything I've ever despised. I'm a drunk; I've started using drugs, something I swore I'd *never* do. I slept with a guy I didn't even know. What's happening to my life? What have I done to make God so angry at me? I was a good girl; I was. I'm not anymore, and I'll never forgive myself for the things I've done. God can't forgive me; I know that. Sue, what did I do to you? Why did you leave me? Everybody leaves me. I wasn't good enough for my daddy; he left. If I would've been a good enough daughter, he would've stayed, but he wasn't happy. He wasn't happy with his life, and that means he wasn't happy with me."

The heavy restroom door opened; Kristin Alexander and Carrie Matthews, the two most popular seniors, walked in. They came to a brisk halt when they saw me glaring in the mirror with tears streaming down my face. A smile crossed Kristin's face; she cut her narrow, slatted eyes toward Carrie and giggled. "Somebody must've told her. I guess little Miss Einstein's not as smart as she thought." Carrie pulled the door back open, and they both walked out laughing and sneering.

I backed against the wall and slid to the floor. Wrapping my arms around my torso, uncontrollable wails broke forth. "Ah, Sue, why did you leave? I could've used your super power just then; please answer me. Momma didn't leave, but she did; she doesn't notice I even exist anymore, and…and…Laurie left me. She promised she'd always be there, that I could always lean on her. Why did she lie to me? I would have rather never been friends. I let her through The Wall, and she doesn't even think about me anymore. My sister has always cared more about her friends. I'm not pretty enough or popular enough for her."

Pounding my fists on the floor, I screamed, "Sue, Sue, where are you? My life is a mess. I don't know how to make it stop; I can't make it go away. I'm trapped in a dark place, Sue, and I can't see to find my way out. I'm tired. I'm tired of fighting. I've been trying to lift this heavy, black cloud off me, but I can't do it. It's not like a regular cloud; it moved in and surrounded me. There's no oxygen in it; I can't breathe. Its weight is heavy. It feels like it's crushing me; my lungs feel like they've collapsed, and Mason, oh, god, I loved him so much. He lied to me, Sue. I gave him all of me. He said he wanted to spend the rest of his life with me. I would have *never* done it if I didn't believe him. Why does he hate me? Surely he must hate me to do what he did to me. How could anyone do that to someone they cared about. He hates me, and I don't know why. All I ever did was love him. I just want him to love me; that's all. He was all I had left, and he left me all alone. The black cloud came and hovered over me while he was there, Sue, but he was strong; he kept it off me. When he left, it descended and wrapped around me, suffocating me."

I clutched my belly and whispered, "Even my baby left me, Sue. It was a part of me and him. I could've had a part of him with me forever, but even my baby left."

My tears ran dry, and I gave up on hearing a response from Sue. I sat on the floor of the restroom until Sheena walked in. She had left class searching for me when I didn't show up. She had seen me get out of Ray's car that morning, so she knew I was there. While walking the halls, she overheard Kristin and Carrie snickering about finding me crying in the restroom. "Aralyn, what's going on?" she asked as she knelt beside me. "Why have you been crying?"

I glanced up at her through red-rimmed, swollen eyes. "They're not gonna let me graduate," I whispered. One last tear trickled down my face.

"Oh, man, come on, let's wash your face and get you home." Sheena pulled me to standing and walked with me to the sink.

Trying to rinse away the pain and guilt, I splashed cold water on my face. Gazing at my likeness in the mirror, I no longer saw a Plain Jane. What I saw repulsed me. "Thad was right; I am ugly," I mumbled. With the ugliness I had become illuminated to me, I yearned to simply be *Plain Jane*.

Hearing my comment, Sheena looked at my likeness in the mirror and asked, "Who's Thad?"

"Just a guy."

Sheena sighed. "Come on, let's get you home."

"How? You don't have a car." I reminded her.

"I'll borrow Daniel's," she answered, and she did just that. She walked past his class and signaled for him.

He approached the teacher's desk and asked if he

could go to the restroom. Ms. Tibbs excused him and handed him a hall pass. He slipped out the door and whispered, "What's goin' on?"

"Can I borrow your car to take Aralyn home? I'll come right back," she assured him.

"Yeah, sure, what's up?" he asked as he reached in his pocket and retrieved his keys.

Sheena made eye contact with him and answered, "Tell ya later."

"Sure thing. Be careful." Sheena kissed him and drove me home.

She asked if I wanted her to stay a while, but I assured her I'd be fine. I just wanted to be alone. After she left, I went to my room, crawled on my bed, and sat with my arms wrapped around my knees. I thought about my life and what had become of it. I pondered if there would ever be an escape for me, but I could see no light at the end of the tunnel. Eventually, I lay down and fell asleep. As I slept, I dreamt of holding a beautiful baby with perfectly shaped full lips in my arms. I looked up and saw Mason smiling at me. It was our child, our baby girl, and she wasn't cursed with my liplessness!

A knock on the door awoke me from my perfect dream. Mom had been invited to spend the weekend in Pensacola with her friend Lydia, so she had already left. I sat up and stretched, a little peeved at being aroused from that dream because it felt good to see Mason smile at me. Grumbling, I stumbled my way to the front door to see who it could possibly be. We had no peep hole, so I had to do things the old fashioned way and open the door. My mouth fell open; I stood in shock looking at Mason.

"Can I come in?" he asked.

Suddenly all the anger I had toward him dissolved. "Sure," I sighed.

Without hesitation he walked in and sat on the couch. "Your mom home?"

"No, she's gone for the weekend." Realizing I didn't know how long I had been sleeping, I asked, "What time is it?"

"It's four o'clock. Didn't you just get home from school?"

"No, I came home early today. I've been asleep."

"You sick?"

"Nah, uh. I just had a bad day."

"So, if your mom is gone for the weekend, that means we're here all alone." He smiled.

"Is that what you came over here for?" I shoved him and turned away from him.

He laughed. "I was just kidding. I came because I wanted to talk to you."

"About what?" I inquired; my hands trembled in his presence as nervousness set in.

"A little birdie told me about you and Mack."

"Oh." I hung my head and wrapped my arms securely around my torso, hiding my trembling hands.

"Are you two dating?"

"No, that was months ago. It was just a one-time thing. I was drunk, *really* drunk. I can't believe I did it. I'll never stop regretting it."

"You regret it? Do you regret being with me?"

I looked into his eyes. I wanted so desperately to be able to say, *yes, I regret ever knowing you at all*, but the coldness in my heart melted away; I couldn't say it. I couldn't tell him I regretted it even though I did. I took a deep breath and answered, "I guess you can't help who you fall in love with; if I could have helped it, I would not have allowed myself to fall in love with you."

Without warning he leaned in and kissed me. His kiss was passionate. I had forgotten how his lips felt and how he tasted. I wanted to push him away, but I couldn't find the strength. It felt so good to have him wrap his arms around me; it felt safe. The black cloud's heaviness lifted from me. He was bearing its weight again, and I could breathe. The forcefulness and the passion in his kiss never let up. He brought his lips to my ear and whispered, "I love you, Aralyn. I've always loved you." My heart felt joy for the first time in a long time. It jumped up and sped to life. I threw myself into his kiss. He slipped his arms under my body; lifting me, he carried me to my room and laid me on the bed. Lying next to me, he asked, "Will you make love to me?"

I couldn't speak; I simply nodded in compliance. I couldn't say no; it had been so long since I had felt his touch and kiss. I had missed him; I needed him.

Afterwards, lying on my bed, he caressed my face. "I'll always love you, Aralyn."

I heard a "goodbye" in the word *always*. Frightened, I propped myself on my elbows and asked, "What do you mean always?"

He traced his fingers over my lips and whispered, "What I mean is you're the first person I've ever truly loved, and no matter what happens, no matter what other person I have in my life, you're the last person I'll ever love this way."

"What are you saying? Are you saying that we're not going to be together?" I panicked.

He hung his head. "We can't be together. That's why I came over here." He tilted his head and gazed in my eyes. "I didn't come for this. I never even imagined this would happen, but when you said what you did, I couldn't help myself." He turned his head in shame. "I came because I needed to tell you something. I came because I'm getting married, and I wanted to tell you in person."

A bolt of shock shot like lightning through my body propelling me to jump from the bed. "*Married*?" I screamed. "What am I to you? A game? An inanimate object you think has no emotions, so you can just play around and toy with it? I *have* emotions; I *have* feelings. How can you make love to me and then tell me you're gonna marry someone else? Who is she?"

Stunned by my response, he sat up and explained, "It's Samantha. She just had our baby, a little girl. She was born three days ago. She was a little early. We decided to wait until after the baby was born to get married. It's set for May 1. I wanted to say goodbye; that's all. I guess I got carried away."

"Well, I guess you did. How could you do that to me? What have I ever done to you to make you hate me so much? Because, obviously, you do. You tell me you love me, sleep with me, and then tell me you're marrying someone else! You're the cruelest person I've ever met! I *hate* you; you're such a liar. I believed you. All those times you said you loved me, I believed you. Was Laila right? Was I just a trophy to you? A virgin for you to conquer? Well, you did it. You have *destroyed* my life. I hope you're happy. Now, get out; *get out!*" I screamed.

Mason slipped his clothes back on and left. He took his lashing without uttering a word. He didn't try to explain any further. When he opened the front door, he turned to face me with his head hung down and mumbled, "Bye, Aralyn."

The light thud of the door caused the room to spin out of control. Watching racing images pass through my mind, I found my way back to my room. I could see Samantha holding a little girl in her arms, the little girl that should have been mine—the little girl that almost was mine. I had just dreamed of her. I saw them walking down the aisle in each other's arms on the one-year anniversary of the day I gave him all of my heart. It was the day I had given him myself. He was getting married on the day I gave him myself. Blackness descended and draped around me, cutting off all oxygen and suffocating me. With nothing left in me to fight it, I gave in.

I scrambled through my cassettes, pulled out my tape of Air Supply, found my hidden stash of vodka, and then thought, *Sleeping pills! Momma has tons of them. The doctor gives them to her to help her sleep.* I dashed back to my mother's room and flicked through her medicine cabinet. I found the object of my desire and ran back to my room. I crawled onto my bed with the bottle of sleeping pills in one hand and the bottle of vodka in the other. *This way won't hurt, and it shouldn't take too long*, I thought to myself. I could no longer endure the pain, the pain of being completely alone in the world. Sure, others existed around me, but that didn't matter—they weren't a part of me. How can someone be a part of you when they barely recognize your existence?

I had been abandoned, plain and simple. Everyone I had ever loved had abandoned me. My dad deserted us all, which caused my mom to turn comatose. Sure, she didn't leave the house, but she abandoned us nonetheless. My sister's world had always revolved around her friends, so when Dad left, she dove into her world of friends and college. My best friend leaving for school instigated the downward spiral of my life. It didn't take long after she left me before my world came crashing down around me. The last one to forsake me was the one I least expected. I had expected Laurie to go on with her life at her new school, but Mason was there with me through all the rest, and his departure hurt the worst. Now I had to face the knowledge that another girl would be spending the rest of her life with him. It was a knowledge that pushed me past the point of no return.

I poured the pills into my cupped palm, brought my hand to my lips, and hesitated. I thought of the hideous creature reflected back at me through the mirror. I despised her. I wanted her gone from my life.

I threw back my head; the pills filled my mouth. I chased them down with the vodka. I shoved my Air Supply cassette in my stereo, fast forwarded to the song that ripped my heart out, took another swig, and laid my head gently on my pillow. Tears washed over my splotchy red face as I listened to the words of "Without You." My eyes were swollen; nevertheless, I managed to close them.

CHAPTER 24

RAY OF LIGHT

Blackness closed in on me; it appeared to be absorbing everything as it passed, stretching its long, cold arms toward me. The words and the music of the song lulling me into my abyss began to fade away, their sounds now muffled by the black hole drawing me into its grasp. It pursued me, and I feared its entrapment. With no escape from the force of its lure (tired of the struggle, exhausted from the fight, weary of breathing in and breathing out), I gave in. Outside of the few moments of relief I encountered when Mason was near, every breath I had taken over the last eight months had been agonizing. Every time he left, the pain intensified. I longed to be free from its grip. I looked into the gross darkness and saw nothing. *Nothingness must be better than this*, I thought; then I realized the arms of the black void already surrounded me, pressing its cold lips to mine and sucking the life force from me as my breathing grew faint. *Even God has abandoned me*, I theorized.

I searched everywhere in the hollow void and found nothing, but even in my nothingness, every wound still ached, every word still cut, and the cavity of my chest still throbbed from emptiness. All of the pain I had felt in life had passed into the darkness along with me. I mused, *even in death there's no hope for me. The Fates have chosen eternal torment for my plight.*

My breathing shuddered and slowed. Sound warbled in and out, gaining my attention. I blinked open my heavy lids. In the distance I saw a small ray of light shining through the darkness. I heard a muffled, distorted voice. The voice brought the light, so I welcomed even the confusion of the distortion. "Aralyn, Aralyn," the light called. "Oh, my god," the voice hollered; I heard the shaking of a near-empty medicine bottle and a glass bottle as it hit my wooden floor. "Please, Aralyn. You have to live," the voice commanded me.

I felt warmth cover my chest. Strangely, the heat radiating from the face of the one searching for a heartbeat soothed the emptiness in my heart. "No!" he screamed. I felt a heaviness pound on my chest, forcing my heart to pump blood to my body. "You can't die," he pled. "I love you. Don't leave me," he commanded. I felt the tenderness of his lips as they pressed firmly against mine breathing life back into my lungs.

"Please don't leave me," he begged.

At that precise moment I felt the most extraordinary feeling I had ever felt. Something wet yet warm landed on my chest as he continued to force my heart to pump. I heard a sniffle and recognized the wetness as a tear; it landed right above my heart. My skin soaked it in. That single tear brought with it love and healing. My heart absorbed the tear; it permeated every fiber and cell, intermingling with my blood. Another forceful thrust came to my chest and pushed the tear through my veins. As the blood ran through my body, I could feel life infusing my being. Those parts of me that had been numb for so long started to tingle; it soothed the aching throughout me. With every breath he pushed into my lungs, I sensed hope. Finally my body reached out and grasped it; I inhaled a sharp breath, breathing on my own once again. My heart beat faintly, but it beat.

I didn't know who the voice belonged to, but I sensed his love wrapping around me as he picked me up. "Stay with me," he whispered as he carried me away.

He must be an angel sent to save me, I thought. Then I wondered, *Are we flying?* The angel kept apologizing to me; I wasn't sure why.

"I'm so sorry, Aralyn. I should've been there. Why didn't I get there earlier?" he fussed.

He must've been caught in a battle on his way to take me, I mused. The ray of light had shined through just in time. The darkness was just about to consume me. *Whoever this angel is, he really loves me. I can actually feel the warmth of it. It's amazing. I've never felt this kind of love before. It's different; it's better.*

I felt his arms wrap around me again. I longed to stay in the comfort of his embrace. My breathing grew shallow, and my heart beat remained barely existent with its soft, slow thrums. Suddenly, the angel left me. Coldness ripped me from his grasp. *No, no,* I thought. *I need him. Where are you taking me?* I saw the darkness closing in on me again, and then I saw no more.

Dark dreamlessness consumed me, yet even the darkness felt peaceful. It wasn't the same as before, when the pain and suffering of this life had followed me—attaching to me like a dark and dreary shadow. The sounds were no longer muffled. I heard the clear, strong rhythm of a heart beat echoing through my mind, and I heard the humming of a lullaby. I had heard that lullaby before; I knew who it belonged to. "Ray," I whispered with a croaky voice.

I heard a chair screech across the floor; Ray grabbed my hand and whispered, "I'm right here."

"Where am I?" I blinked and looked around the room examining my surroundings.

"You're in the hospital," he answered.

"Is my mom here?"

"No, I didn't know where she was or how to contact her."

"How long have I been here?" I asked.

"Since last night," he told me.

Furrowing my brow in confusion, I asked, "How did I get here?"

Still holding my hand, he answered, "I brought you here."

"*You* brought me here? Why am I here?" I asked.

"They think you accidentally overdosed. They had to pump your stomach. They said you flat-lined once. It really scared me."

The memory of the previous night started flashing before my eyes. I glanced away from him. "They think I overdosed?" was all I said.

"Yeah."

"What happened? How did you know I was in trouble? What made you go to my house?" I wanted to understand, so the questions kept flowing.

"Sheena told me she took you home. She told me what happened at school. The band was scheduled to practice after school, so I went, but I kept feeling like I needed to leave and check on you." He shook his head and sighed. "But I didn't." He inhaled a sharp breath. "Anyway, I left Blade's house and passed Mason standing outside his car loading a few things from his house into the back of it. I pulled over and got out to say hi and all. When I asked what he was doing, he told me he was getting a few things to take back to Starkville with him. He mentioned he had just left your house, and then he told me why he had gone to see you. I called him an idiot and took off to check on you." He let out a chuckle and added, "Well, I kind of punched him too."

Never letting go of my hand, he turned his head

and looked to the window, staring into the grey sky. "If I would've left practice like I felt I should, I would have gotten there before you did that." He started shaking his head again like he was disappointed in himself.

"Ray, you saved my life! Don't act like you didn't do enough. Nothing is your fault; it's mine," I assured him. Then I mumbled, "I'm the stupidest person on the face of the earth."

He sat on the edge of the bed and looked me in the eyes. Staring back at him, I saw the glassy redness; he had been crying. He squeezed my hand and commanded me, "Yeah, you are stupid for attempting that; don't you *ever* do anything like that again. Do you understand me? I thought you were gonna die, Aralyn." His hands trembled; to hide that fact, he tightened his grasp.

The strong, gravitational pull in his eyes refused to release me. I couldn't glance away from him in shame like I desired. I peered back through to the depths of his soul and apologized, "I'm sorry, Ray. I promise I won't."

He closed his eyes and sighed. What I had seen when I looked into his eyes was love. Ray loved me. I thought I remembered being in a dark place and hearing a muffled voice say "I love you." Thinking about it, it sounded a lot like Ray's voice, but I wasn't sure. It felt like a fading memory or a flash from a dream. Although I felt the memory slipping away from me, the love I felt coming from the dream man was strong. I saw a much deeper love than I had ever seen in Mason's eyes peering through to my soul. This love was pure, whole, and true, and I knew I loved him too; I just never recognized it before that moment because it was different from anything I had ever experienced.

"Ray, I can't really remember what happened. I mean, I remember what happened with Mason and all, but I can't remember your getting there. I just remember everything going black and being scared. I wanted the pain to go away, but it was still there. I dreamed I was trapped in a black abyss, but then there was a light. It was a small ray of light." As I spoke, I began to remember. "The light was an angel, and he spoke to me. He said he loved me. He asked me not to leave him. It was his strength that forced my heart to continue beating, and it was his life that breathed fresh life into my lungs." Ray sat silently listening intently to my description of his rescue. Revelation hit me; I looked up at him and said, "It wasn't just a dream, and it wasn't an angel. It was you. You were the light that pulled me back, and you cried." I lifted my hand and lightly touched his face.

"Yeah, it was me."

"Thank you," I whispered, smiling at him. "When I was coming to a little while ago, you were humming a song. I've heard you hum that song before. Is it a new one of yours?"

He smiled back and shifted his eyes away from me. "Yeah, it's new."

"Will you sing it to me?"

"Someday, I promise." A huge grin crossed his face.

"Why not today?" I pouted.

"Because, Aralyn, it's a special song. It has to be

the perfect moment."

I poked my bottom lip out; shaking his head "no," he stood his ground. I glanced at him again and realized he wore the same clothes he had on when he picked me up for school the previous day. Reaching out to tug on his shirt, I asked, "Why are you still wearing what you had on yesterday morning? Have you been here all night?"

Glancing down at my hand as it grasped his shirt, he shrugged. "I wasn't going to leave you here alone," he insisted.

"Hey, isn't tonight that gig with an agent listening to y'all?"

"Yeah." He hung his head.

"You are going, aren't you?"

"Nah. I've already called Blade. Your mom's still gone; I'm not leaving you alone," he insisted as he planted his feet in determination.

I felt bad that he was missing out on an important opportunity. "Ray, music is your future; it's your life. I'll never forgive myself if you don't go. This is important to you," I insisted.

"Aralyn, you're important to me. Yeah, music is important to me, but it's not my life; it's not what I value the most."

I couldn't allow him to give up on his dream, so I contemplated what I could do to convince him that he had to go. "How about, if I get out of here today, and I promise not to drink or do anything else, and I go with you. Will you go then?"

He narrowed his eyes and asked sternly, "And you

promise not to touch a thing?"

I crossed my chest. "Cross my heart."

"Okay, if the doctor releases you, we'll go."

When the doctor came in, he informed me I had to undergo an evaluation by a psychiatrist. I cringed at first, but when she came in to speak to me, I found out that it does actually help to talk to someone about the feelings you've locked away inside. It was hard at first, but once I opened up, the words just flowed. It was a very healing process for me, but I knew I had a long way to go. The damage had not been done overnight, and it wouldn't be fixed overnight either. She insisted I schedule a regular counseling session; I agreed to do so.

I was released, and Ray made it to his gig. I had always admired his talent, but for the first time ever, a sense of pride filled me as I watched him play. I begged him that night to sing the lullaby for me, but he refused. He kept promising he would sing it for me one day.

My mother took me to the school the following Monday and made arrangements for me to be able to graduate. I had to work hard to do it, but I determined within myself to buckle down.

Ray and I had been inseparable since my near-death experience. Like a protective watch dog guarding me, he never left my side. After that day at the hospital, I never brought up the confession of love he whispered as I lay dying and neither did he, but I knew it was still there. Although he never reached out and touched me, I could feel the desire to do so as we walked side by side. I figured he didn't want to be a rebound, so I understood.

I accomplished my goal of graduating. I did not graduate with highest honors as I should have; I didn't even graduate with honors, but I graduated. That meant something to me. On that night everything between Ray and I changed. Because he graduated with highest honors, we were seated nowhere near each other. The time came to throw our caps in the air, and we all threw them high. I didn't wait to pick mine up from the ground; I just started running through the crowd of people. I pushed my way past the masses and found Ray. He saw me in the distance and smiled; without a second thought I ran up to him, threw myself in his arms, and kissed him.

"Oh, gosh, I'm sorry," I said, throwing my hand over my mouth. "You're not mad at me, are you? I didn't just cross a line you didn't want to cross, did I?"

Laughing, he kissed my forehead and said, "No." Then he draped his arm over my shoulder, smiled at me, and said, "Come on. Let's go celebrate."

Walking across the field, we passed Kristin and Carrie. I heard Kristin snicker and whisper to Carrie, "Can you believe she's smiling. She shouldn't even be on this field."

Ray tightened his grip around me. I held my head up high and asked, "Okay, what are we gonna do?"

"We're gonna go get a couple of pints of triple chocolate ice cream, go back to your house, and watch a movie."

"Sounds good." I smiled.

CHAPTER 25

LOVE CAN BUILD A BRIDGE

My life slowly but surely pulled back together. I had made up my mind that Aralyn was not dead; she had only been trapped behind the wall she built as a little girl. Through building it, she desired to protect herself by hiding from the hurts and pains life so often shoots at one through the fiery arrows of words, the most powerful weapon an enemy can hold. With them one can rip apart the hopes, dreams, and self-esteem of the most innocent of lives. Spewing out of a vile heart, they often leave destruction in their wake. They stab, they cut, they sever, and they burn, leaving the fragile nature of the human spirit in ruins.

Too often their victims fall and never return. The traps they fall into may be different, but the enemy who put them there is the same. Some fall into a pit of muddy selfishness, covering the beauty that once

289

shined. The slickness of the walls often have them slipping back into the filth. Some fall into a bottomless well of greed, and there never seems to be an end to what they must have. Some fall into the quicksand of anger, hatred, and wrath; the harder they fight to free themselves, the faster violence swallows and consumes them. Some fall into the deep, dark waters of depression. All too often they drown as they give up on trying to find the surface and breathe in the surrounding despair, and then there are those who fall into a cold, dark cave where they entomb themselves in silence. Their only companions are loneliness and hopelessness.

As I pondered the lessons I had learned, I dove back into my poetry. Ray and my life served as my muses. I knew I had survived a war over my life. On the one hand, the dark side of this world had sought to destroy me, and on the other hand stood the side full of life that always remained in my heart even when I could no longer feel it, the side that yearned to lift me from the place I fell and to heal me from the wounds left by words. Sometimes we need someone to be an angel in our life and to bring us a ray of hope. We often need an extended hand willing to reach down to where we have fallen and help to pull us back to our feet, but what we must realize is that we have to make a choice to stretch forth our hand and receive the help, and we must choose to work together with the angel that comes our way. For the angel cannot do it on his own; he will only fall in with us if he tries to lift dead weight. We must climb and fight our way back out and never, never give up.

One summer day as I contemplated the choices I had made in life, I sat at my desk and wrote:

"Broken Path"

A broken path
Spread before my feet
Standing, I pondered,
What fate would I meet?
Does the loom of the Fates
Hold the thread of my life?
If it does,
Will the broken road depict for me strife?
Or is it merely
Stepping stones which lead the way?
Each one full of choices
Throughout the day.
Walking down the broken path,
I lost my way.
Tripping and falling,
I slipped and went astray.
I wallowed in the pit
That below the path lay.
Surrounded by darkness,
I yearned to find my way.
Using all of my strength,
I climbed and I climbed.

Plain Jane

When I got to the surface,
I wondered, what will I find?
Upon a firm, hard rock
I placed my feet;
I chose to walk the path
no matter what fate I may meet.

~ Plain Jane ~

"Don't Give In"

There is an evil that resides
Many times in those by our side.
The words they speak that are not true,
They are the words meant to ruin you.
When the rumors and the lies
From their mouths begin to fly.
As they pass the words along,
Remember that you can be strong.
Don't let them beat you down
And leave you bleeding on the ground.
Harness the strength that lies within.
Stand up and fight—don't give in!
The world can be so cold and cruel,
And wicked people sometimes rule.
Their tongues are sharper than a sword;
They spew out fire upon this world.
They aim their words straight for your heart
With every rumor that they start.
Don't let them beat you down
And leave you bleeding on the ground.
Harness the strength that lies within.

Stand up and fight—don't give in!
So when you feel you can't go on,
Remember I am there, be strong.

~ Plain Jane ~

Ray walked over to the desk; standing behind me, he leaned over and kissed my cheek. I smiled, laid my pencil down, and turned into his kiss. "Wanna watch a movie?" he asked.

"Sounds good to me." I smiled.

We sauntered to the living room, and I plopped down on the couch while he slid the movie he had rented in the VCR. We lay down on the couch together to watch it. My mother had left with Lydia for the weekend, so I knew the temptation that might arise. I turned my body toward his, stretched, and pressed my lips against his. "Ray," I whispered.

"Yeah." He pulled my hair away from my face.

"I know we've been seeing each other for a while and all, but I need to say something."

"What is it?" he asked as he ran his long fingers through my hair.

"It's not that I don't love you or care about you, but I need you to know that things can't go any farther than this." I waved my hand between our proximity.

He lightly traced his fingers over my cheek and whispered, "I know. It's okay, Aralyn. You just need somebody to love you, and somebody who loves you will want to give you what you need, not take what they want. I'm not gonna lie and say I haven't thought about it; I am a guy." He chuckled. "But I don't expect you to sleep with me to show me that you love me. I want to show you that I love you." He ran his forefinger down my nose; when he came to the tip, he gently poked me.

As the words came out of his mouth, I felt the strangest sensation in my heart. An invisible bridge formed in my heart and stretched forth, finding its way to his. When the two came together, it felt as if my heart and his had actually melted together and become one. I nestled into his chest, allowing the oneness to absorb me.

Ray and I both decided to go to the local community college for the first two years. We enrolled at JC in Gautier and arranged to have our classes together. His band had plenty of weekend gigs to furnish him with a small income, and I went to work for my grandpa and my mom at Daisy's. Our lives were moving along smoothly when a choice was thrown my way. On the tenth of October, Ray drove me home. When we pulled in the driveway, we looked at each other and sighed. We both spotted Mason's car pulled in the shade.

"I wonder what he wants," I mumbled, rolling my eyes.

Curling his lip, he grumbled, "Who knows?"

Ray parked the car, and I hesitantly stepped out. Mason sat fidgeting on the front steps. When he saw us both get out of the car, he stood and strode toward us. "Hey," he raised his brow, "you two riding to school together?"

Ray answered him before I could speak. "Yeah, something like that."

Mason stepped forward and reached out to shake Ray's hand. When Ray extended his hand in return, Mason asked, "Do you mind if I speak to Aralyn alone?"

Wide eyed I glared at Ray, searching for help, for a way out, but instead he cut his eyes toward me and answered, "Yeah, sure thing." Turning to face me, he added, "Aralyn, call me when you're ready to study."

I just nodded my head. Ray smiled. "See ya in a bit," he mumbled as he got back in his car. I watched as his car and my way of escape drove down the road. Breaking my focus and glare, Mason interjected, "So, you two drive to school together *every day?*"

"Hmm?" I shook myself free from my trance. "Oh, yeah, *every day!*" I exclaimed with a bubbly voice.

"Can we talk?" he asked.

I crossed my arms and shifted my glare to him. "Yeah, sure. What do you want?" I asked still standing in a safe zone—outside!

"Um, can we talk inside?" He squinted.

Sighing, I answered, "I suppose, if it's necessary."

"Well, I'd like to be able to sit down."

"All right then. Come on in." I unlocked the door, flung the keys on the phone stand, and sat on the chair, careful not to sit on the couch and give him the opportunity to sit close to me. He noticed my distance.

Rather than sit on the couch, he knelt down next to the chair. "So, you graduated and you're going to JC,

295

huh? I figured you be off to an Ivy League school somewhere on the other side of the country." He let out half a chuckle. When I didn't respond to his remark, he asked, "Met any guys there yet?"

I rolled my eyes. "Don't you have a wife? What do you care if I've met a guy in college?"

"We, uh, we're not together. I didn't go through with it. I couldn't. I care about her and all, but I knew I didn't love her. I was only gonna do it because of Carolyn. That's my little girl's name." He smiled. "You should see her; she's beautiful. She has these big, beautiful green eyes."

The light bulb went off. That was it; he wanted me to meet his daughter. He *had come* for a reason; he wanted us to get back together or at least to see if I was available. I figured I should warn him in advance that his story would be in vain. So, I opened my mouth and said, "Mason, I should—"

"Aralyn," he interrupted me. "Please let me talk first. Look, I know you had every right to say all the things you said to me. I'm sorry. I'm so sorry I hurt you the way I did. I just wish we could go back. Do you think we can? I just want things to be the way they used to be between us. You're the person I've always loved. I know I can't take back the things I've done to you, but I can promise to try and make it up to you. Will you let me do that? Will you allow me to try to make things up to you? I know I don't deserve it, but I'm asking for forgiveness."

The entire time he spoke, my eyes never left his. I could see the sincerity in his eyes, and I could hear the honesty in his voice. I sensed true sorrow for the way things had happened in his tone, and I knew if he had it to do over again, he wouldn't make the same mistakes, but I also knew in that moment that if I had it all to do over again, I wouldn't make the same mistakes either.

"Mason, what I was trying to say earlier is that I am with someone. I'm with Ray, and I'm in love with him. The truth of the matter is we *can't* go back. I'm not the same person I was when we met; you fell in love with her, and that's not who I am anymore. The part of my heart that belonged to you died, Mason. It died, and I had to cut it out in order to heal again. Ray has my whole heart; there's no place left for you in there. You were my first love, Mason. I can't change that, but Ray, he's my true love. There's a difference. I hope someday you'll meet someone and learn what that difference is."

His forehead crinkled in pain. "I...I didn't know. When did you? How did you?" he stuttered.

"It just happened. We were friends, and we fell in love."

"Huh, well...I hope that when you think of me, you'll remember the good parts more than the bad." He ran his hand through my hair, leaned in, and kissed my forehead. "Good bye," he whispered; then he left.

I broke down and cried for a fleeting moment; I wasn't sure why exactly, just a buildup of emotions I assumed. I picked up the phone and called Ray. "Can you come over here, please?" I asked.

"Be right there," he answered.

Shortly he pulled up in the drive and knocked on the door. When I opened the door, he could see that I had been crying. He just stood there not knowing what to think or how to interpret the blood-red eyes. Finally I asked, "Are you gonna just stand there, or are you coming in?"

"Are you okay?" he asked as he walked through the doorway.

"No thanks to you, I am. Why did you do that? Why didn't you tell him 'No way!'?" I fussed.

He grabbed my hand, sat in the chair, and pulled me to his lap. I laid my head on his shoulder and sighed. He wrapped his arms around me and squeezed. "So, was he here for the reason I think he was?"

"Yes," I answered. "If you figured that's why he was here, why did you leave me here alone with him? Weren't you scared?" I sat up and looked in his eyes.

"Scared to death! But, Aralyn, I didn't want you to be with me out of any kind of obligation or because you couldn't be with him. I didn't want to stop you from being with him if that's what your heart truly wanted. I wanted you to choose me," he explained.

I leaned over and rubbed my nose to his. "Well, you won by a long shot." I smiled.

He smiled back at me and kissed me. "Good," he whispered.

On Christmas Day Ray showed up at my doorsteps

bright and early. Telling me he had a special Christmas surprise for me, he urged me to climb in his car. Before he opened the car door, he pulled out a blindfold and covered my eyes. He guided me as I climbed in and made sure I didn't hit my head. Clueless as to where we headed, I begged him to give me a hint, but he refused. The car finally came to a stop, and the engine shut off. My door creaked open, and Ray held my hand and led me to a chair. He untied the blindfold, and I opened my eyes. I placed my hands on the small white bench he sat me on and peered in front of me, a small lake and a folding chair in my view. His acoustic guitar leaned against the chair. The sun glimmered over the water creating starbursts of glistening light, a beautiful sight to behold.

"Oh, wow!" I exclaimed.

Ray sat in the folding chair, picked up his guitar, and played the lullaby I had longed to hear; then he sang:

"I Promise"

I see you from a distance
Standing with another guy.
He wraps his arm around you,
And I'm wishing you were mine.
I see you from a distance;
In his hands you place your heart.
If you'd only give it to me,
I'd never tear it apart.
If I promised to love you

And to stand by your side,
If I promised to love you,
Would you be mine tonight?
If I promised to love you
And we would never be apart,
If I promised to love you,
Would you give me your heart?
If I promised to love you
And I sealed it with this ring,
Would you answer with a yes?
Would you make my heart sing?
Cause I promise I love you.
I love you, Aralyn.

He laid his guitar to the side, pulled out a ring, knelt down, and asked, "Will you marry me?"

"Yes, yes, yes!" I squealed, jumping into his lap with such force that we both ended up on the ground.

On July 1, 1995, we had a lovely small wedding. Although my relationship with Laila remained strained, she was still my sister, so I asked her to stand in as my maid of honor. Sheena had been with me through some pretty rough stuff, so I asked her to be a bridesmaid. I drove over to Mrs. Nan's and asked for Laurie's number. I called her and asked her if she would stand beside me as well. I knew things were different between us, but I was so glad to have had the opportunity to get to be close to her when I did.

I was no longer angry at her for leaving. I had come to the understanding that we have to appreciate the times and moments we have with others while we have it. We shouldn't regret being close to someone and loving them; we should be thankful for their sharing a piece of their heart. People's lives often go in different directions, but the imprints made upon our heart while they are with us are the things we can carry into our future; in that way, they will always be a part of us. Laurie had left a huge imprint on my heart. Without her, I may have never created a doorway through The Wall. I would forever be grateful to her for that.

I even called my dad and made peace. I asked him to give me away, but out of respect for my mother, I asked him to please come alone. He complied with my wishes and was thankful for my forgiveness. I learned that it doesn't do any good to harbor bitterness in your heart. People make mistakes; we all do. It doesn't excuse their mistakes to love the person despite them. Daddy was no longer the hero of my childhood; I would always cherish his heroic acts but another man had taken that place.

My wedding day was a good day. Everyone got along. Mom and Dad were sociable to one another. Ray was as handsome as ever although he no longer had his long hair. He had cut it off for a job interview. The band had decided to go to Memphis, and he respectfully declined. I felt bad about that, but he assured me his life was with me.

Many do not understand the traditions in a

wedding ceremony. For instance, feeding each other the cake and drinking from one another's cup is an ancient tradition with significant meaning. It is a part of a covenant ritual which symbolizes partaking of each other's body and blood. It means that the two are no longer separate but one. The importance of this is that when two become one, they share in everything—even in enemies. Ray and I feed each other and drank from one another's cup, and in that moment, Ray's sheer presence caused my enemies, the carved out stones I had used to build The Wall, to crumble. No longer would words be able to penetrate my heart because he was my protector and my shield.

On our one-year anniversary, I sat at my same old desk writing a new piece of poetry. Insisting the ancient piece of furniture served as a Muse, Mom urged me to keep it. A gift, wrapped in silvery-white paper, appeared before me.

Startled, I jumped. "Oh, my gosh, Ray, what are you doing home?" I didn't hear him enter.

"It's our anniversary, so I took off early." He shrugged his shoulders.

"A gift? Now? You don't want to wait until after dinner?"

"Nope," he insisted, shaking it in front of me.

I unraveled the paper and peeled it back to find a beautiful crimson-red journal; around the perimeter of the 6 x 9 book was the scrolled vine of my life; hanging in the top left corner and stretching forth from the bottom right corner were two wilting, white flowers. It was embossed with the inscription *PLAIN JANE* and tied together with a yellow ribbon. "What's this?"

He knelt next to me and traced his long fingers over the cover. "Well, the one-year anniversary gift is supposed to be paper, so I thought I'd get you a journal. It's paper, and it's red, for your heart; also, you were wearing crimson-red the first night I met you." He smiled and wiggled his brows playfully. "You captured my heart that night, you know."

A shy smile inched across my face. "So I hear."

"The scrolled vine and the white flowers are those parts of you that you used to keep hidden behind The Wall, and," he said, tugging on the yellow ribbon and untying it, "the yellow ribbon, symbolizes your intelligence that has always held you together. Now you can write your story and poetry. I've always thought you should."

He kissed me on the cheek and stretched his hand forth to caress my bulging belly, our baby. "Concerning the title and your pen name, I've never thought you were a Plain Jane. Sometimes the way a person sees oneself is formed through false words spoken into their lives, and it's not who they truly are. To me, you are the most beautiful woman in the world, inside and outside, and I happen to think you're even more beautiful pregnant."

"Thank you," I whispered and smiled. I placed my hands on top of his and stared at the rather large bump. We both laughed when we felt a firm kick.

I thought about my life and what I would say. I knew love could build a bridge that could cross over into even the tallest walls which had been built around a heart, and I was certain unconditional love could shatter the strongest of walls. My wall had crumbled, and the beautiful vine that had withered behind it was exposed to warmth, sunlight, and tears of joy that fell like rain. The little girl trapped inside blossomed for all to see. She no longer stared in a cracked mirror hanging above her dresser; she finally found something that revealed her true reflection. The storyboard I had conjured as a small child didn't compare to the reality I now lived.

I decided to start with a poem that best described my early days:

"Me"

Do you see me,
Or do you see my dress?
Do I look confident,
Or do I look a mess?
Am I who
You thought I'd be?
Am I what
You expect of me?
I may be simple,
Ordinary, and plain.
To you I may be no one,
But to me I am Plain Jane.

~ Plain Jane ~

Then I began with the story:

Plain. That was a word I knew quite well. The word described *me* perfectly. I embraced it as a part of who I was. I had eyes, I could see...

Plain Jane

Works Cited

Lauper, Cyndi. "Girls Just Wanna Have Fun." *She's So Unusual*. Portrait Records, 1984.

Club Nouveau. "Lean on Me." *Life, Love, & Pain*. Warner Bros. Records, 1984.

Bon Jovi. "You Give Love a Bad Name." *Slippery When Wet*. Mercury Records, 1986.

Midler, Bette. "Wind Beneath My Wings." *Beaches*. Atlantic Records, 1989.

Cutting Crew. "I Just Died in Your Arms Tonight." *Broadcast*. Virgin Records, 1986.

Van Halen. "Jump." *1984*. Warner Bros. Records, 1984.

Chicago. "Look Away." *Chicago 19*. Full Moon/Reprise, 1988.

Chicago. "Once In a Lifetime." *Chicago 17*. Full Moon/Reprise, 1984.

Air Supply. "Without You." *The Earth Is*. Giant Records/Warner Bros. Records, 1991.

Freaky Friday. Dir. Gary Nelson. Jodi Foster. Walt Disney Productions, 1977.

Beaches. Dir. Garry Marshall. Bette Midler, Barbara Hershey. All Girls Production, 1988.

Mannequin. Dir. Michael Gottlieb. Andrew McCarthy. Gladden

Entertainment, 1987.

Far and Away. Dir. Ron Howard. Tom Cruise, Nicole Kidman. Imagine Films Entertainment, 1992.

Gone With the Wind. Dir. Victor Fleming. Clark Gable, Vivien Leigh. Selznick International Pictures, 1941.

Risky Business. Dir. Paul Brickman. Tom Cruise. The Geffen Company, 1983.

Wheel of Fortune. Harry Friedman. Dirs. Dick Carson, Mark Corwin. Pat Sajak, Vanna White. CBS. WKRG, Mobile.

Matlock. The Fred Silverman Company. Created by Dean Hargrove. Andy Griffith. ABC. WLOX, Biloxi/Gulfport.

The Oprah Winfrey Show. Harpo Productions. Created by OprahWinfrey. CBS. WKRG, Mobile.

The Fantastic Four. DePatie-Freleng. Created by Stan Lee, Jack Kirby. NBC. WDAM, Laurel.

Thriller. George Folsey, Jr. Dir. John Landis. Michael Jackson, Ola Ray, Vincent Price. Columbia Pictures, Paramount Pictures, Epic Records Productions, 1983.

Byrd, Robert. Finn MacCoul and His Fearless Wife. New York: Dutton Children's Books, 1999.

Malory, Thomas, Sir, 15th Cent. Tales of King Arthur. New York: Schochen Books, 1981.

Lane, Edward William. Stories From the Thousand and One Nights. (The Arabian Nights' Entertainments). New York: Collier, 1937.

Cauley, Lorinda Bryan. The Ugly Duckling. New York: Harcourt Brace Jovanovich, 1979.

Montgomery, Lucy Maud. Anne of Green Gables. New York: Grossett Dunlap, 1961.

Bronte, Emily. Wuthering Heights. New York: Bantam Books, 1981.

Peppe, Rodney, ill. Humpty Dumpty. New York: Viking Press, 1976.

Keene, Carolyn. Nancy Drew Ghost Stories. New York: Pocket Books, 1983.

Frost, Robert. "Revelation." The Poetry of Robert Frost. New York: Chicago: San Francisco: Holt, Rinehart and Winston, 1969. Pg. 19.

Schledia Phillips is the author of Plain Jane, Pretty Boy, and Wildflowers. The mother of five resides on the Gulf Coast. She dedicated eight years of her life to working with teenagers as a youth minister and has been invited to speak to high school students and to women's groups. Her goal as an author is to write stories that touch the hearts of readers and to tackle issues such as bullying, abuse, depression, domestic violence, and suicide.

www.ingramcontent.com/pod-product-compliance
Lightning Source LLC
Chambersburg PA
CBHW020406260626
47156CB00007B/2261